PROLOGUE

FOURTEEN YEARS EARLIER

Greenville, Montana

𝒟earest Luke,
　　Words cannot express how much I miss you! Somehow, it just snowed here in Greenville, even though it's still in the dog days of summer. I'm pretty sure that's the earliest snow ever! Mom and Dad are talking about taking a vacation to the Grand Tetons before senior year starts—I worry that'll be too expensive, but they insist! You know how they are.

　　I could sit here for hours, writing you a novel about how much I already miss you. You always told me you don't like to read long stuff (which is good! I should practice being more concise!), so I'll keep it short. I miss most:

- Your handsome face, with its chiseled, always clean-cut jaw-line, dimpled cheeks, and majestically brown eyes, as enchanting as the Missouri River

- Your unshakable faith; I give thanks to God that you and your family are healthy, but I truly believe that with your faith, you would be a modern-day Job
- The way you make me laugh like a hog (I can't believe I'm admitting this!) with jokes about Bozeman

I know you going to college will be the hardest years of our relationship yet, but we've made it this far, and I know the Lord has a plan for us. I can't wait for you to get back here so I can tell you in-person where I'm going to go to college. I thank God daily for Him bringing you into my life. I love you!
Love,
Brooke
P.S. You should try writing me a note sometime! I promise I'll like it, even if you think you're not good at it! :-)

Spokane, WA

DEAR BROOKE,

I miss you too. I don't like being this far away from God's country, but you know what Papaw said—I won't appreciate someone or somewhere until I leave. It's been less than a month, and he was right.

I am not a good writer, but I love everything about you too. You know I will tell you all those things in person soon enough. Unfortunately, Papaw insists I try college for at least one year, but I promise I will be back soon. When I get back, I'm never leaving again, and I can't wait to be with you and start a family with you with God's blessings.

Praise be to God. I love you, and I cannot wait to see you soon.

COWBOY'S HOMECOMING

A WALKER FAMILY SAGA

HOPE VALLEY RANCH SWEET ROMANCE
BOOK ONE

SIERRA HART

HOPE VALLEY PRODUCTIONS

Love,
Luke Walker

1

LUKE

PRESENT DAY

The sun cracked the horizon to the east, blessing the evergreen, mountainous Idaho landscape with a brand new day. Luke Walker, driving his black 2009 Ford F-150, smiled and said a silent prayer of thanks for the chance to come home—even under the circumstances at hand. Once he finished his prayer, he glanced at the clock, just after five-thirty a.m., and then looked at the passenger's seat.

His young daughter, Montana, rested with her head pressed against the car door, her jaw slightly agape. She still wore her light-blue buffalo-covered pajamas, something that Luke would never have allowed if not for the request to be woken up when they crossed back into the state she was named after. Then again, Luke thought, there were many things he never would have allowed that had come to pass. Sometimes, especially with a young daughter, a man had to prioritize and bend a bit.

"Hey, Tana," he said, gently rubbing his daughter's shoulder, careful to keep his eyes mostly on the road. "Taaaana. Tana Tana!"

Montana mumbled something incoherent. She looked *thrilled* to be awake at least a good hour before she normally woke up. With some time at the family ranch, Luke thought, she'd consider five-thirty a.m. sleeping in.

"We're three miles from the border," he said. "It'll be your first time in your state."

"My state?" Montana asked for confirmation, though it took a couple of seconds for Luke to untangle her garbled words.

Luke smiled as he nodded. The news seemed to lift Montana's spirits like a good cup of coffee would for most people, and she straightened up from against the truck door.

"My state," she repeated, almost in awe of herself. "First time ever."

"First time ever," Luke repeated. "I'm sorry it took so long to get you over here. I should have brought you a long time ago to see where Mimi and Papaw live."

"It's OK, Daddy," she said. "My state!"

Montana started bouncing like someone had plugged her into an outlet. Luke just chuckled, then turned his gaze ahead to the road. He had another two minutes before he would dance with Montana about returning home.

Those two minutes, however, reminded Luke that he was not just coming back to big skies, happy ranch life, and favorite dining spots and watering holes in Greenville.

He was coming back to his past, a past that had taken a very different turn from what he thought it would become after high school graduation. He was coming back to people who loved him, yes, but also people who might look at him askance and whisper.

He was also coming back to the real possibility that there would be someone who would hate him a great deal, and he could not fault her.

Lord, I hope you have treated Brooke much better than I ever did. I...

He stopped. He did not feel he had earned the right to pray for anything regarding Brooke's treatment of him.

"Look!"

His daughter's high-pitched cry shook him out of his thoughts. He felt a bit ridiculous; that woman, great as she was, had too much smarts and too much ambition to remain in a small town like Greenville. A remote possibility existed that she had moved to Bozeman, Helena, or Billings; the far more likely outcome was she had launched a white-collar career in some city like Seattle or San Francisco.

Luke wished her the best, hoped that they could be amicable if he saw her around the holidays, and then looked at the welcome sign.

"Three!" Luke and Montana shouted together, counting down the seconds to their crossing over into Montana. "Two! One! We're heeeeeere!"

For a half second, the view changed little; a welcome center on the right had not yet opened for the day, and even if it had, it was like offering someone gum in a line for a rodeo show. Better than nothing, but not worth stopping for.

Then the luscious, green mountains opened up to reveal the vast valleys of western Montana, and even though state boundaries were only on maps, it just *felt* like the world had changed. Luke had never forgotten how much he loved the state—he needed only to look at his daughter—and crossing the state border, even at five-thirty-six a.m., provided him with a surge of peaceful energy.

It felt like all was right with the world; living in these rolling, snow-capped mountains, with the nearest major city several hours away and surrounded by family, friends, and their families, would allow him to live as God would have wanted. He was forever grateful for what his father had done for him and his brothers, forcing them to explore the outside world, but Luke knew as he saw his daughter making up a song about returning to "*my* state" he would never leave.

He had made many mistakes in his past. He had failed many people. He had faced difficulties that would have broken many.

But now, he was fulfilling his promise to the one person he never wanted to fail—he was, indeed, bringing his daughter to the Walker family's ranch.

"Montana, my state, my state, we are here!" Montana continued to sing, drawing a laugh from Luke. Sometimes, a father's job was as simple as letting his child relish in their silliness.

"Can you teach me the lyrics to that, Tana?" he asked with a growing smile, briefly forgetting about the past. "'Montana, my state, my state, we are here?' Anything else I should know?"

"Ummm, I don't know!" his daughter said, giggling.

"You don't know!" Luke said. "Well, why don't you sing about the mountains? Or the bison and elk and other creatures you'll see here? Or the stately pine trees you see outside your window?"

Montana glanced out the window, seeming to try to drink in all the views. *Oh, to have the innocent eyes of a child once more.*

"I'll sing more once I know more about Greenville, Daddy!" she said, as if it was the most obvious thing in the world.

"Fair enough," Luke said with a chuckle.

"What's there?"

"Well, most importantly, the people. Mimi and Papaw. Your uncles aren't here yet, but they'll visit throughout the fall. There are the Chamberlains; they're an even bigger family than us. There's Broo…"

What are you doing?

"Who's Broooo?" Montana said.

Luke chuckled.

"Well, she was a very close friend of mine in high school, but I'm sure she's moved to the big city now. Bigger even than Spokane."

"Woah!" Montana said, as if Spokane might as well have been San Francisco. "What places will be near our home?"

"Well, there'll be the restaurants, of course. There's a great diner, Bacon & Bakin', that Mimi and Papaw went to when they were kids. There's the church. There's an ice cream shop, Green Cream. But most importantly—"

"There's ice cream?!?"

Of course. The two magic words that could make any child sit still during homilies and do their homework without asking twice.

"Yes, yes, but Montana. Tana. Most importantly, remember, the best place of all is what God has given us—this Earth. You won't find a place in all the country more untouched and pristine than Montana. Greenville is just large enough for us to enjoy the comforts of civilization, but not so large that we lose touch with God and our world. I know we did a lot of outdoor activities in Spokane, but there's a big difference between going outdoors and being outdoors."

Montana nodded, listening with rapt attention. Luke gave thanks that he never had to worry about his daughter listening to him. Surely, someday, she would become a rebellious teenager, but he had years before that happened.

And if she was a rebellious teenager, well, at least she'd rebel in his hometown of Greenville, where his teachers would be her teachers, the store owners the same, and the sheriff practically a next-door neighbor.

"Now, kick back and enjoy the show," Luke said. "You won't find anything better than this in the cinema."

JUST A LITTLE OVER five hours later, Luke and Montana saw the first sign for Greenville, MT, just after driving through Helena. Though a straight shot from the border would have only taken about four hours, Luke insisted on stopping multiple times for photos and a chance to stretch their legs.

Montana, bless her, never complained and, in fact, seemed to relish being in her "home state." Even she seemed to sense that something was, indeed, different from eastern Washington and Idaho. She called little pebbles "her rocks" and the mountains "my backyard." The sight warmed Luke's heart, who had wondered what uprooting the little girl's life might do to her.

But what Montana had said was true—as long as she was with Daddy, she would be happy.

Thank you, God, for making me lucky with her.

He held off on sounding resentful and adding *for being lucky with at least one woman.* He'd had so many blessings in his life; one self-inflicted mistake and one heartbreaking tragedy did not justify being resentful.

It all added up to Luke feeling more and more certain that he had made the right choice to come home.

What was also certain, however, was a certain little bugger's voice insisting on stopping for food.

"Daddy, I'm hungry!" Montana said.

"Hi hungry, I'm Luke," he said.

Montana scowled and dramatically folded her arms.

"I'm sorry baby, I'm hungry too," Luke said, still laughing, "but the best restaurants are in Greenville. If you want breakfast food, we can do Bacon & Bakin'. Or, if you want lunch, we can go to a new place. It's called Bison Brothers, and though it's not as old as Bacon & Bakin', it's still become a town staple quickly."

"What do they have?"

"Burgers, barbecue, good ol' meat and potatoes."

The answer seemed to placate Montana, because she unfolded her arms and turned her attention back straight ahead.

"Do they have chocolate chip ice cream?"

Luke chortled.

"We have to earn our ice cream," Luke said. "Tell you what. For the first special occasion here, we'll get ice cream. But for now—"

"Pancakes?"

Well, that settled the answer for where they were going.

"Bison Brothers does not, but B&B does."

"B&B?"

"Sorry, it's what we called Bacon & Bakin' as kids. I'm sure some people my age still call it that."

"You old people!"

Luke stuck out his tongue at her, which Montana reflected back. The two giggled before Luke nodded his head to the left.

"See that? It's Greenville Elementary School. That's where you'll be learning in about one week!"

"Eww, school."

Luke shook his head, but a smile remained on his face. Montana always came home with good grades and high praise on her report card; he could safely say that her smarts had not come from him.

"You may say 'eww,' but I know for a fact your school back in Spokane didn't have a river," he said, pointing to the next feature.

"Woah!"

"It's the Missouri River, and you could paddle all the way to Missouri if you had enough food and water. But even your ol' Daddy isn't adventurous enough to do that."

"Why not?"

Luke chuckled.

"One can enjoy God's world without making a fool of yourself in it," he said.

As they continued the drive down the road, Luke pointed out the coffee shop and the other landmarks. To his surprise, though, there was much that he did not recognize, especially near Montana State-Greenville's campus. He did not need to explain much, since those locations were mostly bars, but it still felt a little unsettling to see his small hometown seem to change so much.

I wonder if she saw any of this.

Focus, Luke. Your daughter.

"And near the end here, up on the right, just before the church, is our first stop of the day," Luke said. "It's a Thursday, and we're not dressed appropriately, so we'll save church for another day. But we'll be going every week with Mimi and Papaw."

Montana, though, had her eyes only for Bacon & Bakin'. And Luke was relieved to see that the storefront had not changed in the slightest; there was still the one large red "B" that started both *bacon* and *bakin'* on the sign over the entryway. Wooden steps led up to a porch, and humorous, homely signs, like "Don't flatter yourself, I was starin' at your horse," lined both the outside walls and the interior.

He opened the door for his daughter and stepped inside. Sure enough, it was exactly as he had remembered from fourteen years ago, albeit a little cleaner and with some new wooden chairs. The color scheme resembled the American flag, and countless photos of God's country hung up all over the walls.

"This place is as much a cornerstone of Greenville as anything else, Montana," he said to his daughter, holding her hand.

At this time of day, later in the morning but not quite time for lunch, they were only one of five patrons in the restaurant. There was an older couple, probably in their sixties, holding hands at a small table near the back, and a younger woman with brown, shoulder-length hair with her back to them in a booth. Luke's stomach briefly flared, but the possibility of this being *the* brown-haired girl was so unlikely, it bordered on absurd.

"Is that… Luke Walker?"

Luke looked up to see the restaurant's owner, Krista Baker, a woman now in her early seventies, coming from the back of the kitchen. Luke's eyes widened at the sight—Mrs. Baker had owned the shop for so long, she had served his parents before they were even married.

"Good morning, ma'am," Luke said with a slight head nod. "Indeed, the one and only."

"Oh my Lord!" she said, throwing her arms out for a hug that Luke happily took. "It's so good to see you! And look at you, all grown up. And you are like a mini-him," she said to Montana.

"Excuse me!" Montana said, drawing a laugh from both Mrs. Baker and Luke.

"Now, Tana, remember your manners," Luke said. "Mrs. Baker, this is my daughter Montana. You can guess why I named her."

"Such a beautiful name," Mrs. Baker said.

She crouched down to talk further to Montana, which gave Luke a chance to look back over the restaurant once more. He felt watched. He turned his gaze to the woman with the brown hair, and his stomach flared with nervousness and excitement.

It was none other than Brooke Young.

2

BROOKE

The instant Brooke heard the name "Luke Walker," the hair on the back of her neck stood up, and it became impossible to lesson plan for the first month of the school year.

She tried to push out all the memories of their three-year relationship in high school, both the good and the bad. There was far more good than bad—but unfortunately, the way it ended made that one bad moment far outweigh much of the good that had transpired before then.

And now... he had a kid?

She turned in her booth as Mrs. Baker said something about a mini-him. She had tried so hard not to turn, hoping that if Luke was just in for a visit to his old spots, he wouldn't stick around for food. She could go back to preparing lesson plans for her second-grade class.

But a comment about a child, she *had* to see this.

She turned. A part of her felt a strange sense of relief. This child was far too young to be conceived right around the time they had broken up; if she suspected he had cheated on her during those few months of long-distance dating, she did not think she could stop herself from perhaps even cursing, let alone feeling the strongest anger of her life.

But a part of her also felt jealousy and, strangely enough, sadness. *They* were supposed to be having kids together; they were supposed to be starting a family once he got back from school. Now, fourteen years had passed since she had last seen him, and that had been time enough to have a daughter.

And, in the name of all that was good, she chided herself for thinking as much about a married man, but he looked even more handsome than back in the day. That Luke was hot and fun, fit but not yet a man; this clean-cut man had some ruggedness to him, some lines on his cheeks and in his eyes that suggested someone who had gone through some hard times, yet still retained his strength and vigor.

She was about to pull herself from looking at him when he looked her way.

Time seemed to freeze. Though she had moved on with life once she had recovered enough from their breakup, seeing those strong, toughened brown eyes brought her back to her youthful, wistful days at Greenville High School. She could still remember losing herself in those brown eyes as his hands respectfully wrapped around her back. She could still easily recall how warm everything felt when…

When he kissed her.

She turned back to her plate and papers. She did not need to be thinking about what it was like to kiss a married man, even one as handsome and with as much history as him. She had a job to do, and the opportunity to return to her hometown and do what she loved, even under her family circumstances, was not one she could compromise in the name of immature lust.

Lord, give me the strength to focus on what matters and not to covet him. He has found his happily ever after. I trust in your plan to help me find mine.

She held her breath for a couple of seconds, anticipating that

Luke might come over and say hello. But when she saw Mrs. Baker returning to the back of the restaurant and heard Luke and his daughter sitting down at a table near the entrance, she exhaled all the tension out of her.

Well, most of it. But enough of it she could focus on her lesson planning and goals for the upcoming year.

First, she wanted to push her kids to learn basic writing and organization skills. Though she had not learned how to write creatively until fourth grade, she had spent enough time at UCLA to see how kids in more urbanized and affluent environments learned faster. She saw no reason she couldn't bring their drive to learn faster and willingness to take on higher standards to Greenville's students.

Second, she wanted to spend at least one thirty-minute session with each of her kids per month, going over their academic progress and getting a sense of how they were doing. The best teachers Brooke had ever had did more than just teach multiplication tables or how to write a thesis sentence; they built true relationships based on genuine care and compassion.

Third—

"Excuse me, Brooke?"

Oh, Lord, she thought as her heartbeat ramped up. She drew in a breath, put on her best smile, and turned to Luke. He stood there with his daughter. At least she was adorable.

"Luke Walker," she said, trying her best to keep all emotion out of her voice. "I never thought I would see you again."

She supposed her words, as flat as they may have been, did not hide how she felt.

"That's fair," he said with a level of regret that surprised Brooke. "I came over here because Mrs. Baker said that you're now teaching second grade up at the school?"

"Yes. I'm making lesson plans now," she said, gesturing to her papers.

"You're going to be my teacher!"

The young girl's exuberance was impossible not to smile at, and it would have been rude and unprofessional to discourage her excitement at school.

But... first she'd dated a Walker, and now she was going to teach his progeny?

"Why yes, I am," Brooke said, hoping her smile was as genuine as possible. "What's your name?"

"Montana! Daddy said I'm named after home!"

Home. Not Spokane. Here. The smile Brooke wore was natural as she turned her gaze to Luke for an explanation. She had to focus her eyes on his cheek or nose, lest she feel all sorts of emotions for a married man. *Much less one that broke your heart all those years ago.*

"I always knew I'd come back at some point, and this place has given me almost everything good in my life."

Almost.

Not her mother.

But just as Brooke was about to ask something about Montana's mother, she noticed Luke did not sport a ring. Curious. But also something she did not dare to ask in front of someone seven or eight years old.

"Daddy, where's the bathroom?"

"If it's in the same place as before, it's just past the kitchen counter on the left," he said, looking at Brooke for confirmation.

"It is," she said, and without asking for any help, Montana pulled herself away and headed straight for the restroom. "She's fearless, huh?"

"She's got my streak of independence," Luke said with a chuckle.

Brooke let the words hover for a few seconds.

"I know," she said, and this time, she did not mask her emotions. The coldness of her response immediately put Luke back on guard as he wiped the half-grin off his face. He cleared his throat and nodded questioningly to the other side of the booth.

Brooke did *not* want to deal with this right now. She needed time to process and think about how she'd handle things like seeing him after school, at parent-teacher conferences, and school events. Being put in a booth after fourteen years of no communication felt like a test from the Lord, unlike anything short of what her mother was dealing with right now.

But if nothing else, as a professional teacher, she needed to act like an adult to the parent of one of her students. And so she gestured for him to take a seat, but she waited for him to speak. She was curious, perhaps in a judgmental way, about what the first personal words would be to her after fourteen years. "I'm sorry?" "I know I messed up?"

"How have you been, Brooke?"

That was what he started with? A question as if he'd just seen a college roommate? Not a woman he swore he'd marry someday?

Brooke had to draw a breath from lashing out with a lengthy, insult-riddled response.

"Fine, now," she said. "I see you have been better than just fine. I'm not sure why you're back in town, seeing as how it hasn't given you everything good in life."

"The good parts it hasn't given me are gone," he said, rubbing his ring finger.

Was he rubbing it in? No, he didn't even seem to realize what he was doing. He didn't sound resentful, but he also didn't sound like he was desperate to win whoever she was back.

Brooke drew in a breath. Luke had made his own choices, and he would live with whatever consequences they brought.

Right?

"Hmm," she finally murmured. "How long are you in town for? A year? Or are you back for good?"

Luke pursed his lips and gave a small smile.

"Probably permanently," he said. "I will never pretend to predict the future, but Papaw's not doing great. Mimi can handle some of the work on a short-term basis, but the time when my brothers and I will need to assume operations and ownership is sooner rather than later."

"Oh."

Brooke felt a pang of guilt. As much as she resented seeing Luke right now, she would never utter anything harsh against Mr. or Mrs. Walker. His brothers, maybe they could be goofy and overbearing, but those two were impeachable.

She did not know much about Mr. Walker's condition, but granted, she herself had also only moved back this summer, and as far as she could tell, none of Luke's brothers had come back to town.

It also told Brooke she needed to stop pretending that she could act like this meeting had never happened or that she'd only have to tolerate Luke for a short period. Like it or not—mostly not—she would have to be back around him a lot more.

"It seems like so much has changed about this town," Luke said. "I was driving in, and—"

"It's growing and evolving," Brooke said, happy to have a relatively neutral topic to talk about. "You know how Bozeman used to be this secret that only a few people knew about, making it mostly safe for those of us who were born and grew up here? Well, it's quickly becoming the hot spot to move to. Fortunately, that makes us the new secret cool spot. Growing enough to add some new places, but not so rapidly that it's an additional California city."

Luke chuckled at that. She didn't know how much they still agreed on, but one thing they both loved was being a part of country living; her time at UCLA and Los Angeles had shown her she never wanted to live in a big city again.

"You don't seem to have changed, though," Luke said, a small smile forming at the corners of his lips. "You're still the same smart, sweet girl that I... from back in the day."

Oh, how that made Brooke swoon. She felt a burning excitement in her gut, and her arms felt weak. A compliment from Luke Walker could still make Brooke want to melt where she was, needing to be picked up by Luke.

And then she realized that was a problem in itself, and she quickly steeled herself.

"Thanks," she said, though she could not help the smile that formed, even though she repressed it quickly enough.

"Daddy! Can we order now? I'm starving!"

Brooke had not even noticed Luke's daughter returning from the bathroom. Luke laughed and pulled his daughter into a gentle headlock, rubbing her head.

"Yes, we can, and we can even get some food to take back to Mimi and Papaw's," he said. "Just don't eat it all at once."

"I won't!"

She stood back up and hurried to the booth. Luke met Brooke's eye one more time, and gosh darn it, no matter how much she told herself this was a bad idea, she kept his gaze and welcomed the feeling.

"It was good to see you, Brooke," he said. *Are you about to... ask me...* "I'm sure I will see you around."

A part of Brooke felt disappointed. But no, this was for the best. She forced most of herself to be grateful she would not get hurt again.

"Yes, I'm sure you will," she said.

Luke nodded his head and walked back to his daughter. All this encounter had done was create a thousand more questions.

Why did Luke have a daughter but not a ring on his finger?

Why did she both hate seeing him and feel the same rush of excitement as before?

Why was she equally conflicted about having young Montana in her class this fall?

And most of all, what would happen next?

No, Brooke thought as she turned her gaze to her papers. That ship had sailed. Even if Luke was single and looking, even if Montana became her teacher's pet and the model student, she needed to focus on what mattered most in her life—her mother and her work.

The chance to marry Luke Walker and start a family was over.

Right? *Right, Lord?*

3

LUKE

$\mathcal{A}$lthough Luke had intended to take his time at Bacon & Bakin', the sight of his first love had made his stomach roil with so many emotions that he changed course.

"Tana," he said as he sat down in the booth. "Why don't we get this food to go so we can see Mimi and Papaw sooner?"

"But I'm hungry, Daddy!" she pouted. "And you won't let me eat in the truck."

"It's fine. You can eat in the truck."

"Really?"

Lord, what was the sight of Brooke Young doing to him? There were few rules that Luke was as strict on as not eating in his truck; he'd wanted to teach Montana the need to understand what would inevitably get dirty through hard work and what needed to remain pristine and clean. And now, he was throwing out that rule like bread covered in mold.

"Yes, it's fine," Luke said. "But just this once. We've driven a long way to see your grandparents, and then we won't have long drives like this for a while."

"OK! I'll be clean, Daddy."

"I know you will, Tana," he said with a smile. "Now look at the menu and figure out what you want."

He already knew the answer—chocolate chip pancakes. But he needed a moment to process what had just happened.

Brooke Young. His first love. The woman he was sure to marry. Even when he left for college in Washington, he was sure they would make the long-distance challenge work. His parents had been through far more tumultuous challenges, and their marriage had *never* suffered.

And then… he and Brooke just kind of crumbled.

If he thought long enough, Luke knew he could find rational reasons why their relationship had failed. The distance had proved more difficult than he thought. As soon as she discussed the idea of going to UCLA, the distance became an even greater issue, to say nothing about what Luke thought of the dangers of her going to Los Angeles, though by that point, they were already all but done. As discussions about career plans began, with Luke wanting to develop skills for further developing the ranch's business ventures and Brooke wanting to become a teacher, it became evident that if they remained together, someone was going to make a difficult sacrifice.

But those were all just excuses. Luke knew if he had truly been a good man, he would have prioritized his love for Brooke above all else. He would have sacrificed the superficial desires for their future, and he would have made it work.

Instead, they broke up, he moped through most of college, then he met Chelsea, and—

"Daddy?"

Luke came out of his head and looked at his daughter. Embarrassed that he'd gotten so distracted in her presence, he apologized and looked down at the menu.

"Were you thinking about Mommy?"

Luke sighed. *Time and place, Montana*, he thought. It wasn't that he hadn't had the hard conversations with Montana, but he didn't like Brooke being able to overhear everything.

Actually, he didn't know how he felt about that. The only thing he knew for sure was he needed to get to his parents' ranch as soon as possible; the other emotions he could figure out later.

"A little," he said, "but let's save that for later, OK, Tana?"

Montana nodded. Luke could always tell when she was hiding something because her nods, instead of swinging like a pendulum, went up and down once and stopped cold. Normally, he'd say something.

But today, he just mussed her hair, smiled, and said he loved her.

A few quiet minutes later, Mrs. Baker brought out their food in to-go boxes. Luke left two twenty-dollar bills, more than enough to cover their meal, but he wanted Mrs. Baker to have some more—for all the times she had provided extra sides and drinks to him and his brothers, he still owed her way more.

Just as he got to the exit, he glanced back at Brooke. Lord, she was still so beautiful. Older, but more graceful and stronger.

She turned her head, and he hurried to his truck before he gave the wrong impression.

But then again, was his actual impression not that he still liked her? That a part of him still wanted to return to the good old days?

IT TOOK ONLY fifteen minutes to get to the Hope Valley Ranch, but those fifteen minutes were enough to put Luke's soul back at ease. There was just something about being along a straight road, having plains around you, snowcapped mountains in the far distance, and almost no houses in between here and there that made it so special. The further out you went, the further away neighbors got.

Luke had always loved the town of Greenville and its inhabitants; Mrs. Baker was far from the only name he would come to reacquaint himself with in the coming weeks and months. But he also loved the isolation of the two-thousand acre ranch and how it kept his family close.

Maybe it explains why Brooke came back. She may not have grown up on a ranch, but...

Luke shook his head. But unlike at the restaurant, Montana didn't say anything to interrupt him. Perhaps she was thinking about her mother or her teacher. Though she could be plenty exuberant, as most eight-year-olds were, Luke also knew she was ultimately more likely to turn into a reader than she was a speaker.

"Here we are," Luke finally said as they turned left on the ranch.

"Wow!" Montana said, as it hit home that this was not only her first time in her home state, but visiting Mimi and Papaw in her home state.

He had tried to explain the sheer size of the ranch to her, but some sights could only be experienced. He loved the look on her face at the stone pillars, the wooden beams, and the ornate arch, almost creating the appearance of entering an old church. Luke would never dare call the ranch holy, but if anything secular came close, this was it.

Thank you, Lord, for bringing us back here, he thought silently. It was good to be home; not to be at the house he lived at the time, and not to be in the residence he paid rent or a mortgage on. This was *home*.

But then he saw dilapidated, brown grass down the road, and a frown formed on his face.

"Oh, look! Sheep! And horses!"

Luke laughed, grateful for the distraction from the unusual

sight. To him, the sheep and horses were as much a part of the ranch as silverware was as part of a kitchen—they mattered and needed tending to, but they were just a part of life. *To see the world as a child does...*

"That's Storm," he said, pointing to a black horse grazing close to the truck. "Your Uncle Jesse got her as the oldest in the family. Now that he's working in Wyoming, though, she's kind of a family pet."

"Can I ride her?"

"At some point, I'm sure we can make it happen," he said, knowing full well Jesse would never say no to his little girl, despite doing so to most everyone else.

"What about the sheep? Do they have names?"

Luke chuckled.

"Most of them, no," he said, "as we have too many of them to keep count. But there is one we call Benny, because he's different."

"Different?"

A series of memories flashed in Luke's mind at the many instances that someone would yell at Benny and laugh in the same breath.

"Let's just say 'the dog ate it' may turn into 'Benny ate it' if you don't do your homework for Ms. Young."

Montana laughed at the joke. Luke smiled, both at her reaction and how Brooke's name brought back a warm feeling. He tried to fight it, telling him he needed to treat Brooke as his daughter's teacher and nothing more, but that was a battle he knew he'd lose with great frequency.

"Benny would be an old man now. Most sheep don't live past twelve years old, and he's going on fifteen now. So he may be past his chewing days."

But knowing the good Lord had a sense of humor, old Benny probably hadn't finished his chewing days.

They pulled up to the homestead, and though Luke tried his

darndest to keep his face neutral, he couldn't help but notice that cracks had formed in the wooden facade. Such cracks did not signal the impending doom of the house, but they did suggest that, despite what Mimi and Papaw had said on the phone, Papaw's condition was bad enough to prevent him from repairing relatively simple problems.

"It's so beautiful," Montana said. "You grew up in this home, Daddy?"

"Sure did," he said. "My four brothers and I. It was crowded."

"Five of you!" Montana exclaimed. "That would be crazy!"

"It was!" Luke said as he thought about how, depending on his father's condition, it was likely to be crazy again soon enough—and not in a fun way.

He parked the car to the right of his father's 1993 Dodge Ram 1500—a fact that he couldn't believe, for it suggested the vehicle still worked—got out, and walked around to help Montana with the drop down. He was pleased and a little relieved to see that despite the potential for crumbs and chips, he saw very little food particles on the ground.

They walked up to the front door and knocked.

"Mimi? Papaw?" Luke said before he opened the front door gradually. "It's Luke and Montana! We're home!"

"Hello, Luke!" his mother shouted from the kitchen.

Montana didn't wait, rushing through the house to hug her grandmother. Luke's heart warmed at the sight; for as uncomfortable—or perhaps just unexpected, not uncomfortable—seeing the old face of Brooke was, seeing this old face and Montana's reaction reminded him he had done well coming home.

"Hi, dear," she said as she kissed Luke on the cheek and hugged him tight. "Papaw's upstairs taking a nap. Although you can peek your head in and say hello if he's awake."

"Sure thing," he said. "Montana, will you catch Mimi up on how the drive was?"

His daughter instantly agreed, none the wiser that he did not want his daughter to see his face when he saw what he expected to see.

"Wait just a minute," Mimi said. "You said you were going to be here this morning! It's almost noon! Did the geese cause a traffic jam at the river?"

Luke chuckled. Such a traffic "jam" had only happened once, but it had become his mother's go-to question when someone was late.

"We stopped to take photos since it was Montana's first trip down I-90," he said, "and we stopped at Bacon & Bakin.'"

"Oh? Did you see Mrs. Baker?"

"I did," Luke said, drawing in a breath, "and Brooke Young."

His mother, in the process of stirring what looked like shredded chicken, paused and turned a curious eye toward Luke. She had always been good about not prying too much into their relationship, but this was different.

"And?" she said with a budding smile.

"And we talked. Nothing more."

"Hmm," Mimi said, nodding her head once—just like Montana did. "I've seen her around in town the last couple of months. She's never with anyone, you know. You should pay her a visit."

Luke laughed a little too loudly for that one.

"You laugh, dear, but your brothers are out of town, and most of your high school friends haven't moved back yet. She may be your only outlet to escape the elder Walkers."

Luke laughed again, this time coming from a mixture of hope, nerves, and unease. He wasn't sure what the predominant emotion was.

"I'm sure I'll be talking to her again since she's teaching Montana this school year," Luke said, "but we can talk about that more soon. I need to go see Papaw."

He kissed his mother on the cheek once more, then moved

to the stairs as Montana and Mimi started talking about all the sheep and horses on the ranch. He held his breath as he went to his parents' bedroom door and knocked.

"Come in, son."

He heard his father, but it lacked almost none of the strength it usually had. *The lung cancer's taking away everything he has...*

He pushed open the door.

And to his surprise, Papaw was standing, opening the curtains to the bedroom, fully clothed. His face was a little more gaunt than usual, and cancer treatments had taken away his hair, but the face of dying, he did not have.

"What?" he said, his voice raspy. "You think I'm going to let cancer keep me in bed all day like a teenager? As long as the good Lord says it's not time to go, I'm not going to waste his gift."

"Papaw," Luke said.

Unsure what more to say, he went over and hugged his father. The embrace lasted a little longer than usual, each patting the other on the back more than once. For a moment, Luke thought his eyes might be getting moist.

But then his father pulled back.

"Write your eulogy for me when I'm actually dead," he said, drawing relieved laughter from his son. "And besides, it won't do me any good to teach you how to run this ranch when I'm lying in bed."

"I know, but—"

"No buts, son," his father said. "Build for a new life, be present with the living, and celebrate those who God blessed with life now gone."

Luke nodded.

"Now, what's this I hear downstairs about you running into that old lover of yours?"

Luke sighed. It was going to be quite the year ahead.

4

BROOKE

As Brooke left Bacon & Bakin' about twenty minutes after Luke and Montana left, she looked to the right at St. Luke's Church.

As a child, she and her parents had attended every Sunday at nine a.m. The only justification for missing church was a contagious illness, and she was expected to make up for it on a weekday service. But attending church, for her, was far from an obligation; it was her refuge, a space that she had found solace in both as a place for prayer and for speaking to the local pastor, Pastor Paul O'Connell.

Prayer and Pastor O'Connell had gone a long way to helping her pull out of the depression she found herself in after her relationship with Luke ended. Pastor O'Connell, especially, had shown her that the way out of her funk was not to "go have fun" or to "date a lot of men" but to find God and to find peace within herself. Moreover, she had learned to forgive Luke, or at least she thought she had.

Seeing him, though, with a daughter of his own left a lot of unanswered questions and unclear emotions. She considered stepping into St. Luke's for a brief prayer, but she needed to get home to her mother. So instead, she said a quick prayer in the car, hoping for a resolution on how best to handle Luke and her own emotions and feelings the next time she saw him.

Unfortunately, she did not get an answer to her prayer by the time she got home. She would have to wait until later.

BROOKE PUSHED OPEN the unlocked door to her and her mother's small home. She looked at the photos of her childhood and wistfully smiled. Her father was a pilot, and he still cared and loved for her mother, but her recent medical needs meant he could not retire—which, unfortunately, meant he also could not be home for long stretches of time.

She then saw the photo of her graduating from UCLA, just a couple of short months before she would go work for Teach for America at an urban school in Sacramento. The experience had been one of the most difficult experiences of her life, from a professional and cultural perspective alike. But it had also honed her patience even more and taught her how to overcome seemingly impossible obstacles.

Like how Luke and I...

She shook off the thought and went to the kitchen, where she saw Lola, the caretaker that helped her mother when she or her father were not home.

"Hey, Lola," Brooke said. "How's Mom?"

"As fine today as I've seen her in recent months," Lola said. "She seemed to remember most everything, and the only moment she got irritable was when her morning waffles didn't have enough syrup on them."

"Think that would make most of us irritable," Brooke said, the kind of joke that got polite but not exaggerated laughter. "You remember school starts this Monday, and Dad won't be home until September, so unfortunately, I may need you to stick around longer."

"That's fine! It's what you brought me here for."

Brooke smiled and silently thanked the Lord for giving her mother a good caretaker. She had never expected being in her early thirties and having to care for her mother so relatively early in life, but all things considered, they were making the most of it.

"Then I'll see you at seven a.m. next Monday?"

"Yes," Lola said.

Brooke handed her a check for the week's services—an amount that would leave her with no spending money, but thankfully, with the mortgage on her parents' house paid for, no student loans due to scholarships, and only a small car payment, she wasn't in the worst place financially. Lola thanked her, stepped outside, and left Brooke to collapse on the couch in exhaustion.

For the next several minutes, Brooke lay on her stomach, trying to make sense of her feelings on the matter. She tried to remain as objective as possible as she ran through everything.

First, yes, Luke had been polite in front of her. His daughter seemed to like him. He did not have a ring on his finger. He had shown some regret when her voice suggested her frustration with him. If he was pretending to be distraught over how things ended, he was doing a darn good job of it.

But all the objectivity she could muster vanished as her emotions overcame her.

He'd promised her he'd start a family with her, and then by Christmas of that letter, they'd broken up!

He said that he would tell her so many things in person, and she was still waiting fourteen years later!

He'd said that he'd come back soon, and only the eternal Lord thought of fourteen years as "soon enough." What a bunch of malarkey!

Brooke calmed herself down. The solution seemed obvious, didn't it? She would treat Montana the same as her other students. She would treat Luke like any other parent in the town. And she would move on with her life, caring for her mother and trying to find love with someone that wouldn't lie to her.

But he didn't lie to you, did he? Things changed. You were the one who initially suggested ending things.

Suddenly, just treating Luke "like any other parent in the town" didn't work as well as she had hoped. She was surprised to find herself so emotional that her eyes welled, but she stopped herself from actually crying. No, tears were not for situations she just needed to get a hold of.

She rolled onto her back, closed her eyes, and prayed.

"Dear Lord, I know you have much more important things to handle. But please, give me the grace to deal with Luke with dignity and honor. Help me help Montana reach her full potential."

She paused, hesitating to speak, but knowing in prayer, she needed to reveal her full truth.

"And give me the courage to know if there's any reason to give him a second chance. In your name, Amen."

She opened her eyes. As if on cue, she heard her mother calling for her. Feeling better after her prayer, Brooke rose off the couch and walked down the hallway to the living room. Though the master bedroom and Brooke's bedroom were all upstairs, they had turned the living room into a makeshift bedroom because of her mother's stroke.

Mom sat against her bedrest, reading a cozy beach novel with her right hand; her left had lost its use and, according to the doctors, would not likely regain its capabilities in the near future. She had a smile on her face, confirming what Lola had said. Some days, she would scream; on her worst days, she would curse in ways that would make Brooke blush. She knew in those moments that it was not her true mom uttering such foul language, but it still brought her to tears.

"Hello, Brookey," she said, using her affectionate nickname for her only child. "You look like you've had quite the day."

Brooke saw no reason to lie to her mother. Not only was it wrong, anything embarrassing that Brooke would admit to would likely be forgotten shortly after. She never intended to manipulate or trick her mother, but it gave an additional layer of comfort in admitting things.

"I saw Luke Walker at the breakfast diner. He's... he has a daughter. But he's apparently single."

She wondered how her mother would react. To her surprise, though, her mother appeared saddened by the news.

"I know your relationship ended poorly, but Luke was always a good man. I never heard that boy curse or forget to hold the door for you. I doubt he had a child out of wedlock."

Mom grimaced.

"Have you talked to Pastor O'Connell about it?"

"No, I wanted to get home to you. But I probably will at some point."

"You shouldn't have been in such a rush to see an old lady like me," her mom said, putting her book down to wave with her good arm.

"Mom, you are my—"

"Priority one, I know, dear, I know," she said, "but you can't be spending your entire life revolving around me. The good Lord has blessed me with a wonderful husband and you. This," she said, gesturing to her body, "is merely an ailment of my physical body that was bound to turn to dust at some point."

Though Brooke was a woman of faith, it still never felt good to hear her mother talk so casually about dying. She had heard through the town that Luke's father was in much worse shape; that was a man who was probably not going to live through the end of the year. Her mother had obviously suffered a debilitating stroke, but it didn't foretell an impending death any time soon.

"So, are you saying I should give Luke a second chance?"

"I'm saying you should spend enough time around him to see if he's worth having a second chance," her mother said. "If he's not, then you should spend enough time around other fine young men to find someone to start a family with. You won't get married to any of these nurses, you know."

She laughed at her own joke. Brooke gave a short chuckle, happy to indulge her mother if it meant a temporary reprieve from her pain.

"Even if I do that, though, you know I will not leave you here by your lonesome self while Dad is gone."

"Bah! Lola more than entertains me while you teach. And when your father is here, well, I have enough things to stay on top of that absent-minded fool."

Her mother smiled as she joked, and Brooke knew full well everything said was endearing.

"You're here for the night; that's fine. Just be open to the Lord's will. Sometimes, it may be the very thing we think we don't want."

Brooke nodded. She still could not wrap her head around *him* being the one that He wanted her to have.

But.

But if they could overcome their past, process it, and put it behind them… if they found true fulfillment, not the lust rush of teenagers, in each other… if, if, if…

It wasn't impossible to imagine a happily ever after. And for right now, Brooke figured that's all her mom wanted.

"Just put something on besides HGTV," she said with a smirk. "You and Lola have made me watch that channel so much it's turned an interest into boredom!"

This time, Brooke's laugh was genuine.

DAYS PASSED, but Brooke did not see Luke again. Not on Friday, when she went to the school to prepare her classroom for the first day of classes; not on Saturday, when she spent her last free day hiking Helena National Forest; and not on Sunday, when she took her mother to church before grabbing ice cream at Green Cream.

Her mother never made any further mention of it, although Brooke was a little surprised not to see Luke at the Sunday service. It was plausible that he would go to an earlier service than nine a.m.; in a town full of country folk, the seven-thirty a.m. service was always well attended compared to the city services.

Nevertheless, with Monday morning came the first day of school. As Brooke got into her red Nissan Rogue Sport, she told herself to compartmentalize her feelings. Her kids and only her kids deserved her full attention today, at least until about four p.m. At least on the first day of second grade, it wasn't like she was going to teach economics or advanced mathematics; she always made the first day about catching up on everyone's summer, explaining goals for the year, and introducing new kids.

Which included Montana.

Luke's daughter.

But far from drawing a sigh or a swallow from Brooke, she smiled at the opportunity to test herself.

She pulled into the parking lot of Greenville Elementary at six a.m. sharp, making sure she would be awake to greet the students when they arrived. Sunrise had not yet hit, but there was more than enough light for her to see.

And with that light, she saw Luke Walker leaning against his pickup truck, his daughter in the passenger's seat, reading comfortably.

5

LUKE

*A*wake for a good hour by that point and with Montana comfortably distracted by a book, Luke had his arms folded and one foot on the truck's sidebar. He knew no other parents would be here this early, and even if they were, who cared? What was wrong with a parent who loved their only child so much they wanted to chat briefly with their teacher for the year?

Brief chat, my Lord, he thought, chuckling at his own half-lies.

Brooke caught his eye almost the instant he pulled into the lot, so he remained where he was, not wanting to give the impression of an angry parent. She pulled up and parked about three spots to the right of his truck, forcing him to come around —but also allowing her to stay close to him and watch him as she prepared to get out. However she wanted to do it, Luke would work with.

He'd waited almost fourteen years to have a deeper conversation with her again; what was another fourteen seconds?

When she finally got out, the first thing Luke saw was just how beautiful she was. The morning skies illuminated her luscious brown hair and her matching brown eyes, but it was the way she was dressed—professional, with black slacks and a red top, yet also eye-catching. Her kids, of course, were too young to think of her as anything other than "Ms. Young," but to Luke, oh, Lord have mercy.

"What the heck are you doing here so early, Luke? Shouldn't Montana be taking the bus with how far you have to drive?"

The second thing he noticed was her harsh tone. But it wasn't genuinely harsh; no, it sounded like someone puffing their chest up to sound tough, but in doing so, making it obvious they were hiding something.

"Normally, yes, but given what we've been through, I'm taking the father-daughter time while my parents are still running the ranch," he said. "I came here to talk to you. Or, if you don't have time, to ask you to join me for some afternoon fly-fishing, a hike, or just a walk around town."

He said those words with a lot more certainty than he felt. His father had taught him all his life how a raised chin, shoulders pulled back, and a lack of tension went a long way in making your words sound real.

But in reality, Luke feared rejection.

It wasn't the kind of fear that kept him up at night, though different thoughts about Brooke accomplished that anyway. Rather, it was like the little devil in his head, nagging at him in quiet moments that there was another shoe to drop at some point. That little demon would remind him that because of their past, it wasn't if but when the shoe dropped.

Luke just hoped that he got to spend long enough with Brooke that he could bend over to catch that shoe before it fell on their second chance.

"You came to talk to me before sunrise outside my school," she deadpanned. "Do you know how many bad news reports start with that setup? 'An angry parent stood outside his child's school today, prepared to be anything but the teacher's pet. More at six!'"

Luke's smile grew at that joke. For a millisecond, a smile also formed on Brooke's face, but she suppressed it.

"How can I have anything to talk to you about your teaching skills when you haven't even had the first day? And besides, Montana wouldn't stop talking about you after Bacon & Bakin'."

"Really?" Brooke said, her face softening instantly.

"Yes. But I'm not here to talk about her. I'm here to talk about us."

His face pulled taut. Hers did the same, albeit without malicious intent.

"Let's just tackle it straight on," Luke said, drawing in a breath. "I know I made some awful mistakes fourteen years ago. I know I promised you things that have never come to pass. I know I made you believe we were to be forever, and we didn't even make it to Christmas. I am sorry for that, Brooke. I do not know how well the fourteen years have treated you since, but I know I started it off on the wrong foot for you."

There was much more Luke wanted to say. He wanted to tell her about why he was a single man with a daughter. He wanted to ask her on a date—not just to catch up, but to try to rekindle that fire. He could play it cool and pretend that he was not really attracted to her, but he had not gotten Brooke in the first place by "playing it cool."

And besides, how could he tell his daughter that God favored those who knew how to balance caution and boldness when he did not exhibit the latter?

"Luke," Brooke said, drawing out his name.

Several seconds passed. Brooke looked at a car driving by on the main road, but the car did not turn in. They were alone and would be for at least the next ten to fifteen seconds. Luke would have loved to know what was going on inside her mind.

"I don't think I can say this enough, Luke," she said, "but you *crushed* me all that time ago. I appreciate you came here to apologize. But what would you do if I came to you and apologized fourteen years after I forgot to call you back? What would the Lord think?"

"It depends on if you were genuine or not," Luke said. "I know you have a lot of questions. But understand, this is my first time back in Greenville since that summer, that last time we were together. I could have emailed, texted, written, I know. But that's not the same as looking into your eyes and expressing the truth. A text takes no courage but a few seconds. Coming face-to-face and seeing your eyes, with all their beauty and sorrow and hope for joy... that's what I was waiting for."

At least Brooke was not pushing him away. Luke felt the next words catch in his throat, so he simply stopped talking. Brooke sighed.

"You are genuine, aren't you?" Brooke said.

Luke nodded, again deciding against saying anything.

"Here's the problem," she said before taking a deep breath and exhaling slowly. "You seem sincere. You're still handsome. But..."

6

BROOKE

THIRTEEN-AND-A-HALF YEARS AGO

*B*rooke had just finished her final exam for her penultimate high school semester. She felt certain that she had aced her calculus exam, and with news from the day before that Montana State-Bozeman would offer her a full ride if she wanted, the future felt as open as it could have been.

But all she wanted to do was cry.

It had been about a month since her relationship with Luke had fallen apart, but this wasn't just any relationship falling apart. No, this was much worse than when she and Bryan ended their middle school relationship, something that barely qualified as a "relationship," considering they had never even held hands.

He was *the one*.

Brooke was so darn sure of it. They'd dated for the past three years with nary a fight—even the moments that could have gotten tense often dissolved into laughter—and Luke was unabashed about the idea of marriage. The only thing—the *only* thing—that prevented him from proposing before he left for college was his father's insistence that he see the world a little before coming back home.

And who was she to complain? Her father, a pilot, had said the same thing. She knew neither father meant "see other people" when they said "see the world." Her mind had brimmed with curiosity about what places like Hawaii, France, and Italy were like.

But apparently, that had been the curse to end their love.

And what's worse, she had been the one to end it.

She told herself that she may have said the words, but his lack of communication, his distancing, and his prioritizing other activities in Spokane meant he had frayed their knot enough that it had to be cut. She repeated them over and over at night and while studying.

But it did not take away who had been the one to say, "I can't do this."

As she stepped out of her high school, with only one semester left before going to either Montana State-Bozeman or somewhere in California, she headed for her dad's truck. He was flying somewhere in Asia, and he trusted her enough to drive it within the confines of Greenville while he traveled. She welcomed this because it meant that neither parent had to see her so distraught.

When she got into her dad's car, she could no longer hold it in. She burst into tears, sobbing uncontrollably. Nothing could comfort her; there was no more school, no more exams to distract her from the emotions bubbling inside of her.

She thought of what could have been. She wondered if there might be another chance down the line.

But this pain... it was unimaginable. It almost felt sinful to say, but the death of her grandparents had hurt less; they had made it to their late eighties and had repeatedly said they did not fear death, and in fact welcomed a chance to see the Lord. There was no such solace here.

When Brooke eventually looked up, she saw some of her classmates also streaming out of the school, having finished their exam a few short minutes after her. Brooke did not waste any time turning the truck on and getting the heck out of the lot. She didn't want anyone's sympathy or pained looks.

She just wanted to drive.

Daddy, forgive me, she thought as she just started driving north up 287. She had no destination in mind. She just… drove.

She got as far north as Helena before she turned around. She still didn't have a destination; it was just as likely she'd drive all the way to Yellowstone before she turned back around for Greenville.

All the same, there was something soothing, if not comforting, about being out on the road and seeing the glory of God in the open skies and the Montana terrain. She felt extraordinarily blessed to spend her whole life here, and even though she agreed with her father about seeing the world, she knew no matter what happened in college and right after, she would find her way back here eventually.

Her long drive allowed her to see things she had not noticed before, such as small off-trails for hiking, the way the Missouri River flowed, or even where elk and bears crossed the road. She wasn't expecting such sights to provide some divine revelation, but she was not looking for one. She just needed to be alone.

She never made it all the way to Yellowstone; she didn't even get as far as Bozeman. In fact, she only drove about two miles south of the east side of town, with the newly built Montana Motel about half a mile east of the church setting the furthest boundary before turning around. There was one person she did not mind seeing in this ragged, beaten-down state.

Pastor O'Connell.

She pulled into the church parking lot, grateful that there weren't any other cars there but the pastor's. She wiped the tears still left in her eyes, cleaned her cheeks as best as she could, and cleared her throat. She stepped out of her father's truck, walked up to the chapel steps, drew in a short breath, and gently pushed open the doors.

Inside the chapel, complete with stained glass windows from back to front showcasing the fourteen stations of the cross, Pastor O'Connell cleaned some of the pews, a task he welcomed to feel more attached to the church. His hair had started to gray, but he still looked youthful despite having been a pastor Brooke's entire life. She had heard her father joke about Pastor O'Connell being "ninety in the mind and nine in the face" and though she hadn't gotten it when she first heard it, gray hair aside, she certainly understood now.

Brooke took only a couple of steps forward before Pastor O'Connell turned around.

"Brooke Young?" he said, surprise on his face but calmness in his voice. "What brings you here, my child?"

Brooke opened her mouth to speak, only to realize how ridiculous her request would send. Pastor O'Connell dealt with real tragedy—the death of grandparents and children, marriage struggles, and crises of faith. What was a silly high school breakup to someone who literally dealt in life, death, and the afterlife?

"Nothing," she said, forming a weak smile. "I just came to pray."

"And what did you come to pray about?" he asked, still sounding so kind.

Brooke sighed.

"Luke and I are no longer dating, and, I know it's silly, it's just high school and college kids, but I can't…"

She trailed off as she saw genuine sorrow on the pastor's face.

"You care?" she asked.

"My child, pain is pain. Grief is grief. It is not my job to judge on God's behalf, but to meet each parishioner at their level. If this is what is causing you great anguish, please, speak.

Do not fear that your problems are too small or petty; we all were once your age."

A warm smile followed, as if Pastor O'Connell knew nothing was more likely to drive away a teenager than the phrase "once your age." That self-awareness and the trust Brooke had in him kept her there, and she started to speak.

"I was so sure we were going to be married," she said, "and now, he stopped speaking to me so much that I felt I had no choice but to end it. I... I don't want to blame him for the end, but it felt like I have no choice. And I can't help but feel abandoned."

Her voice cracked near the end of her words. Pastor O'Connell came over, gently put a hand on her shoulder, and waved her over to the pews, where they sat side-by-side.

"God never has, is not, and never will abandon you," Pastor O'Connell said. "Certainly, find refuge in Him and the Bible. But even in seeking refuge in Him, we may still feel sorrow and pain at what has happened."

Brooke sobbed, but at least she did not turn into a tearful mess like she had in her father's truck.

"I know that such a task may seem impossible, but I would ask that, in time, you find it in your heart to forgive him."

"Forgive?"

"Do not mistake forgiveness to mean permissibility. We can forgive someone while not condoning their actions. We can forgive someone while setting boundaries to ensure that we do not get harmed or that they do not repeat the same mistake."

We can forgive someone while setting boundaries. Pastor O'Connell continued to speak, but Brooke honed in on those words as if they were the path to freedom for the pain she felt. She could forgive Luke. And then she could set boundaries to make sure she never got hurt again.

But... how?

Any attempt to say "I forgive you" would be the most disingenuous thing she'd ever said or thought. The boundaries part was, surprisingly, just as difficult; that she would just throw up a fence around herself and say "never again" to Luke felt so final, so cold. So sad. She'd been his everything, he hers.

But this pain... Lord, it hurt worse than *anything*.

"... come see me after service on Sunday, OK? Brooke?"

"Sorry," she said, shaking her head. "I... I am sorry."

Pastor O'Connell put a reassuring hand on her shoulder again.

"Believe me, you are not the first person to get lost in their head as I speak," he said with a gentle chuckle. "Think about what I have said, and if you have any further questions, come and see me after service on Sunday."

Brooke nodded.

"I will leave you to pray," Pastor O'Connell said as he rose. "I will be cleaning here. You are welcome to stay as long as you need. Find strength in the Lord, Brooke."

With that, the good pastor did exactly as he said, returning to the pew he had been cleaning. Brooke lowered the kneeler before her, knelt forward, and folded her hands.

"Lord, I vow to always follow your ways. I vow to always be faithful to you and follow your will."

She hesitated for a half-second. It seemed somehow *wrong* to say what she was about to say. But her heart ached so much; the mere thought of what had happened could bring her to tears. Pastor O'Connell's words had placated her at the moment, but now, sitting here, she could not help herself.

She needed to set boundaries.

"And I vow never to return to Luke."

Unless your will suggests otherwise.

7

LUKE

*L*uke had an idea that he had caused Brooke pain when their relationship had ended. He did not dispute the idea that his actions had put her in a spot where she had to be the "bad guy" and end their relationship. Almost nothing she had said was unexpected.

But that she had prayed to never fall into a relationship with him…

That hurt Luke more than anything since he'd made the fateful decision to return to Greenville, Montana.

"Brooke…"

He swallowed after hearing the story. He needed to act quickly. Other cars had entered the parking lot, and while they all maintained a respectful distance from Luke and Brooke, he knew they would talk.

"Look, I'm not here to ask you on a date or for a second chance. That was true even before you told me what happened that December day. And I'm not going to beg—I know you're better than that. I'm just asking for you to talk. Right now, probably not a great time. But what time do you get off?"

Luke could see the long look of doubt on Brooke's face. He

braced himself for a rejection or for a scolding, and he wondered how he'd find someone else worth pursuing in this town. He loved the town and his place in it, but—

"I can talk at five p.m.," she finally said.

A long silence formed. Luke had to fight to avoid smiling; he did not want to come across as manipulative. But the prospect of spending time with her excited him.

"Fly-fishing up the Missouri?" he asked. "Actually, I know you were never a huge fan, we can—"

"Fly-fishing would be good," Brooke said, much to Luke's surprise. "But you have to promise me you'll do it somewhere quiet and remote. If we're going to talk, it's just going to be us. I don't want any of Mrs. Baker's regulars or the other teachers to be eavesdropping."

Luke was not about to argue with those terms, especially since he knew how far north he had to go to avoid the worst of the fly-fishing crowds. Plus, it being a Monday made it all the easier.

"You have yourself a deal," he said. "I will meet you in the parking lot at five, and you can follow me from there?"

Brooke nodded.

"Great," Luke said, followed by a long pause. "It's... good to see you again, Brooke. Truly."

"Don't forget your daughter."

Luke chuckled. Already, she'd moved on to her professional duties. But that was fine. He would have a chance to address her personal concerns in a little under eleven hours.

"Right," he said, "thanks, Brooke."

"Mmhmm," Brooke said as she turned and walked toward the school, though Luke absolutely noticed her taking more than one look back as he turned around and helped Montana out of the passenger's side of the truck.

Luke couldn't stop smiling. God truly was good. Even if this never led to anything romantic, even if Luke did nothing more than shake Brooke's hand at a parent-teacher conference, at least he had gotten a second chance.

Not a second chance at love, not a second chance at happily ever, but just a second chance to talk. If more followed, well, Luke would not pretend he didn't hope for that. But right now, he just thanked the good Lord that Brooke saw enough to meet with him once again.

"Thanks for your patience, Tana," he said as he opened the car door. "Daddy needed to talk to Ms. Young about some things."

"Do you love Ms. Young, Daddy?"

Luke laughed out loud, not expecting such a blunt question. Then he stammered over his words, struggling to answer without sounding hyperbolic or dishonest.

"In a way, I suppose," Luke said. "But Ms. Young is her own woman, and she is not with me. I need you to promise me you will not say anything about this to the other kids, and I need you to promise me you will respect Ms. Young and do as she says."

"I promise, Daddy."

Luke smiled as he mussed with her hair. He wasn't worried about his daughter getting made fun of for Daddy spending time with the teacher; he just wanted to keep the town gossip to a minimum as long as he could. And as for obeying Ms. Young, well, respecting teachers and elders was a given in the Walker household.

"Now you have a good first day of school, make some friends, and I'll see you at three, OK? When we get back, Mimi and Papaw are going to make sure you do any homework you may get."

"Eww, homework already?"

Ahh, still a kid, Luke thought with another laugh. Practically anything right now, it seemed, could get him to laugh.

"I said that you may get, not that you will get. Now get on with yourself. I love you, Tana."

"I love you, Daddy."

Montana headed to the school doors, paused to make sure no cars were coming, and then disappeared into the school. In a little under two hours, second grade would begin.

It was hard for Luke to decide what was more improbable—that his little girl had already finished kindergarten and first grade or that fourteen years had, in some ways, felt like fourteen weeks.

∼

LUKE SPENT the day handling small tasks around the ranch, including helping repair some of the damage at the house. His father, feeling spry that particular day, participated, though he became winded more easily and could not handle some of the more difficult tasks. It was difficult for Luke to see his father, the strongest man he knew in every sense of the word, have to delegate so much of the labor.

But his father's sense of humor did a wonderful job of keeping the worst of the feelings at bay, such as when, upon not being able to go up a ladder, said, "you ain't ready to handle this inheritance. Get your butt up there." It also, for better and for worse, did a good job of keeping Luke distracted from five p.m. that afternoon.

During the day, he also put in phone and video calls to his four brothers—Jesse, Weston, Sawyer, and Carson. He used the calls as a chance to explain the truth—that their father was in worse condition than he or Mimi was letting on, but that he still had his sense of humor and was relatively far from death's door. All the brothers expressed little surprise, for they all had grown up with the same stoic father and the same mother who pushed anxiety out the back door.

COWBOY'S HOMECOMING

Unfortunately, Luke also knew that it would be difficult to get everyone back together under one roof. Jesse and Weston would come, no problem. But Sawyer was set to deploy to Eastern Europe in the coming weeks, and Carson... well, Carson unfortunately kept his distance from the family.

Nevertheless, once it came time for Luke to pick up his daughter, he put concerns about his family for the next day and headed to school. He promised himself that he would not speak to Brooke unless she spoke to him in the pickup line, not wanting to put any extra attention on her. Knowing the town, word had probably already spread, but there was no reason to accelerate it.

The line moved quick, but Luke supposed he should have expected as much. Here in Greenville, even with the population "boom," the town still had not surpassed two thousand residents; Spokane, where he'd stayed after graduation, had almost a quarter-million people. It made sense that Luke would be picking up his daughter less than fifteen minutes after arriving.

And wouldn't you know it? The good Lord just happened to put Brooke on traffic duty for the end of the day.

"Montana Walker, right?" she said when Luke pulled up.

"Yep, just her."

Luke swore he saw a smile forming on Brooke's lips, like she felt silly asking the question she already knew the full answer to, but he played his part as well, waiting for her to come out. She emerged a few seconds later, but to Luke's concern, she did not wear the usual smile she usually did.

"Some kids made fun of her name," Brooke said as she opened the truck door and helped Montana in. "She's a great kid and listened very well. I'll make sure the kids get punished."

"Understood. Thank you, Ms. Young."

Once more, the two exchanged a smile that, from the outside, simply looked like a friendly teacher-parent interaction. Both of them, Luke understood, knew better.

51

Once Brooke shut the door, Montana sighed.

"Hey, Tana," Luke said. "Do you wanna talk about it?"

Montana shook her head once. Interesting. It meant she did, but wouldn't admit to it. Luke thought about trying to prod more out of her but thought better of it. He decided that if Montana had still not said anything by the time they pulled under the entrance of Hope Valley Ranch, he would ask her.

For now, though, he stayed quiet as he drove his daughter back home. His heart ached for his young daughter to have a rough first day, especially since she had moved to a brand new school where she knew no one. It was great that Brooke liked her and that she was closer to family than ever, but at some point, Montana would look more to her peers than her elders.

He got as far as Grocer's Market, the local grocery store, roughly two-thirds of the way home, when Montana finally spoke.

"They said it's stupid I'm named after the state," she said, looking out the passenger's side window.

Luke had a feeling at her birth that someone, somewhere down the line, would make fun of her name. What he knew—and what he did not say—was he could have given her any name, from as plain as Jane to as symbolic as Montana to as exotic as Ilona, and bullies would have still found something to make fun of.

"How do you feel about your name?"

"I love my name, Daddy," Montana said, quietly drawing an enormous sigh of relief from Luke. "But I don't understand why they don't."

Luke nodded and took a few seconds to form his thoughts. He had always felt like his parents, as great as they were, had given him cliche answers to tough questions in his childhood. The issue with having a stoic father and an avoidant mother was that in tough times, there was no acknowledgment of the toughness.

"Sometimes, there's not a good reason," Luke said. "People do bad things, and even if we knew exactly why, it doesn't ease the pain. I'm sorry you had to experience this on your first day."

"It's OK, Daddy."

"Thank you, Tana, but it's OK to say it hurts," he said. "Just remember this. I named you Montana because of what the name stands for. Strength. Beauty. Grace. Faith. The people of this state love this place, and we are humbled and grateful to God for being here. Kids will not always understand that, but the more time they spend here, the more they will."

Montana looked at her father. She wasn't smiling yet, but the pain in her eyes seemed to have receded.

"It did hurt, Daddy," she said, "but Ms. Young told them to stop, and then she told them if they kept misbehaving, they'd have to do extra homework. That got them to stop!"

She laughed, giving Luke permission to do the same.

"Well, I'm glad Ms. Young stopped things before they worsened. She always…"

He exhaled slowly.

"She always had a way of making sure things didn't get out of hand."

I can't say the same for myself. But at least there's five o'clock today.

"Are you going to see her later? Are you two going to fall back in love?"

"Oh, Lord," Luke said with a laugh. "We've got a long way to go before that happens. But never say never."

"I will not ever say that word."

Luke chuckled again. Montana laughed with him. For at least the hour, all was right.

He could only hope the same good fortune would carry over to five o'clock.

8

BROOKE

Too early in the school year to have assignments to grade, yet not wanting to return home when Lola had promised to watch her mother until seven o'clock at the latest, Brooke remained in the school classroom, reading a mystery novel to pass the time.

She had other options, of course. She could have gone out with some childhood friends who had never left town, like Clara, who owned the bookstore down the road, or like Danielle, who was a real estate agent set to take over her mother's agency when she retired.

But they would ask questions about why she had popped in and why she would need to be somewhere else at five o'clock. And when they learned that Luke Walker was back in the picture, Lord help her. She couldn't decide if they'd be excited for her to have a second chance at that handsome, rugged, charming man… or if they'd cuss his name and promise to protect her from him at all costs.

After all, she wasn't the only one who had dated a Walker before.

Thankfully, none of the other teachers or administrators at

Greenville Elementary stayed around as long as she did, and the few that asked questions accepted her answer of wanting some alone time. Most knew about her mother's condition, and the few that didn't weren't prone to prying into personal lives anyway.

At ten minutes till five, Brooke tucked her book into her handbag and headed for her car. As she thought about the date, she realized that she'd agreed to fly-fishing without water boots or even any fishing equipment. She did not like the idea of relying on Luke to provide that equipment, but that was better than skipping out entirely.

Yes, it would have avoided the potential of getting hurt more, but the only thing stronger than Brooke's fear of getting hurt was her fear of failing to live up to a promise. Nothing was more important than her word—so her parents had ingrained in her from the earliest days she could remember.

She put her handbag in the trunk of her car—she didn't need to take that much precaution in Greenville, but living in Los Angeles had forced some paranoid habits on her—and turned around. Before she could even lean against the trunk, she saw Luke's black pickup pulling into the parking lot. She couldn't miss it; his car was the only one coming into the school grounds at this hour.

He pulled up beside her and rolled down the passenger's window.

"Mind if I give you a ride?"

"Given that I'm not sure exactly where we're going, sure."

Luke nodded, turned off the truck, and hurried out to open the door. He wore a brown button-down shirt, dark black jeans, and black boots. Brooke wasn't sure if Luke remembered, but she had always commented that she liked him in darker clothes than the white shirt and light blue jeans combo others preferred.

He put his hand out, and for the briefest of moments, Brooke hesitated to take it. No, holding his hand as she got in did not commit her to marrying him.

But…

She grabbed it, and goosebumps popped up on both her arms. She had to suppress a grin as warmth enveloped her, her arm tingling with excitement and possibility. *Get it together, Brooke. It's not a date, it's a chance to talk over some casual fly-fishing.*

But as much as she could control her thoughts, she could not control these reactions, both a concerning and a curious sign.

Luke shut the door behind her, and as he walked around, it hit Brooke that she was about to experience many "first time since" moments. This was the first time since 2009 that she'd sat in Luke's pickup truck. Being in California for so long had meant she had not ridden in pickups often, and she forgot how tall and how powerful she felt sitting in a beast of a vehicle like this.

Where else would she feel tall and powerful with Luke? *Careful, Brooke.*

Luke opened the door to his side, let out a satisfied "ahh," and revved the truck to life.

"When's the last time you went fly-fishing?" he asked casually, the way people made small talk before jumping into much bigger and more important conversation points.

Brooke shook her head.

"Probably with you, sometime that summer."

That summer before things fell apart.

"That summer," Luke repeated with a sigh. "I suppose there's no beating around the bush anymore."

He gulped. Brooke felt like she was going to throw up. She braced herself for the worst possible news—that he'd cheated on her in that first semester in college, that he'd fathered Montana out of wedlock, that he'd done something terrible, probably illegal, that forced him to distance himself from her.

"First, it can't be said enough, Brooke. I'm sorry for how things ended. I messed up. I put you in a bad spot, and while I knew things were bad, I never thought they were so bad, you'd make a vow to God that you'd never return to me."

Brooke wanted to say that vow was said in a moment of emotions, that she was no longer sure how to feel about that—how many men and women, not just in Greenville but throughout history, had made questionable or even immoral prayers to God?—but for now, she stayed silent, believing that was the best way to learn what she could.

"Growing up on Hope Valley Ranch made me many things. It made me a Christian man, it made me a self-reliant man, and it made me a learned man. But unfortunately, it also made me a boy eager to be free. And I don't mean the good freedom, where you escape oppression. I mean the secular, indulgent kind of freedom."

Brooke kept her eyes straight on the road, but out of the corner of her eye, she could see Luke gripping the steering wheel so tight, his hands were turning red. He wasn't sharing this story because it relieved him.

"When I got to Spokane, a part of me rebelled and wanted nothing to do with the life I had come from. I wanted to drink. I wanted to party. I didn't want to have to think about getting up before dawn, ordering tags and Ivermectin, or, and I hate to say this, going to church on Sundays. I wouldn't say I lost my faith, but I didn't work to keep it alive."

He shook his head. Brooke silently empathized, for while she hadn't lost her faith, she, too, had struggled in the aftermath of the breakup. Faith had been her refuge, but she hadn't gone without moments of weakness.

"The adult thing to do, of course, would have been to express this all to you. To communicate that I wanted to be a little indulgent, to escape what I felt was a suffocating lifestyle, and to figure out how I could better do that. Instead, I did the opposite.

I stopped talking to you, and when I did, I barely spoke to you. I... darn it!"

He slammed his fists on the wheel. Brooke held out a hand and placed it on his arm, reassuring him. Luke slowly regained control of himself.

"I suppose in some respects, I became the man I am today because I went through that period. After that first year, I found my faith again, limited the drinking to only three a night on weekends, and did well in my business administration degree. But all of it, *all of it,* was self-inflicted. And it would have been one thing if that damage was only to myself. But it wasn't."

With an empty road ahead of them, Luke looked at Brooke. His face was both as vulnerable and handsome as she had ever seen it. No longer did it hide the "hot boy" look he'd had as a teenager, but instead featured the weathered yet wise face of someone much older.

"I'm sorry, Brooke," he said. "It's all probably too much to overcome to even be friends, never mind anything more. But now you know."

Brooke took several moments to process what Luke had just said.

On one hand, who could fault the classic story of the child who goes to college and "lives a little?" Even she attended a few parties when she went to UCLA and had too much to drink. She'd never kissed anyone she didn't go on at least five dates with—much to the frustration of many impatient boys—but she couldn't pretend she didn't flirt with a few.

But she had done all that while she was single.

It was tough. She appreciated Luke's vulnerability and his confession of that semester, but every time she wanted to lean a little further into how she felt about him, she recalled the pain of driving on this very road aimlessly, of sitting in the church and begging *not* to have a second chance.

"Thank you, Luke," she finally said, not wanting to be rude.

"I… I'm not sure what to say today. It's all still fresh, and seeing you brought back a lot of memories."

"I know, and probably most of them were bad."

"Not necessarily," she said, a warm smile forming. "We did date for three years, you know. You don't stay with someone that long if you don't have any good memories."

Luke's smile mirrored hers.

"Oh, shoot!" he said suddenly, hitting the brakes and turn signal rather abruptly. "This is the spot, right here."

"Where?"

"You have to park and walk probably half a mile, but the walk gives you privacy," he said as he pulled over into an unmarked, seemingly half-abandoned parking lot that had more potholes than parking spaces. "If there's anyone here, there's more than enough space. And since we're the only vehicle in this lot, I'd say the odds are good for God being the only one to hear us chat. So, shall we?"

"We came this far, didn't we?"

We came this far…

Brooke shrugged off the words as she got out of the car, meeting Luke at the back as he gathered his supplies. As prepared as his father was for all their trips, Luke handed her some wading boots and a rod. He grabbed a tackle box and his own wading boots as they began the hike down the trail.

"Wait, wait," he said, walking quickly back to his truck. He reached in, grabbed something, and pulled out a black cowboy hat.

And Lord, that cowboy hat was like the blackberry topping on a delicious chocolate cake. Her attraction to how he looked had never changed, but him putting that hat on turned him from an attractive man into the archetype of a *cowboy*. She did not dare open her mouth, because if she did, she knew she was bound to say something that would give the wrong impression.

Then again, depending on how things went, maybe it was exactly the impression she wanted to send.

She shook off the apparent contradictory thoughts, doing her best not to ponder which of the two was truer, and followed him down a trail. The trail did not look well-defined, but they also obviously weren't the first to take this route. For as much as Luke had talked in the car, he remained silent.

Brooke wondered if that was the first time he'd said everything to someone.

Actually, speaking of... there was one person in this play called life that she still knew nothing about.

They reached down to the river, and true to Luke's word, there was no one else around. The river flowed at a steady pace, one that definitely had a direction but not one that would sweep even a child over the age of eight under. Though Montana weather could change on a dime, but so far, nothing suggested anything other than clear skies.

"Beautiful," Luke said as he helped Brooke hook a fly onto her rod. "I didn't do this much back in Washington. Glad to be feeling like old times."

"Agreed," Brooke said, almost without considering the implications of her agreement. "There's one question I have left, though, Luke. At least for right now."

Luke nodded. She could see on his face he already knew the question, but he didn't stop her from asking it.

"What's the situation with Montana's mother?"

9

LUKE

Luke knew *that* question would pop up at some point. It wasn't like he could hide Montana's existence, and even if he could, why would he hide the best part of his life?

He just wished it hadn't happened on the first... meeting? Conversation? *Date?*

Today was about apologizing for past mistakes and how badly he had hurt Brooke. He wanted the focus to be on their past so that, well, their future might not be so tense and cold, even if it wasn't as... as it was. Bringing in Chelsea brought up the possibility for conversations he wasn't ready for.

"I met her in college," Luke said.

"When?" Brooke said tersely.

She thinks I cheated on her.

"Not until junior year," Luke said. "She was a freshman. I had no idea who she was until that year."

That seemed to placate Brooke, who had handled everything so far pretty well. This, however, was a ticking time bomb, with a very uncertain question of if Luke could effectively defuse it.

"And we just dated for two years. I... Do you really want to know all of this?"

"Yes," Brooke said again, tersely.

But why?

Luke hesitated. Brooke would only be asking so many questions if she cared, and she would only care if she wanted to be back with him, right?

He bit his lip, using the casting of his line as an excuse to think in silence for a few seconds. Ultimately, he returned to what he always did in tough moments—his faith that the truth was the path to freedom. *Lord, I hope that holds true in this case.*

"After two years, we got married. She wanted kids immediately. I told her she should wait until she graduated college so that we could figure out our living situation before we introduced anyone. We both kind of got our way. She got pregnant but didn't give birth until about two weeks after graduation."

He pulled in a breath. The next question, he knew he wouldn't be ready to answer.

"And what happened to her?"

No.

That was not something he was ready to go back to. He'd gone through what truly felt like hell. Just the thought of retelling that story caused his heart to pulse uncomfortably fast.

"I'll tell you more later," he said.

"Luke, come on."

"No, Brooke, it's not something I'm ready to discuss."

"I want—"

"I don't care what you want. It's not any of your business, and that's final."

He paused. Lord, he'd never snapped at Brooke before like that. What had gotten into him? She asked because she wanted to know. She had her own anxieties.

He drew in a breath.

"I will tell you someday if you are still curious," Luke said as he focused on his breathing, trying to steady his heartbeat. "But it's not something I'm comfortable going into on just a whim. I went through a lot, and I had to keep a strong face for Montana throughout. If it makes you feel better, she's not going to come back into the picture. I promise you that."

Brooke looked apologetic but also relieved. Luke was realizing Brooke still had feelings for him, even after everything that had happened. As much as this helped to calm his nerves, he knew he had to tread extremely carefully.

For as painful as the first breakup had been, who knew how brutal a second would be? Or worse, how final such a breakup would be?

"Sorry, Luke," Brooke said. "I just… I just wanted to know. I didn't realize it would be so bad."

"It's OK," Luke said, coming back down. "Like I said, I will tell you someday. Just… not today."

He drew in a breath. He reminded himself where he was—with the first love of his life, out at the river, fly-fishing while his daughter was with his parents. God had truly treated him well, even with what happened to Chelsea.

He always has a plan. It's up to me to trust Him.

"I'm happy to answer any other questions you have, but I think we might as well catch some fish while we're here, huh?"

Brooke smiled. Though the sun was still another couple hours away from setting, with the late afternoon glow, she had almost developed a gorgeous sunset look with the sun directly behind her. Though he had to admit, the black slacks and red top with wading boots did look slightly ridiculous.

But who else was Brooke, if not the woman who cared less for how she looked and how she dressed than she did for what she was doing and who she was doing it with?

"I would like that," she said. "Remember, I just moved back here this summer as well. I'm experiencing my second chance with Greenville almost as much as you are."

Aren't we both, Luke thought.

~

As a child, Luke had always loved to flyfish for hours on end. With the late start to the fishing, the drive out, and Brooke's insistence that she get home to take care of her mother—something she did not elaborate on—Luke begrudgingly ended their expedition after only an hour.

It was far from enough time to catch anything, but Luke just reminded himself if he wanted to flyfish to actually catch fish, he would have come out here right at sunrise. The only thing he wanted to catch, he would not admit to himself. Not yet, at least.

They headed back to the car, laughing about jokes about Washington, but Luke knew both of them had things to say that neither was even hinting at. It was one thing not to touch on obviously sensitive subjects like Chelsea or Mrs. Young; it was another for there to be feelings between the two that went unspoken. But at least it made things fun, and the shared experience told Luke that this was far from the last time they'd interact. *Small-town living has more than one perk.*

Luke helped Brooke into his truck. He knew, as her wading boots went inside, Montana would have questions about why Mrs. Young got to get the truck dirty but she did not. They were the type of questions an eight-year-old did not let go of easily, but all things considered, Luke was happy to have to answer them.

Once more, on the car ride back, conversation remained light, discussing when they'd next make a trip to either Yellowstone or Glacier National Park. Luke thought about asking what Brooke had been up to the past fourteen years, but satisfied with how this had gone, he refrained from going any deeper. And as it was, this was not a date, so it did not matter.

Right?

He pulled into the school lot with Brooke's car still there, no one else in sight. Though Brooke was more than capable of getting out herself, he hurried out of the driver's side, opened the door, and helped her down. Maybe it was a little old-fashioned, perhaps even too much so, but Luke would wait until Brooke said something otherwise.

She was not, both with her words and her body language.

"Dang it," Luke suddenly said. "Your wading boots."

Brooke laughed at the silly oversight. Luke played up the part of forgetful man, much to Brooke's delight, pretending he had also forgotten her bag in the back of his truck. He reached back, saying "gosh," and "darn it," and "ya dummy, Luke," as if he were a pious sailor, and handed her bag over.

"It's OK!" Brooke said, but she was laughing so much that even Luke joined in. *Just like old times.*

"Well, today has been more than OK," Luke said as their laughter came down. "I…"

They made eye contact, and Luke struggled to know what to say—or what to do. A date? Casual conversation didn't have deep gazes or emotionally charged moments like this. But to go back there…

All the pain that was possible, all the heartache that could come, all the mistakes he could make…

He gulped. He took two steps forward. Luke was not close enough to kiss her, but if they both extended their arms, they could hold hands. Luke was tempting a lot of fate here, but he trusted the Lord would make sure that "fate" favored his boldness.

"I had a great time, Brooke."

Even that sounds like the end of a date!

Luke bit his lip from saying anything more. He did not want to pressure Brooke into calling this anything other than two people with a lot of history catching up. He was realizing that would be, at best, a severe misrepresentation and, at worst, an outright lie, but he had not been the one hurt.

Luke hurt, for sure, but he was the one who started all the pain. The recipient needed to forgive the aggressor before the aggressor could push for a second shot.

"I did too, Luke," she said. "You seem like you've changed."

Luke gulped. A compliment? It was said that way.

Flirting?

"Montana has forced me to grow up and remember my faith a heck of a lot more," he said with a chuckle.

"She might just be the best thing that's ever happened to you."

"There's no might in that."

As much as Luke saw an opportunity to make a flirtatious remark, something like "no, you are," he agreed with her. Nothing in this world filled his heart—and, yes, sometimes drove him crazy—like his only child. He was curious where this was going, but if Montana stepped in at any moment and said Ms. Young had done something to hurt her or drive her away, Luke would end it right away.

How fortunate, then, that the good Lord had ensured the two of them got along just fine so far.

Then Brooke took a step forward. Now the two of them were close enough to put their hands on the other's shoulder; still not close enough for a kiss, but more than enough for a hug to lead to that. *Fourteen years, and I still remember that cherry lipstick she wore and the way her hands ran through my hair as we kissed.*

Luke swallowed.

Brooke raised a hand, as if—

"I should go," she said suddenly, dropping her arm. "My mom's going to need me home soon. Shoot, I'm probably already late."

Luke bit his lip in disappointment, but the disappointment

was short-lived. What a blessing it was to be standing here and not have Brooke Young hate his guts. What a blessing it was to have just spent an hour with the first woman he ever loved and be able to leave this meeting on good terms.

But though Luke did not want to put pressure on Brooke to think of this as a date, he could not refrain from saying something.

"I understand," he said, "but let's just not wait fourteen years until the next hangout."

Brooke roared with laughter, putting her hands on her knees. The joke, Luke thought, had not been funny, but the magnitude of her laughter said it all.

There was an opportunity there they both wanted, but that both needed to tread carefully with.

"I don't think that will be an issue," she said. "Make sure Montana does her homework, OK?"

"She's a much better student than I am. You needn't worry about that."

"OK," Brooke said. "Good seeing you, Luke."

"Same," Luke said, tipping his hat.

But they could not do the whole "step together into something more" dance, and though Brooke hesitated for just a split-second, she then pivoted on her foot and walked back to her car. Luke, not wanting to look the part of a creep, tipped his hat one more time and made his way back to his truck. By the time he got there, Brooke had already begun backing out, and Luke used the chance to let out the biggest sigh of relief he'd had since Montana's birth had gone off without complications.

There was something there.

All those old feelings that came back when he saw her at Bacon & Bakin' had a real chance to be discovered.

There was still the conversation about Chelsea, which would not be easy for either of them. Especially since everything had happened in the last couple of years, there would be genuine questions about if Luke was ready.

If Brooke was named Brittney and Luke had met her in line at Grocer's Mart, not fourteen years ago, the answer would have been "probably not."

But Brooke was Brooke, they had met fourteen years ago, and while Luke didn't know how fast things would move, he knew that with one Brooke Young, he was willing to walk down that path once again.

He closed his eyes and prayed.

Lord, give me the strength to treat Brooke Young well, he thought. *Give me the wisdom to recognize and respect her desires and wishes, and give me the courage to pursue love if the opportunity arises.*

Amen.

10

BROOKE

Brooke's whole body shook as she returned to her car. She had come *dangerously* close to kissing Luke, and she hadn't even found out much about who the mother of his child was!

A million thoughts ran through her head as she turned on the ignition of her vehicle. She didn't want to just sit there, though, and have Luke wonder what in the world she was thinking as she wasted gasoline. So she gave the appearance of heading home, and in fact, pulled south out of the parking lot toward her mother's house.

But instead of taking a right into the neighborhood before Montana State-Greenville, she kept going straight and turned into the parking lot where the two town doctors and dentist had their offices, knowing by now they had all gone home and would not have any evening visitors. Just in case, she pulled to the far end of the parking lot, her vehicle still far from the road, but her license plate and herself were unlikely to draw notice from any passersby.

OK. So.

She was still attracted to him. There was no denying that.

But she knew she needed to have self-control, and she had confidence in that; Los Angeles had many beautiful men who were also without her values, and she had never struggled to say no to a second date or even a first date in such spots.

But this was so, so, so very different.

There was nothing "on paper" that suggested them dating wouldn't work. Heck, they'd already done it once! And what split them apart wasn't Luke being himself, it was Luke *not* being himself. When he was... gosh!

But the question...

What in the world had happened with the mother of his child?

Divorce?

Death?

Those seemed like the only two realistic probabilities. Brooke supposed she could have just vanished off the face of the Earth, not confirmed dead, but as much as Luke breaking up with her had hurt, she did not think he would have gone for someone that unstable.

Unfortunately, "divorce and death" left a lot to the imagination that she did not dare to venture into. Any conjecture on her part would have been disrespectful.

But it left a question that she could think about.

Did she want to be a mom to Montana? Would that not be the inevitable outcome of this?

Wait.

Mom.

She shook her head. Thank goodness she'd had this realization only about five minutes after passing by her home instead of thirty minutes. Luke may have excited her, but the thought of him could not cloud what she needed to do for her mom.

Not that she imagined Luke ever, *ever* forcing her to make such a decision, but if it came down to being with her mom or being with Luke, she would choose her mom. Luke would find someone good for him eventually; but no one could both live in Greenville and care for her Mom like Brooke could.

She pulled into the house's driveway at about twenty after six, certainly later than she'd intended, but not so ridiculously late that Lola would leave in a huff. Brooke pulled out an extra twenty-dollar bill from her wallet, fully aware that Lola would try not to take the money. She walked up to the house, and just before she opened the door, she heard her mom shout.

"Who is Brooke?!"

Brooke bit her lip, trying to push back her eyes from watering before she even stepped through the door. Today was a bad day; these were the days that tested Brooke's faith and strength. Luke could have proposed to her, and this still would be a test of her commitment.

Believing after a few moments she had pushed back an early onslaught of tears, Brooke opened the door and heard Lola, bless her, gently explaining that Brooke was her mother's daughter.

"Oh, Brooke!" her mother exclaimed.

It still wasn't a great day, but that at least promised Brooke it would not be the worst ever. On those kinds of days, her mother had almost no mind, asking constantly where she was, who Brooke was, and why she was here; no answers could reassure her, and nothing but sleep and prayer would return her to a state merely ten percent better, let alone with full memory.

Brooke stepped into the living room and smiled.

"I'm sorry I'm late," she said, walking over to Lola and placing the twenty in her hand. Brooke stepped back before Lola could shove it back in, leaving her mother's caretaker to begrudgingly nod her thanks. "I had a meeting run a little late."

"A five o'clock meeting on the first day of school?"

Lola's voice carried no suspicion. In fact, it almost sounded like the voice of hope. Lola had probably only heard of the name Luke Walker in passing; Brooke had never told her the story. Nevertheless, anyone under the age of thirty-five who was single and attractive would draw curious eyes for having a weekday meeting at five o'clock on the first day of their role.

"OK, maybe it was something more than that," Brooke said with a smile she kept small, aware her mother could snap at any second. "But it was good. Lola, thank you for staying late. I'll try to schedule such work meetings on the weekend going forward."

"Nonsense!" Lola said with a gentle wave of her hand. "If you can only do these meetings on weekdays, do what works for you. It's a gift to spend time with your mother."

Brooke sighed. Lola was truly the best; how did the good Lord bless her so well?

"You are kinder than I would be, Lola," Brooke said. "Go buy yourself dinner at Bison Brothers or at least something at Green Cream on your way home. You've earned it. I'll see you tomorrow?"

"Yes, sounds good," Lola said as she gathered her things and wished them a good evening.

Once the door shut, Brooke turned back to her mother. There was indeed recognition in her eyes that this was her daughter, but how much else she would remember was anyone's guess. There were some bad days when her mother had the impossible accomplishment of recalling what Brooke's father wore on their second date to the state fair, yet couldn't remember that same man's first name.

"I'm sorry, Brooke," her mother said, as if trying on the name. "I know it's you. But..."

Not Brookey. Just... Brooke.

"It's OK, Mom," Brooke said, keeping her voice stable. She'd dealt with many days like this; surely, she could handle another one? Especially after such a wonderful afternoon?

"What did you do today?"

COWBOY'S HOMECOMING

The question was not framed like her mother knew the answer. *Lord, please give me the strength and compassion needed.*

"I had my first day of teaching the second graders. They all mostly behaved. A couple of them bullied a girl named Montana about her name, but the warning of extra homework got them to behave."

"Oh, good, you know how kids these days need a reminder to behave."

That was another thing her mother did on bad days—complain about the upcoming generation. Brooke had her own concerns, of course, but her experience showed that, at least in Greenville, the kids were well-behaved.

"But the real good news," Brooke said, recognizing her mother may not even remember this conversation tomorrow, "was that I saw Luke Walker."

"Hmm."

She doesn't recognize the name today.

Brooke drew in a breath.

"We dated for three years in high school. He's back in town now. We…"

Went on a date? No, that wasn't a date. At least, not officially.

"We spent some time together fly-fishing. It was great."

That felt like the most apt description.

But unfortunately, it was not enough for her mother to remember anything more.

"I'm sure he was a fine young man," her mother said. "Are you going to see him again?"

"I hope so," Brooke said. "My mind is telling me to go slow. He has a child, and he has some past with an ex-wife that he won't talk about. She could have died tragically, or they could have had a bitter divorce."

"Maybe he murdered her!"

Brooke actually stifled a laugh, as awkward and almost uncomfortable as her mother's exclamation was. The worst thing Luke had ever done was prioritize riding horses with his brothers one Saturday over her; she could not imagine him becoming a murderer.

But it reinforced the need to go slow. Brooke knew little about Luke from the last fourteen years. She had a better chance of replacing Pastor O'Connell at St. Luke's than he had of being a murderer, but it wasn't impossible to think he'd become jaded, cold, or manipulative for his daughter's need in some other fashion.

"I don't think it's that," Brooke said as she tried not to laugh, fearing it would embarrass her mother. "I think something extremely difficult happened. In any case, Mom, my mind is telling me to go slow. But my heart wants to pick up like we last dated fourteen days ago, not fourteen years. He's become a man now—a real one at that. He's still handsome, and he's still a faithful, Christian cowboy. I feel like a teenager."

"You don't want to feel that way, young lady."

Brooke swallowed. The tone was harsh, but the words were correct. As a teenager, Brooke could get away with not listening to her mind—that was called young love. As a thirty-year-old woman, she had to feel *and* think.

Still, she had to be careful not to swing too far in the other direction, lest she turn into a computer trying to predict love.

"I understand," she said. "I just wanted to tell you the good news. No one has made me feel like this in a long, long time."

Since Luke himself.

"I don't want to let myself get too carried away, but… it's not impossible to think that he's the one."

"Just be careful, dear," her mother said. "Put your faith in God and let Him decide what happens."

Incoherent or not, that was the best advice her mother could have given. Before she saw Luke again, Brooke knew she needed to speak with Pastor O'Connell. She'd gotten so caught up in the moment she'd forgotten the very story she started her meeting with—that of vowing never to return to Luke.

She felt reasonably sure that God would see that as an emotional moment, one spurned by a broken heart, not one of genuine intent. But as much as she held strong to her faith, doubt plagued her, and she needed someone wiser like Pastor O'Connell to guide her.

And if nothing else, given that Brooke otherwise needed to focus on a successful first week of school, it would give her time to let the heart settle and the mind to do its job. She just wouldn't have time to see Pastor O'Connell until Saturday, maybe even at Sunday service. One week was nowhere near enough to figure out questions about love, but it was enough to prevent her from rushing into the wrong ones.

Even if, as her mind ran over all the rational reasons this was a good idea, her heart still pulled her into wanting to see Luke again.

"I promise," Brooke said.

She took her mother into an embrace, kissed her on the forehead, and grabbed a mystery book for her. She then lay on the couch next to her, turned on HGTV, and exhaled.

It was time to relax and let God work His plan.

11

LUKE

"Benny! No!" Luke hurried out of his truck, past the front porch of his parents' house, through their kitchen, and onto their back deck as he saw a sight he would have laughed at if not for it being his daughter.

Benny the sheep was, as had happened many times before, eating paper.

"Hey! Hey!" Luke said, chasing off the sheep. Like a dog who knew it had messed up, Benny shrunk away and hurried off the porch, moving as fast as its senior citizen legs could take it. "Dang sheep," Luke said.

But any concerns he had were quelled as Montana giggled.

"He really ate my papers!" Montana said, her giggle turning into laughter. "I didn't think he really would!"

Oh, Lord, did she actually dare him to do it? Luke turned, arms folded, an exaggerated look of grief on his face. Montana knew immediately he was not serious, and his hyperbolic expression only caused her to laugh harder.

"Well, I suppose it's best to do it on day one than when you are studying for a test," Luke said with a sigh. And really, he couldn't be too mad, not with how the afternoon had gone. "But now you know one of the house rules. Don't let Benny near your papers!"

"I know!" Montana said, still somehow laughing. "But it's so funny!"

"Is it?" Luke said, raising his hands like claws. He and Montana both knew what that meant. "You know what's really funny?"

"No, no tickles! Daddy!"

The two of them burst into laughter as Luke crept from behind and tickled his daughter. Montana ran away, even bumping into Benny, which drew a startled bleat from the sheep. Luke had to laugh at the sight—it was like his daughter was getting one back on the sheep!

"OK, OK," Montana said, but she was still giggling, so much so that she had to pause to catch her breath. "I will make sure Benny doesn't eat my homework!"

"Good girl," Luke said, coming over and mussing with her hair. "Otherwise, Daddy's going to make you do it twice over!"

"Nooooo!"

Montana leaned into her father's leg, and Luke leaned over and kissed her on the forehead.

"Real question, was that actual homework?"

"No. It was just a sheet we were supposed to fill in about ourselves. Like what's our favorite food and that kind of thing."

Luke nodded.

"Tell you what. You tell Ms. Young that you will give your answers in front of the whole class."

"I will?" Montana said, sounding nervous.

Luke wasn't doing this just to be funny, though. He knew that life on a ranch often required a loud voice and the ability to use it to command attention. Montana may not have been getting ready to check on the cattle, pump water out of wells, or call to the sheep soon, but the quicker she could develop skills without Luke seeming like an overbearing father, the better.

"It'll be good for you," he said, "and if Ms. Young doesn't accept that, tell her Daddy made a mistake with his goat. She will understand."

A glimmer of recognition crossed Montana's face.

"What did you do with her, Daddy? Did you kiss her?"

"Lord!" Luke said with a laugh. "No, no, I did not. I just... caught up with her. I've known her longer than you've been alive."

But what I would give to kiss those lips once more, to be in her arms once again. Heavens...

"Wow!" Montana said. "OK, Daddy, I'll do my best."

"That's all we can ask for, Tana," he said. "Now just keep a closer eye on Benny, would ya?"

∼

THE FIRST WEEK of school passed, and life seemed good in the present, even if his father's lung cancer seemed to sap just a percent of his strength every single day.

In quiet moments, Luke overheard his daughter singing the song she'd first belted in the car, "Montana, my state, my state, we are here!" It brought him immense pride, for it told him whatever bullying and teasing may have taken place on the first day was no longer a concern. At the very least, she had learned to brush it off and take joy in her name.

Not a day went by where a part of Luke didn't want to reach out to Brooke to see how Montana was doing. He knew better than to believe that was his real reason, and now, at thirty-two, he refused to behave like an awkward teenager afraid to ask the question of interest. But since he did not want to pressure Brooke into anything, he had no choice but to not to contact her at all.

It wasn't comfortable sitting with the discomfort and impatience. It wasn't just a nice line to say no one had made Luke feel this way; even Chelsea, as much as he had grown to love her, just hadn't had the same spark at first. Chelsea was special to Luke in her own way, but by the path of life, she could not claim to have been his first.

Thoughts of Chelsea were also never too far off. He knew what she'd said to him near the end of their time together. He knew she had wished him nothing but the best, even through the hard times of their marriage. But still, he knew there would be questions if he went to Brooke this quickly.

Or maybe "this quickly" was subjective, and he was overthinking things.

If it involved Brooke, probably.

Luke gave thought to reaching out to Brooke that Saturday, with school done for the week and Montana having a Mimi-Papaw-granddaughter "date" out on the more remote parts of the ranch, but he again held back on it. He wasn't sure when he would reach out, even though every part of his heart begged for "when" to be "now," but he only knew that God would tell him when the right time was. God would differ between desire and love, and He would tell Luke when it was time.

Saturday came and went; in the evening, Luke cooked a delicious chicken-and-biscuit recipe that his grandmother had passed down through the Walker generations. Many had considered such a plate more of a Southern staple than a Montana specialty, but when they took the first bite of the shredded chicken and the buttered-up biscuits, no one gave a second thought to if it had come from Mississippi, Montana, or Mars. It provided a wonderful opportunity for Luke to sit down and spend true quality time with his parents and daughter, something he hadn't gotten the chance to do for an extended period since coming home.

But once again, he thought about Brooke. She had come over

to their ranch many times in their more youthful days for dinner, and she herself had had the chicken-and-biscuit combo, albeit cooked by Mimi. He wouldn't quite call her a staple of their weekend dinners, but it happened enough Luke could easily recall certain conversations or encounters.

Their second encounter, wherever it happened, would not take place here at the house. Luke craved that chance—and depending on Papaw's condition, it might happen sooner rather than later—but that was a step only to be taken once feelings really blossomed.

Still, as Luke went to bed Saturday night, all felt wonderful. Maybe not perfect, for there were things to strive for, and he, as a man, was sinful and far from perfect, but he had certainly been in worse places.

Lord, thank you for bringing us home. You could not have put us in a better spot. Amen.

~

To show his thanks, Luke awoke Montana for the seven-thirty a.m. service at St. Luke's. Mimi and Papaw had woken around five a.m., and Luke, even without an alarm, had only slept in until about six, but for Montana, it was a struggle to be up before seven. Still, Luke could take pride in how she was learning to be a good Christian, and she did not complain as he knew so many kids might have about church.

A part of Luke hoped to see Brooke at this service; it would give him a safe way for her to become reacquainted with his parents and for her to see Montana in a setting outside the classroom. But he snuffed out the thought quickly, aware that he went to church to give thanks to God, not to have a serendipitous romantic encounter. Even as a teenager, he had not dared cross that line.

She was not at this morning's service, which was for the best.

Pastor O'Connell gave a sermon about how "thy neighbor" was not just the literal neighbor next door, but all of humanity. Even those who got under our skin, Pastor O'Connell said, deserved love and God's grace. If anything, they most needed it, for it was easy to love those who loved us.

Luke couldn't quite call it the most profound sermon he had ever heard in his life, but he found Pastor O'Connell engaging, and he reminded himself to talk to Montana about it later that day.

Service ended at half-past eight, and they briefly paused outside the church to speak to Pastor O'Connell. The pastor greeted them all warmly, even kneeling before Montana.

"I should have told this to you last week, but you know what? You are the most well-behaved child in church I have ever seen," Pastor O'Connell said, to the delight of Luke.

"Well, you're not boring!"

That drew a laugh from all the adults, including Luke. Their conversation remained casual; Luke knew at some point he would need the pastor's advice about coming to peace with his past, especially if he and Brooke became something more, but until that "if" became more definitive, there was no reason to rush.

They headed home right after, skipping a donut run due to Papaw feeling especially tired. All seemed well and normal this Sunday.

And then, as they got to the entrance of Hope Valley Ranch, they saw a gray truck parked right outside the entrance. It had been years since Luke had seen the man standing with a cowboy hat at the front of the truck, but he recognized him right away.

Bryce Chamberlain, head of Sunrise Ranch, several miles down the road.

Luke had only told Montana the Chamberlains existed, nothing more, for they didn't concern her. But now, as a grown man, Luke knew that the Chamberlains, while good, faithful

Christians at their heart, also had long had eyes for Hope Valley Ranch as a possible expansion point. Tensions never became violent or even verbally aggressive.

But, there was always an undercurrent of a weary eye, Mr. Chamberlain perhaps wondering—hoping, even—that Luke and his brothers, having all moved away, had taken their father's advice too well. Luke always imagined Mr. Chamberlain hoped that he and his brothers had explored other pastures so much they wouldn't return.

"Good morning, Howard," Mr. Chamberlain said, calling out Papaw by his real name. "How are you today?"

"Well enough to give thanks to the Lord and kick a horse into motion," Papaw said, only rolling down the passenger's side window. "How can I help you, Bryce?"

"I was just coming to check in and see how things were at Hope Valley here," he said, nodding toward the pasture. "Luke, is that you? My, how you've grown."

"Thank you, sir," Luke said, trying not to reveal his suspicion in his tone.

"I see that you've come and helped spruce up the ranch a bit," Mr. Chamberlain continued. "I was getting worried. Your father is a great man, but he's a prideful one. Doesn't look to take my offer to help."

"You know I don't need it, Bryce," Papaw said, his voice also measured.

"Understood. Well, Howard, Luke, if you need anything, you know Sunrise Ranch isn't very far."

Luke nodded. Howard did as well, and Luke didn't wait for Mr. Chamberlain to get back into his truck before driving the rest of the way to the homestead.

"That was a bold move," Luke said, no longer willing to hide his tone. "I half-expected him to be waiting for us at the homestead."

"He's bold but not stupid," Papaw said, all the humor in his voice gone. "He knows opportunity is coming soon. He knows you boys have done exactly what I asked of you."

He sighed.

"But we must remember what Pastor O'Connell said. It's easy to love our neighbors when they are how we want them to be. We can still love our neighbors even when they don't get the message."

"And what message is that?" Montana said from the back.

Luke couldn't decide if it was blissful or concerning that Montana had asked such a question. But when he saw the wry smile forming on his father's face, he knew what he felt.

"That Hope Valley Ranch will forever be in Walker hands, and that nothing short of God's will can change that," his father said. "Are there any Chamberlain grandkids in your class?"

Montana thought for a second and then shook her head no.

"For the best," his father scoffed. "They are good people. Bryce, Mary, and their six boys. You just need patience with them."

Luke nodded. It wasn't the first time he'd heard his father say such a thing.

He also knew that it wasn't the only thing he'd need to pray to God to have patience for.

12

BROOKE

Sunday was a good day for Brooke's mother. She woke up alert, asked, "How are you doing, Brookey?" after Brooke had brought her coffee, and showed no hesitation about going to church. She didn't remember everything Brooke had said about Luke that prior Monday evening, and Brooke still couldn't decide if that was for the best or not.

All she knew was that she had only run into him in the pickup line at school, and it drove her far crazier than she ever would have guessed not to speak to him outside of getting his daughter.

Every time she saw him pull up in his truck, sporting that cowboy hat, she felt like she was seeing him come to her house to pick her up for a date. Her mind might tell her that was the past, but her heart would replay the experience every single time. It didn't help that the more she thought about it, the more she realized Luke might just be her best option in Greenville, second chance or no.

She'd had a couple of suitors since she came back to Greenville. The funniest was the college students there at summer school who thought they were hitting on a "cougar."

She couldn't decide if she was flattered or embarrassed, but she did not entertain them any more than politely telling them they needed to see her as a woman, not a prize, and they needed to find someone their own age.

There had been one Chamberlain boy whom she recognized by face but not by name, but she had long been conditioned by Luke to see the Chamberlains as more cunning than courteous. He never got past talking to her in line.

And after that?

It was Luke or do long distance in Bozeman or Helena. And even though Bozeman and Helena were much, much closer than Spokane or Los Angeles, the rule was simple. If Brooke couldn't complete the drive in under an hour, she couldn't continue the dating.

But even if this was a city the size of Los Angeles, and every man over the age of thirty was a cowboy with strong family values and a love of the great outdoors, Brooke still felt sure she'd feel this way about one Luke Walker.

In that regard, the weekend almost brought her a sense of relief. She didn't have to worry about seeing him before and after school. She didn't have to be self-conscious about if she was treating Montana Walker any differently than the other kids. She could just spend time with her mother, go for a solo hike when her mother napped, and not have anything heighten her senses.

Sunday morning, then, was a mixture of feelings from the week and Saturday.

On the one hand, her anticipation grew that she might see him at Sunday service. She had not seen him at the nine o'clock service the week before, but maybe that first weekend was skipped out of a need to adjust to being home.

But on the other, she went to Sunday service intending to speak to Pastor O'Connell, and seeing Luke would do her no favors for keeping her head on straight.

SIERRA HART

As it was, she did her best to listen closely to Pastor O'Connell's sermon about loving everyone as our neighbor. She couldn't completely remain present, but her mother's occasional whispered question ensured she would not stray too far from the present.

Once the service ended and Pastor O'Connell recessed to the front door, Brooke turned to her mother.

"Do you mind staying a bit after?" she said. "I want to talk to Pastor O'Connell about something."

"Of course, dear," she said. "Is it private?"

Brooke nodded.

"I can wait in the car."

"I can't let you do that, Mom. It's going to rise into the eighties today."

"Oh, hush, you act like I've never been south of the border. Turn on the air conditioning and let me be. I'll just read or nap."

At least if Mom was pushing back, she had her wits about her. So Brooke nodded, helped her mother stand, and guided her to the back of the church. Outside, she greeted Pastor O'Connell, who moved to her mother's right side so she could use her good arm. It was small moments like that which made Pastor O'Connell such a valuable part of the Greenville community.

"May I have a word with you after I drop my mom off at the car? She insisted she be alone."

"Of course, my child."

Brooke thanked the pastor and helped her mom into her car.

"You're sure?" she asked one more time.

"I'm sure I'm going to drive off myself if you don't talk to the pastor," she said. "I might even just drive to Hope Valley Ranch myself at this rate."

"Mom!" Brooke said, mortified that her mom seemed to know her not-so-hidden secret.

But Mom shut the door with her good arm and waved as if

saying, "Goodbye, shoo, go do what you need to do." Brooke sighed but smiled; it was like her mother had developed more spunk in response to becoming less physically capable.

She headed up the steps to the church to see Pastor O'Connell shaking hands with what sounded like a visiting family member of Mrs. Baker's. The cousin stepped aside, and Brooke had her privacy and her spiritual mentor.

Now, the hard part.

"My child," Pastor O'Connell said warmly. "What is it you wanted to speak about?"

Brooke drew in a hard breath. This didn't feel like a conversation, but confession.

"Do you remember how, about fourteen years ago, I came in here in tears about the demise of my relationship?"

"Yes," Pastor O'Connell said without hesitation.

That surprised Brooke, although when she took a second to think about it, she knew people swore the pastor had a perfect memory.

"Well, all your advice was wise," Brooke said with a nervous smile. "I found refuge in God and the Bible. It still hurt after, but He helped me feel better. And, even more so, I forgave Luke for what happened. Or, at least, I thought I had."

"You don't?"

How did the pastor always ask such questions without sounding like a judgmental, overbearing authority figure?

"Oh, I did, I do. In fact, as you know, he's in town. I... I went fly-fishing with him about a week ago."

She waited for what seemed like the inevitable arching of the eyebrow, a curious glance, a smile of hope for the two young adults. But Pastor O'Connell made a living out of helping people through such innocuous moments; compared to other encounters he had undoubtedly heard about, this was likely to be relatively minor.

"And how do you feel about everything?"

Brooke sighed.

"A part of me still has feelings for him. But this is why I'm here. Not because I need help forgiving him. But because…"

Gosh, it was almost embarrassing to admit. She'd asked God for something that was unnecessary and, at worst, sinful.

"I prayed to God right after to make sure I never returned to Luke. And now I want to be with him."

"Hmm," the pastor murmured.

Several tense seconds passed. Brooke half-expected Luke to pop out from the side of the church to say that he had said a prayer asking Brooke to come back to him. The Lord certainly didn't hold tournaments to see whose prayer would win out, but…

I'm going crazy.

Gosh, Luke, why do you do this to me?

"First, the Lord hears all our prayers, but He may not answer them as we wish," the pastor said, a common but still very true response. "Do you remember exactly what it was you said?"

Brooke could recall with clarity as clear as the Missouri River.

"I said, 'I vow never to return to Luke.'"

She gulped.

"And then, I didn't say it out loud, but I thought, 'unless your will suggests otherwise.'"

Pastor O'Connell smiled.

"I think you have answered your own question, my child," he said. "Throughout history, many used the name of the Lord as justification for murder, for conquest, for much worse. Man is fallible and sinful; just because we utter the words 'Lord, I pray' does not mean we have good intentions. Certainly, you did not wish for his downfall."

"Never have."

"That is good to hear. All of this is to say that trust in God's will. The full story is yet to be revealed, but let's just say if

COWBOY'S HOMECOMING

fathers and pastors can understand that what temperamental teenagers say may not hold up over the years that follow, I'm sure the good Lord does the same."

They both shared a short laugh at that. Brooke felt immense relief, even as she considered how silly everything had probably sounded. Sure, some in the town might have strong words about their reunion, especially among her girlfriends.

Even so, there was much to be said for having the confidence and understanding of the most important person in her life outside her parents. *And, perhaps, someone else in the not-too-distant future.*

"Thank you, Pastor O'Connell," she said. "If you'll excuse me, I'm afraid my mother will run out of books to read if I take too much longer."

∼

THE BURDEN of explaining the situation had lifted, but with late afternoon plans set up, there was still one party that could make her feel uncomfortable with this evermore likely return to Luke.

Her friends.

At about three in the afternoon, with a couple hours before she'd have to prepare dinner for her mother, Brooke relished the chance to have some coffee at The Homestead. As a coffee shop in between the K-12 schools on the north side of the river and the university just south of it, The Homestead served a wide range of clientele, from the teenagers gossiping about who was dating who to the overworked college student preparing for exams to the sheriff looking to make conversation in this very peaceful time.

It was also an anomaly—perhaps the only place, outside of Montana Motel and Bison Brothers on Friday and Saturday, that stayed open after eight p.m. on weekdays and nine p.m. on weekends. The store owner was a retired Army veteran who was simply called Jon; rumors swirled about Jon's service, with the most exaggerated stating he had played a critical role in Vietnam.

But what mattered most to Brooke and her friends was not whether Jon had served in Vietnam, Desert Storm, or Afghanistan, but that the man was among the most content businessmen they had ever seen. The store could not have been making a huge profit, but Jon never talked about expanding the store or "corporatizing itself," in Jon's words. Brooke, Clara, and Danielle all knew that the store would remain an icon of Greenville, would not replicate into something inferior in the future, and would be the place that their kids would someday study at.

Brooke arrived first. The Homestead had a rustic interior; much like Bacon & Bakin', there were numerous "funny" signs, like "A cup a day keeps sleeping through sunrise away" and "Live, Laugh, Love? Try Smell, Taste, Drink." There weren't many seats, maybe six tables designed for two people and two tables with room for four, but that seemed to be on purpose, for there were at least ten picnic tables outside The Homestead. Even in the dead of winter, Jon wanted to encourage people to enjoy the great outdoors.

She ordered her usual, an iced coffee with extra brown sugar syrup. Clara Reed arrived next, waving to Brooke before making a beeline to the counter; she teetered ever so slightly on eccentric, and that showed up in her drink choices and her ownership of the local bookstore. Fortunately, The Homestead did indeed have dragonfruit smoothies in stock, a recent addition that was more popular than Brooke would have ever guessed.

Danielle Hazel, whose family was the de facto real estate "mogul" in town, was the last to arrive and kept it simple—black coffee with nothing added. Together, the three of them had made quite the dynamic in high school. Brooke, the cheerful, playful one who loved to write, volunteer, and hike; Clara, the quiet yet sweet one who could recite just about any line from any book from the last four years of English class; and Danielle, the whip-smart, sharp woman who often kept the more whimsical impulses of Brooke and Clara in check.

It was her that Brooke was most curious about.

"So, ladies," Clara began with her bubbly voice, "did you know that I got that Yellowstone mystery author to come up from Bozeman? Richard Dangerfield?"

"That can't possibly be his real name," Danielle said with a smirk.

"It's the name he used to communicate with me!" Clara retorted. "And it's a huge get for the bookstore. We haven't had many author speakers in the last few years."

"How did you pull that off?" Brooke asked.

She was painfully unaware of what Clara and Danielle had done. Clara had never left town, which surprised both her and Danielle, for they would have assumed the most open-minded and curious of the group would have road-tripped across the country by now. Danielle had gone to the main Montana State campus at Bozeman, but she had been quite studious in preparing to eventually take over the Hazel Home Realty agency from her mom.

Distance, it seemed, had not only cost her a romantic relationship with Luke. But unlike with Luke, where that distance was at the forefront, she was trying to fake awareness with her friends; she was too embarrassed otherwise.

"He grew up here, and while he went to Vanderbilt, he said God's country has always called him home. He'll go anywhere in the state. Except Billings."

All three of them got a chuckle out of that.

"And you, Danielle?"

"Business, in theory, is good," she said, "except that a lot of the people and groups that want to buy land aren't from here. They're transplants from Washington and California."

All three of them grimaced, even Danielle herself.

"Is it that bad?"

"Being on the inside, I see the worst of it, so most properties will remain local to Montana. But this town is losing its secrecy. Bozeman is becoming too expensive for many."

Brooke sighed. She supposed all the new additions of the last few years didn't happen by mere accident. Like everything in life, there was a price to pay.

"And Brooke?" Clara asked.

Brooke talked before a smile enveloped her face.

"It's a boy, isn't it?!" Clara said, her voice a half-scream, half-question.

"Not just any boy," Brooke said. *So much for trying to keep this a secret or slowly unveil it.* "Luke is back in town. And..."

"You still have feelings for him," Danielle said, her tone neutral.

Brooke nodded. She waited to see the reaction from her two closest friends.

She did not expect *no* reaction at all.

"What? No surprise?"

"The Chamberlains keep making noise that Hope Valley Ranch might be available for sale soon because of his dad's condition, so I'm not surprised he's returned," Danielle said.

"Who approached whom?" Clara asked.

"I was eating a late breakfast at Bacon & Bakin' when he came up to me. He..."

Did she tell them about his daughter?

No, not yet. She needed to get more information out of them about how they felt.

"He was the one who made small talk first."

"Not a surprise there," Clara said.

But after that statement, a strange silence fell over the table.

Brooke always struggled to read Danielle; that girl had been well-trained by her mother not to reveal her emotions until she was ready. Clara looked ready to burst at the seams with *some* emotion, but Brooke was too unsure of what.

"Is this… good news to you two?"

"He broke your heart fourteen years ago," Clara said. "You were inconsolable throughout Christmas."

It was the quietest Clara had gotten all conversation. But then her voice rose.

"I know you got better, Brooke, but that was because you put him behind you. Do you really want to go back to that? Do you really want to get hurt?"

"We're more mature now," Brooke countered. "And I'm not saying we will definitely get back together. We haven't even kissed."

"It's always more painful the second time," Danielle said.

Both Clara and Brooke looked at her in confusion, though Clara seemed to register recognition about something Brooke knew nothing about.

"You remember Paul, my second high school sweetheart?"

Brooke nodded.

"We broke up after graduation, since he was staying in town and I was going to Bozeman. Even at that short a distance, I knew it would not work; I was too focused on school. But when I graduated and came back, he courted me. I thought it was a bad idea; I loved Paul in my teenage ways, but he and I were on different paths. But I gave it a shot."

Danielle sighed. She was trying to play off the breakup as simply part of her personal history, not a part of her, but it sure seemed worse than she was letting on. *Probably because Paul was nothing more than a rebound.*

Her real love was Weston.

"You break up once. It's bad, but at least there's usually a clear reason for it. You break up a second time, and there's something even more final, more painful about it. Like, you broke up, you fixed things, and it *still* wasn't good enough."

Brooke knew there was always a chance—perhaps even a likelihood—she and Luke would not work out a second time. But to hear Danielle sound so pained about something that sounded relatively benign gave Brooke pause. Was she ready for that kind of pain if things fell through?

Could she even fathom what kind of pain she would feel if, after all was said and done, she and Luke still wouldn't work?

"I am lucky. Work keeps me quite busy," Danielle said, although Brooke wasn't really sure if Danielle believed her own words. "It prevents me from thinking about past partners too much. And truth be told, enough time passes by, and what was once too painful to spend time in becomes a simple footnote in your story. But the pain never quite goes away."

"We love you, Brooke," Clara interjected. "Are you sure you want to even entertain the option?"

Brooke sighed. She had been sure after seeing Pastor O'Connell. But her two closest friends would never lie to her.

"He does seem like a changed man," Brooke said. "He's got a daughter now. He's seen life outside of here, and he came back, so—"

"He has a kid?" Clara said. "I'm sure the kid's great, but now I have questions."

Brooke bit her lip. She wished she hadn't said anything. But she needed to hear this, she knew.

"I'll answer them now," Brooke said. "The kid is great. Luke was married. I don't know the situation with his ex-wife. It was too painful for him to recall when we went fly-fishing. I don't think he did something to her. I think something happened to her. But that's all I know. And that, yes, I'm still attracted to him."

Danielle and Clara didn't hide their concerned glance at each other.

"Just be careful," Danielle said. "If we saw Luke, we wouldn't trash him. He was a good guy, and I am sure he has matured. But two people can be good people and still hurt each other. In fact, it's that exact care and love for each other that can make the hurt so bad."

"Yeah, the more you care about him, the worse you can hurt. Just be careful, Brooke."

Brooke, again, sighed. They were right.

But Pastor O'Connell had also been right. *Trust in God's will. The full story is yet to be revealed.*

"I promise I'll be careful. I can't promise anything else."

13

LUKE

Monday, Tuesday, Wednesday, and Thursday morning came and went. Luke picked up his flirtations in the dropoff line, drawing a subtle but coy grin from Brooke. Montana was not oblivious; more than once, she made songs about Daddy and Ms. Young sitting in a tree, k-i-s-s-i-n-g, and so on.

But through it all, Luke refrained from pushing to the next step. He needed to see something more, something to suggest that he could indeed ask for another meeting with Brooke. He knew there was something there, but he knew that there was far more in the rearview mirror that didn't just vanish overnight. He trusted the Lord to show him when the time for patience had ended and when the time for action had arrived.

Thursday afternoon provided him just what he hoped for.

~

AT THE PICKUP line from school that day, he noticed that even as he was a good six or seven cars behind the official pickup spot, Brooke was eying his truck. This far away, in this public a venue, he did not dare to blow his horn or lean out the window, but he certainly would not let the opportunity pass by. Not when he'd waited this long.

When he finally pulled up, Brooke had her arms folded, a sly look on her face, with a piece of paper in her hand. Luke rolled down the window.

"Hello, pretty lady," Luke said.

"That's Ms. Young here, thank you very much," Brooke said, but the smile remained on her face. "Did you know your daughter is a better writer than you?"

"Is that much of a question?"

"I suppose not," Brooke laughed, "but she has a unique craft for her age. She writes so well, I think she has a gift that could use some refinement."

Luke nodded, curious to see where this was going. He would do anything for his daughter, but he had to admit if she had strong creative skills, he would not have known where it came from, for neither he nor Chelsea were especially talented there.

"When I lived in Sacramento, I used to offer tutoring to the kids. Many couldn't even afford to eat out, so I didn't charge them, and I don't think it would be fair to start now."

"Brooke, ahem, Ms. Young, you know—"

"Look at this and decide when you want Montana to get lessons."

Brooke looked over her shoulder. Goodness, the way her brown hair flowed in the air, it was unfair how even simple movements like that could make Luke feel sixteen all over again.

"Here she comes. Luke..."

She didn't finish her words. The look in her eyes said it all. *Your daughter has a gift, but that's not the real reason I'm giving you this note.* "Hey, Montana," Brooke said, now fully back in her role as Ms. Young, second grade teacher, "be sure to tell Daddy what you learned in school today."

"OK!" Montana said excitedly as she got into the truck with

Brooke's help. Brooke waved to them both as she turned away, leaving Luke to decide what he wanted to do next. "Daddy, have you ever heard of 'show, don't tell?'"

"Um, yes?" Luke said, his thoughts still with what had just happened. "Why don't you explain it to Daddy so that he makes sure you understand it?"

"Of course! 'Show, don't tell' means that instead of writing something with passive verbs, you show it! So like instead of saying 'Ms. Young is nice,' I could say 'Ms. Young wrote me a note about my writing!'"

Show, don't tell.

Something about that phrase resonated with Luke in a way it never had in English class. However, he could not quite pinpoint what it was, so he turned his attention back to his daughter.

"And what did that note say?"

"Ms. Young said that she gave you the same note!"

"Oh?" Luke said, looking down at the folded paper in his lap. "Well, Daddy has to drive us safely home. I promise to read it."

"OK! She also teaches me before and after school and during lunch. She says I'm really good at it and just need more practice. She even said if you were OK with it, she could come over and tutor."

Luke's stomach flipped. Her, coming to the ranch to tutor? It was a wonderful gift for Montana, and it spoke a lot about the type of person Brooke was to put aside their past to help nurture youthful talent.

It also was…

A sign to take the next step.

It had to be, right? Brooke could have easily continued to mentor Montana from the comforts of the school, asking Luke to come an hour later if Montana wanted even more tutoring time. To offer to come to his ranch… and Brooke had to know that meant his parents would start asking questions. His brothers would start asking questions.

Luke had prayed to the good Lord for a sign to press forward and see what might happen. He'd exercised more patience than he ever had to wait almost two weeks for another chance to see Brooke. Well, it sure seemed like he had gotten his prayer.

He just wondered if the Lord had attached a catch somehow. Maybe Brooke wasn't really doing this as a hint to Luke? Maybe she really did only want to teach Montana?

But Luke knew he was just making excuses to avoid getting hurt worse. The Lord had given him an opportunity—he needed to be bold and take it.

"We'll have to check with Mimi and Papaw when we get home to make sure it's OK," Luke said, "and I will need to speak to Ms. Young to understand what all we're getting into. But I will certainly see if it's possible."

"Yay! Thank you, Daddy!"

Luke smiled. Even if it didn't work out with Brooke, it sure felt good to see his daughter so excited.

But it sure seemed more likely than ever it was going to work out with Brooke.

Luke continued to pepper Montana with questions about her day and what she was learning with writing as they headed home. Montana's enthusiasm for various lessons, like "use active verbs" and "use strong adjectives," intrigued Luke. He had never considered himself a writer—he needed only to think of how short he fell when his writing compared to Brooke's—but if his eight-year-old daughter could learn to write, why couldn't his thirty-two-year-old self?

They got home about fifteen minutes later, with Montana running in the house to say hello to Mimi, Papaw, and hopefully Benny at a safe distance. Luke remained in the car, unfolded the paper, and read the note.

"*Dear Montana,*

I am amazed at your writing skills! You have a unique gift that many people will come to appreciate. If you would like more help, please see me before or after school or during lunch. You can also inform your father that I would be happy to help you on weekends—you should enter some writing contests with your skills!

Best,

Ms. Young"

Short, sweet, and genuine. Luke couldn't recall any teachers who had helped him like Brooke was offering, but he also had never put himself out there as the most gifted or motivated student.

He needed to be careful here. If he messed things up, he feared what would happen to Montana's chances at private tutoring. He knew Brooke better than to think she would take out any anger or heartache on his daughter, but it was much tougher to take away something once it was given.

But...

He could not wait.

He pulled his phone out of his pocket. He checked the note again—Brooke had scribbled her phone number on there, a 406 number like all people of Montana had. Even after over a decade away from her, the number came back to him almost instantly, with him easily able to remember the last four digits once he saw the first three.

He drew in a breath. *Lord, I hope I am interpreting your signs right. I hope I am following your will. Give me the strength to do her right this time.*

He pulled up her contact name, having never deleted it in his phone, and called her. She answered on the second ring.

"Hello?" she said, sounding like she didn't have his number still saved, although Luke could still hear kids talking in the background.

"Brooke, it's Luke Walker."

"I know," she said, warmth returning to her voice. *So she did keep my number saved. Or she just knew I would call. That's nice.*

"I am looking here at the note, and it says you would like to tutor my daughter on weekends at the ranch," he said. "Brooke, you didn't let me finish in line, so I'll say it here now. I don't feel right doing this without payment."

Brooke laughed.

"Luke, if I wanted to do anything for the money, I certainly wouldn't have gone into teaching. Trust me when I say that seeing young kids developing their talents, especially in writing, is the best form of payment. God gave me the gift of teaching; using that gift is reward enough."

Maybe so, Luke thought, but God didn't pay her bills or for anything she did with her parents or friends. Still, he thought better of contesting the point, especially on the phone when Brooke could easily hang up at a moment's notice.

"You really think she's that gifted?"

"Absolutely. Most kids in second grade are learning to write sentences. She's learning how to write good sentences and put them together. I won't say the word 'precocious' without more time with her, but it wouldn't surprise me."

She must have gotten that from Chelsea, Luke thought with some sadness. It felt like there was some sort of irony to Brooke maximizing the talents Chelsea had given his daughter, but he didn't want to dwell on the subject too long.

"Well, it's a deal then," Luke said.

"Sounds good."

Take it to the next step, Luke. You got the surface reason for calling her out of the way.

"I think we should discuss this further in person," he said, the words sounding confident, but his body tense with excitement and nerves. "What's someplace near you we can talk?"

"How about The Homestead?" she said.

It took a second for Luke to realize she meant the coffee shop near the school, not the homestead on his property. Luke wasn't much of a coffee drinker; life and work on the ranch kept him plenty awake, especially during the pre-dawn hours. But Brooke could have said "a foot under the Missouri River," and he would have said yes.

"Sure, would you like to meet after service on Sunday?"

Brooke hesitated for just a second.

"I think we attend different services. But I can do the early morning service on Sunday. Why not?"

As soon as the question got asked, Luke realized it had been a dumb suggestion. If privacy was the goal, the two of them meeting at the church to go to coffee was the worst idea possible. Plus, he didn't want Montana being distracted by Ms. Young being there, even though in a town as small as Greenville, it was virtually impossible not to run into teachers in public.

Plus, his parents would surely say something, and Luke couldn't pretend not to notice her or not talk to her after church. That would just make things worse.

"Actually, I think The Homestead doesn't open until nine on Sundays. So we'd just be kicking rocks for half an hour after. Why don't we meet there for brunch? They have breakfast foods."

Thank you, Lord, for making sure we don't worship you at the same time.

"That works for me," Luke said.

A silence fell as both Luke and apparently Brooke struggled to decide what to say next. Were they still going to play the game of keeping it coy? Could Luke ever be consistent in when he flirted and when he played innocent?

"Great, then I'll see you then. Talk to you later, Luke."

Brooke solved the problem for him. But her sweet, excited tone was not lost on him.

"Bye, Brooke."

The line ended a short while later. He turned his eyes back to his actual homestead, only then realizing that Mimi and Montana were staring at him through the window, quickly turning away when they realized he was finally looking back at him.

Luke chuckled. He was starting to think the idea of secrecy was ludicrous; the sooner he gave up on it, the more easily he could see if the Lord was blessing him with his desired second chance.

14

BROOKE

*B*rooke got to The Homestead at about ten minutes until eleven, making sure to grab her and Luke a table inside. In a normal situation, she would have preferred to be outside, but until she and Luke were ready to be one way or the other, she didn't want passing eyes to start asking questions.

Of course, they probably already were.

She informed the barista she was waiting on someone and sat in her seat, barely able to control her fidgeting. She knew discussions about Montana would last, at most, ten minutes; she knew Luke knew that; she knew Luke knew she knew that. It felt like things were very much coming to a head, and just as she had at church that day, she prayed for the strength to make the right choice, whatever it may be.

Even though a part of her very much had a preference for what the right choice would end up being.

Five minutes later, she peered through the window at the front of the store and saw Luke's truck pull up. Her heart started beating faster as she took in cooling breaths. But when he stepped outside the truck and sported a white cowboy hat, a

COWBOY'S HOMECOMING

royal blue button-down shirt, and dark blue, almost black jeans… Lord help her.

She reminded herself it was the same Luke as before. She just needed to talk to him as a person and not as a symbol or an idea. Of course, that was easier said than done when Luke wasn't looking like John Wayne in the twenty-first century.

She stood up when Luke walked through the door, flashing that full-tooth grin he loved to bear.

"Hello, Luke," she said.

As he approached, it suddenly occurred to her she had not anticipated how he might greet her. Handshake? Hug? Nothing? All the times before, he'd been in a car or at a distance. Yet…

He opened his arms, and without thinking about it, she fell into his sturdy chest, resting her head against his rock-solid shoulders. Luke had always been on the stockier side, especially compared to the other schoolboys, and not much had changed in that regard in the last fourteen years.

Except he also smelled like he had applied some sort of cologne he certainly had not worn in high school, and heavens, she had to pull away before she got swept up in the intoxicating allure. In some regards, it was already too late.

"Good to see you," Luke said. "Good choice with the green top."

"Yeah?"

Brooke, of course, had agonized over her outfit choice, having to find the balance between being appropriate for church yet beautiful, yet not inappropriate, to catch Luke's eye. Luke had made all that agonizing worth it with a mere six words.

"I didn't think you'd notice a woman's outfit," Brooke teased.

"As a single dad, I have no choice but to have a little more awareness," he said with a chuckle as he took a seat.

He seemed so much more at ease than Brooke did, but she reminded herself that it had taken him over a week for him to ask her out again—and even that was a stretch of an interpretation. Surely, he felt some nervousness too.

"How is that going for you?" Brooke asked, meaning it as innocuous but quickly realizing she'd jumped headfirst into the heaviest possible content.

"Well, having a sweet daughter who listens to me—so far—has made it a heck of a lot easier," Luke said. "And she's got a wonderful teacher willing to mentor her, so I only have to worry about her sixteen hours a day."

"You're funny," Brooke said as she saw someone walk by with an iced coffee, making her realize they had not ordered. "Would you care to join me in line?"

Luke nodded yes, and the two stood about five people behind the register. Through it all, Brooke gravitated toward Luke, almost unable to control herself, as if she were a planet trying to break free of the sun's gravity. More than once, the two of them brushed arms when one turned to look at the other, and every single darn time, Brooke got goosebumps despite it being a relatively warm August Sunday.

Luke ordered an iced green tea, while Brooke got herself her usual, an iced coffee with extra brown sugar syrup, although today she asked for it to have extra *extra* brown sugar syrup. Luke cocked an eyebrow, as if implying something, but he made it just even "worse" when he said nothing at all. She was in line, and she could barely contain herself.

She pulled out her purse to pay, but Luke put his hand gently on her arm and pushed it back down. Heavens, those goosebumps again! And the way his eyes gazed into hers.

"I've got it," he said.

Brooke could only weakly mumble, "Thanks," so enraptured by his eyes and his cologne that she couldn't say anything more. Luke made easy conversation with the barista, and it occurred to Brooke what was happening.

She had inadvertently given him some sign that said she was

beyond any doubt into him, and he had shifted from cautious to confident. She had seen this once before, on about their third date in high school. Up to that point, Luke, as a younger boy, had mostly shown bravado, but she could see right through it.

After she had wrapped her arm around his waist, however, and told him how much of a good time she was having, everything had changed. He showed no fear in pulling her in for a kiss that night, for holding her close, for telling her he was going to see her again—not that he *wanted* to see her again, but that he *would*.

The sign obviously here would have been less subtle, but they also weren't kids anymore. Luke did not need so obvious a sign as her arm around him to shift.

Well, the only question then was when, not if, he would try to kiss her.

The thought was exciting.

Calm yourself, Brooke. He still hasn't told you about what happened with Montana's mother.

The two of them stood waiting by the pickup counter, and Brooke found herself strangely quiet. The thought of Montana's mother, though passively raised mere minutes ago, now hung over her excitement like a storm cloud mere minutes away from overtaking an otherwise sunny day.

"Brooke?"

Luke's question shook her out of her head. She felt stupid for feeling so high one second and so self-loathing the next. Was she thirteen or thirty?

She took in a breath. Yes, she was still attracted to him. Everything so far had made her want him.

But that question had to be answered. It's not that divorce automatically took Luke off the table, but she needed the full story. Unfortunately, a part of her knew she was also going to verify the story later through some stalking online.

"Sorry, I…"

No, get to it.

"Luke, I don't want to beat around the bush any longer. I have to know the answer to the question you didn't want answered."

Luke's smile faded, a serious expression overtaking the handsome cowboy.

"I had a feeling you didn't come here just to talk to me about tutoring Montana," he said, then a chuckle came forth. "To think we're in our thirties now, yet we both make the other so nervous we can barely talk."

Brooke also chuckled back, relieved he had not snapped as he had the last time.

"I suppose there's no point in hiding anything, since you'll never meet her," Luke said with a sigh. "Let me take you back to that fateful weekend in April 2019. Montana was just speaking in complete sentences, but she didn't fully understand what was going on. It's probably for the best."

Luke nodded to the table they just came from. They both sat down. Brooke folded her hands, leaned forward, and listened.

"That day was the saddest day of my life."

15

LUKE

FOUR YEARS EARLIER

The beeping of the Holter monitor in the Spokane hospital told Luke that his wife was still alive as of seven a.m.

The spacing in between the beeps told him that would not be the case for much longer.

He held his daughter in his arms as he looked down at the emaciated face of his wife, Chelsea, stricken by an aggressive form of breast cancer that, despite being caught "in time," had sapped her of her energy, her will, and soon, her life. The sight nearly put Luke to tears, and the only reason he did not cry was because he knew he needed to stay strong for Montana in this darkest hour of their lives.

But whatever strong face he put on, whatever stoic lines he wore, masked the boiling rage he felt inside.

It was the closest he had ever come to renouncing his faith and God. He had prayed every night on end for Him to help turn the tide, for Chelsea to recover, but it never got any better. In fact, her deterioration was agonizingly slow, a process of dying that spared no mercy. Sometimes, Luke couldn't help but feel like the Lord was treating him like Job, punishing him in every way just to see how long a man could remain faithful before cracking.

The only reason that he remained in his faith was because of the email correspondence he carried on with Pastor Paul O'Connell back in Greenville. He did not like nor trust any of the local pastors, and Pastor O'Connell had a way of hearing about Luke's doubts without judging or condemning him. The good pastor's empathy and sorrow gave Luke small breaths of gratitude against a tornado of grief and despair.

Now, with his wife probably unlikely to make it to Easter Sunday, Luke had no choice but to make peace with the matter.

"Daddy," Montana said. "Is Mommy going to get up?"

The question nearly brought Luke to tears. How did you explain to a four-year-old that no, her mother was never going to get up again? You could say she was going to heaven and that she would be in a better place, sure, but four-year-olds had an unfortunately curious way that made explaining things more challenging.

"Not here," Luke finally said.

"Where?"

Luke took a second to answer. So much time had passed since Chelsea's last beep that he wondered if the moment of death had come without them realizing it.

But no, her heartbeat had just slowed, apparently below thirty beats per minute. The doctors had said she was no longer in pain, but who knew how true that was? At least she was not awake.

"In heaven, with Jesus and our Lord," Luke said, though he could not bring himself to say the words with anything more than a flat line.

"Will she come to visit us?"

Luke bit his lip and bowed his head. He drew in a slow, deliberate breath. He was losing the battle not to shed tears in front of his daughter.

"In your thoughts and in your prayers, yes," Luke said.

"What about at my birthday?"

That finally brought Luke to tears. He had to sit down as he held Montana, and the two embraced each other.

No, Chelsea would never be at any of her daughter's birthdays. She would never see young Tana go to prom, graduate from high school, meet her soulmate, or bear children of her own. She would never see some of the smaller but still meaningful moments—her first sports championship trophy, a report card with high praise from a teacher, or the simple joy of riding horseback at sunset.

Luke couldn't even consider what his future held right now. He was too grief-stricken at knowing that Tana would have to grow up much faster than she would have otherwise. And who knew what sort of consequences Chelsea's passing would have on their daughter in five, ten, twenty years? He was no psychologist, but he had read enough in the last few months to know that what happened at a young age carried through one's life.

"Daddy," Tana said. "It's OK. You'll be there, right?"

Luke squeezed her harder, groaning.

"Of course," Luke said through sniffles. "Daddy will always be there for you. All your birthdays, all your celebrations, all the good and bad times. I will be there for you."

Montana nodded, and then she started to cry. The two let their tears flow freely into each other's shoulders.

"Luke?"

Luke raised his head and looked over. To his incredible shock, Chelsea was awake. She had not moved—in fact, it looked like she struggled to open her eyes, let alone to speak. Her voice was the weakest he'd ever heard, a volume that Luke was almost surprised he had heard.

"Chelsea?"

"Mommy?"

"Oh, my family," she said. "Come, sit in bed with me."

Luke walked Montana over to her mother's right side, reminding her not to lean on her mother and put weight on her. Montana easily complied, resting on her elbow and looking into her mother. Luke crawled over to Chelsea's left side, making for a very cramped but loving space.

"I'll always be with you," Chelsea said. "Tana. Be good for Daddy."

"I will," Montana said with multiple head nods.

"Luke," Chelsea said.

She was so weak that she could only turn her eyes, not her entire neck. Luke sat up so he could better look into her eyes.

"I will always love you," Chelsea said. "You have a long life ahead."

"Chelsea, don't worry about me."

"I can't help it," she said, and the smallest of smiles formed. "Do not stop living. Be a part of God's world. If that means... finding someone else. That's OK."

"No, Chelsea, I took a vow to love you in sickness and in health. I'm not leaving you."

"Until death do us part," she added.

Luke wouldn't have this conversation right now. No! His wife was in her last moments, and she...

She wasn't asking him to find someone else now. Not even close. Just to be open to God's will down the line.

He couldn't fathom such a world. Sure, Chelsea was not his first, but she was the one he had married. The idea of finding someone else...

He couldn't do it. He simply could not do it.

"I will *always* love you, Chelsea," he said, "whether you are here on this Earth or not."

"I know," Chelsea said, and she weakly raised her hand. Luke took it in his before she exerted too much strength. "There's always room for more love. Never stop loving."

Luke leaned forward and kissed his wife on the lips. He sniffled some more. Chelsea smiled.

"I love you, Luke. Tana, I love you."

"I love you, Chelsea."

He pulled her into his arms and did his best to control his breathing.

"Mommy?"

But Chelsea did not respond. Though the Holter monitor showed a spike a second later, showing Chelsea's body still lived, no more words came.

"Let's lie here quietly, Tana," Luke said. "The good Lord is about to take Mommy home. Let's be here for her when that happens."

∽

At six p.m., nearly eleven hours later, the doctors said that Chelsea Walker, just twenty-six years old, had passed away.

"Is she gone?" Montana asked.

Luke bit his lip and nodded.

"Yes," he said, deciding he didn't have it in him to lie or make up something stupid.

Montana looked at her now-deceased mother. She kissed her forehead and then bawled. Luke cried as well. He kissed Chelsea one more time on the forehead, declared, "You're in God's hands now," and stood up and picked his daughter up as tears streaked down their cheeks.

Luke walked into the hallway in a daze as other nurses and doctors entered the hospital room. He slowly pulled himself together, but all that meant was he felt numb, not pain. Montana continued to bawl her eyes out, the weight of the moment having just hit her.

That final conversation with Chelsea was still too raw to

think about in any detail, but as he went to the hospital window and looked out over Spokane, one thought came to him.

He could not stay at the home he and Chelsea had bought in Spokane.

He loved the house; it was a four-bedroom house on the outskirts of suburbia, with plans to use the fourth room for a second child. The views, though not quite as majestic as Greenville or even Bozeman, still provided him with a clear view of God's great blue sky.

But so long as he lived there, he'd never be able to fulfill Chelsea's final request—to continue living, to be a part of God's will and His plan. Every morning would entail waking up to a bed without his wife, to living a life built for a family as a single father. He couldn't even fathom dating anyone else right now, let alone marrying someone else and starting over, but even if that never came to fruition, he had to be a strong, present father for his daughter.

There was only one place he could do that.

The place that he truly considered *home*, not just a house to live.

Greenville, Montana.

There would be some logistics to work out, and Luke understood it would not happen overnight. He knew that there would be months, perhaps even years, of grieving and moving slowly ahead. He would have to return to Washington occasionally to bring Montana to visit Chelsea's parents, so it wasn't like he could put this part of his life entirely behind him.

But Greenville was *home*. It was where Mimi and Papaw were. It was where all the places that brought him comfort, from the obvious like Yellowstone National Park to the local like Bacon & Bakin', were. And it was where Luke knew, as he had matured from his initial craze of a freshman year, that he would eventually return to.

"I miss Mommy already," Montana said on his shoulder, still sobbing.

Luke brought her down to the ground and knelt before her. He drew in a deep breath.

He had months to explain to Montana that they'd be moving back to Greenville. She had long expressed interest, anyway, in seeing the state that she was named after. That all could wait.

"I do too, sweetie," Luke said. "Always love and remember her."

"I will."

Father and daughter embraced, aware that, though as painful and deeply wounded as each was, by relying first on God and then on each other, they would eventually learn how to continue living.

16

BROOKE

Brooke didn't even bother to hide the tears that came down her face by the time Luke finished recounting what had happened with Montana's mother.

Luke had clearly told this story before, perhaps to his parents or brothers, because though his voice wavered in a couple of spots, he maintained his composure and never shed tears. But she could see the pain in his eyes when he recounted Montana's reaction.

A part of her felt guilty for having judged what *might* have happened so harshly. She'd assumed Luke had cheated on her, had Montana out of wedlock, or had a bitter divorce and fled home.

None of that had happened.

Luke had been a good man throughout, and he still was a great man. He'd been given unbelievable tragedy—to say nothing of Chelsea herself—and yet, he was still a man of God, a great father, and, presumably, a disciplined ranch hand, if not the outright rancher of Hope Valley Ranch now. True, their relationship had ended on rather brutal terms, but no one was perfect, especially at eighteen years old.

"Luke..." Brooke said, wiping away tears from her eyes. "I'm so sorry. I'm so sorry I pushed you to recall... that moment."

"You have nothing to apologize for, Brooke," Luke said. "Anyone that gets close to me is going to know that story. It's as much a part of me as Montana. You were going to learn it eventually."

Brooke dabbed away another tear. Then a thought came to her she hated for thinking, for it seemed so selfish after such an extraordinarily tragic story, but she could not shake it.

Was Luke truly over Chelsea and ready to date again?

Brooke had no hard feelings about the possibility. For goodness' sake, Chelsea had bore him Montana and helped raise her for the first four years of the young girl's life. To lose someone like that, and to do so relatively recently, would have broken well over ninety-nine percent of men, and no one would ever fault them for being cracked beyond repair.

But even those who did not break still had cracks and scars, and Brooke couldn't help but wonder if Luke picked those scabs in private, keeping the wound fresh and ultimately preventing a second chance at love from entering his life.

No, it wasn't her place to ask such a deeply personal question at this point. To some extent, she trusted Luke would not be pursuing her this much if he still was in the throes of grief and despair. But she knew that attraction was an intoxicating power, one that could cloud any man or woman if not properly accounted for.

And unfortunately, the only way to lift that veil and discover unresolved feelings beneath was to get so far into courtship that it hurt the other person. In this case, Brooke.

"What are you thinking about?" Luke asked.

No, Brooke could not confess what she'd just been thinking about. That would definitely slam the door on any potential opportunity. She'd just have to trust in God's will.

"That you are one heck of a brave man," she said. "Montana is an extremely well-behaved child."

"She is a good kid. I got lucky," Luke said. "I might even call her precocious, but I'm not sure exactly what that means."

"It means she's smarter than smart, and in her writing skills, I would agree," Brooke said with a smile.

Luke smiled back at her and leaned back in his chair, letting out a tension-relieving groan. Luke was definitely in a strong place, all things considered, but the groan worried Brooke a bit.

Then again, if Luke had completely and utterly moved on and was entirely indifferent to losing his first wife a mere four years ago, wouldn't that also say something about him? Something much worse than the possibility of being a little hung up on her still?

"Can I ask another question?" Brooke said as the question came to mind.

"Sure."

"You mentioned in the story that you knew as soon as… everything happened that you'd be coming home. Yet it didn't happen until this past month. How come?"

Luke chuckled.

"Well, I did say I figured at the time there'd be some obstacles, and sure as heck, there were," he said. "First, I needed to give Montana time to grieve. The first time I mentioned moving to Greenville, she threw a fit and said she'd never leave her Mom. When I framed it as coming to be with Mimi and Papaw and in *her* state, she eventually came around. So then we had to put the house up for sale, and that was early 2020. You might remember, though, some things happening in the world around that time."

"How could I forget?" Brooke said with a chuckle. "All those virtual classrooms, Zooms, staying at home… I thought more than once about coming here myself, just to be outdoors, long, long before my mother ever needed my help."

Luke nodded knowingly. Montana would not have been in kindergarten at that point yet, but all the restrictions had surely made raising her that much more difficult.

"It all made selling the house much more difficult, as I didn't want to sell it to some online company. I wanted to sell it to a family that would actually live there. This happened around the fall of 2021—much, much later than I expected—and by that point, Montana had started kindergarten. I did not want to uproot her in the middle of the school year, so the plan at the time was to move in the summer of 2022."

Luke sighed and laughed, a sign this story wasn't nearly as heavy as the one that preceded it.

"I got talked into staying in town by Chelsea's parents for one more year, but I knew it was a mistake. By the end of that school year, I made it very clear to them and to Montana that she had one more summer with her friends in Spokane, and then we were moving here. They eventually got the picture, only asking that Montana see them twice a year. Tana herself was sad for a bit, but also excited to see the state for the first time."

"Quite the whirlwind coming home, huh?" Brooke said.

"I was half-expecting Tana's grandparents to kidnap her and refuse to release her unless I promised to stay in Spokane," Luke said, but he said it as a joke, without malice. "Once we started the drive over, everything fell into place perfectly. Chelsea's parents even met us the morning of our departure and wished us well."

"And you said Montana never felt sad about it?"

Luke shook his head.

"The thing about eastern Washington in general, not just Spokane, is that it looks more like Texas and Oklahoma than it does Wyoming or Montana. That's not to say there are no mountains, there certainly are, but it's just not the same. I think when she saw how beautiful going east was, it became a much easier decision for her. Plus, she thinks Mimi and Papaw are the greatest thing ever."

Luke chuckled.

"I think she's learning, though, Mimi will not bake her apple pie every single night like she did when she was visiting."

"Every night?"

"Mimi loves to play the part of grandma who spoils her grandkids. What can I say?"

Brooke and Luke laughed together.

"So you're really set here," Brooke said, even though she knew the obvious reason. "You're truly home for good?"

"Yep," Luke said without hesitation. "We'll make the drive to Spokane twice a year to visit Chelsea's parents, and I'm sure we'll go travel somewhere in the summer. But yes, this has been, is, and will be home."

That warmed Brooke's heart.

It just left the question of if Luke's heart and spirit were also here, or still quietly back in Spokane with his deceased wife.

But still, Brooke did not dare to broach that topic. For now, conversation had become light and joyful once more, and such a heavy topic would need a more appropriate, private venue than here.

"Put it this way, I'd sooner build my own ranch from scratch than move anywhere else, let alone Bozeman."

That drew a laugh from Brooke, who had forgotten one of Luke's many quirks.

"I forgot how much you joked about Bozeman."

"That big city?" Luke said with a mischievous grin on his face. "The place that's becoming San Francisco, Montana?"

"Oh, stop, it's not that bad!" Brooke said, playfully hitting his arm. "You make it sound like it's become an urban wasteland; it's still a quaint town of only about fifty-five thousand people!"

"Compared to less than forty thousand when we were in

school, with a good chunk of those being college kids across the state."

But still, the two laughed. It felt good to laugh. It felt great to see Luke seemingly having moved on from the conversation of just a few minutes ago.

"By the way, do you have plans for the rest of the day?" Luke asked.

"It's the Lord's day, of course not," Brooke said, even though she knew there were times, as a teacher, she had no choice but to work on Sundays. "Why do you ask?"

"Well, I didn't move back here just to sit in coffee shops, you know," he said with a smirk. "Let's say we go for a hike? At least this way, you won't need wading boots."

Brooke leaned back in her chair. She would need to get back to her mother at some point. She could also picture her mother giving her grief for cutting time with Luke Walker short because of her; her mother would insist on spending all day with Luke if the young man wanted it.

"I say I like that idea," Brooke said. "You'll have to drive, though. I want to see what Luke Walker thinks qualifies for a good hike."

∼

Luke ended up taking Brooke to a trail called Highview Vantage, a trail that she did not recognize. That was an impressive feat, considering that Brooke felt like she knew almost every trail in the area. The drive had taken them further south, closer to, ironically enough, Bozeman, and she liked to stay central to Greenville or north, but it still surprised her.

"Impressive," Brooke said as Luke put his truck in park.

"I used to live here too, you know," Luke smirked, fully aware of what Brooke was implying. "You're not the only one who loves getting outdoors."

He swung around the truck, opened the passenger's door, and offered his hand to help Brooke off. Once more, she felt the surge of goosebumps and excitement coursing through her as her hand folded into his. The first time, there had been a wave of "what ifs" that filled her mind.

Now, though, it didn't seem so much "what if" but more "when?"

"Come," Luke said, eventually pulling his hand back, "the trail to the highest point is only about twenty minutes."

Along the way, Luke and Brooke only passed one solo hiker, a man in his mid-fifties that neither of them recognized. The solitude made Brooke feel even more certain that something was going to bring them together.

Was it going to be a kiss?

Fourteen years had not done much to make Brooke forget how electric Luke's kiss was. He never pushed boundaries, yet there was something just so exhilarating about it that made it impossible to move on from. Maybe that was exactly it—all the college boys and the city men wanted only one thing, which Brooke would only provide with a ring and a vow to God.

Luke was of the same faith and background, and so he knew where the line was, yet still touched and kissed her in all the space up to that line, at times literally causing Brooke to shiver.

Stay cool, Brooke. Remember, you need to go slow too.

He's changed, but so has his life. And you yourself need to make sure you're ready, never mind if he is.

But the thoughts felt like a nagging aunt more than a genuine conversation with herself. She knew full well if the opportunity came to kiss him, she would not pass it up.

Brooke distracted herself by asking if Luke had found any decent hiking trails in Spokane. He said that "decent" was the key word there, for while they existed, they didn't provide the same physical challenge and serenity as this state. He said he always tried to be grateful for being in Spokane, but he also always ended his prayers by asking for a chance to return home.

"I wish the good Lord hadn't put me through so much to get back here, but I suppose it makes me more grateful to be here then," he said.

"That's how I feel about Sacramento," Brooke said. "I tried to be grateful to be doing something very different from what I was used to, but in the end, all it did was accelerate my return home."

"Yeah? I've told you my story. What happened with you?"

Brooke nodded and began, though she knew her story would not have nearly the same emotional weight as Luke's did.

"Well, after we broke up, I got into UCLA with half-tuition paid and Montana State with a full ride," she said. "I truly did not know what to do, and nightly prayers did not seem to give me a clear answer. In the end, I took to advice what my father told me—that the more time I spent away from home, the more I'd grow to appreciate it."

"Funny, that's what my father said," Luke added with a smile that faded rapidly, perhaps aware that advice had split them apart.

"My first semester was terrible," Brooke said, thinking as she spoke just how similar her and Luke's story was. "I wanted to come home and transfer. But a long phone call with my mom kept me there. She told me that while she, indeed, thought Montana State in Bozeman would've been better, she said I had made a commitment to try something new, and that as much as home was home, if I wanted a healthy career, UCLA would be the better bet for that."

All the same, though, Brooke wanted a healthy *local* career. She did not care about trying to become a millionaire or launching her own tech company. She just wanted to have her own source of income and live happily.

"So I did that for four years and graduated before going to

work in Sacramento as a teacher. That was easily the hardest professional job I've ever had."

"Oh?"

"There's just so little resources," Brooke said, drawing in a breath. "Many of the kids were so poor, they could not afford lunch or even basic pens and pencils. I cannot tell you how many times I dipped into my own pocket to provide for them. But…"

She sighed.

"At some point, it honestly became too much. I had a two-year contract there, which I finished in the summer of 2016. I wanted to come home then, but my parents said I should still be out and about. They said teaching allowed me to go anywhere, so if there was a city I wanted to live in, I should."

"And I take it there was?"

Brooke nodded.

"I packed my bags and started teaching third grade in Utah."

"Utah? How interesting."

"It was the closest thing I felt I could get to Montana while being some distance away. It had beautiful scenery, a culture of values, and I wasn't too far from Montana. I did that for a few years but never quite fell in love with it. Then, this past spring, my mom had a terrible stroke."

"Oh, Brooke," Luke said. *He didn't know?* "You kept saying you had to care for your mother, but I didn't realize… should we be closer to home right now?"

"She has good days and bad days. Today is a good day. But for the first few months, it was rough. My dad needed to keep flying to support her, but I couldn't leave until the end of the school year. Thank heavens for good neighbors and Lola, her caretaker. But we knew we couldn't depend on our neighbors forever, so I got to move back in with her."

She drew in a heavy breath. Again, the parallels between

their paths seemed remarkable, yet somehow overlooked despite it staring right at their faces.

"Like you, I'm sure, I wish I was returning home under better circumstances, but—"

"I'm sure the Prodigal Son also wished he returned home under better circumstances, but we should be grateful that this town still welcomes us back with open arms," Luke said. "And we should be grateful that, just like the parable, there are good things waiting for us."

"Like what?"

Luke smirked.

"More like *who.*"

Oh, Lord have mercy.

"We're almost at the top. Come on!"

Luke broke out into a quickened pace, which Brooke struggled to keep up with. She was in shape and slender, but Luke used his body for a living out on his family's ranch; that was a very different kind of being in shape. When she caught up to him about thirty seconds later, he stood with his hands on his hips, overlooking the beauty of Montana.

From here, she felt like she had stumbled upon a slice of heaven. She could see Greenville to the far north, a more smattering of small buildings and dots. To the west, she could see Helena National Forest in all its glory. And, of course, Big Sky Country had its name for a reason, as Brooke felt like she could see all of heaven up above.

"Isn't it something?" Luke said.

Brooke nodded.

And then Luke did something Brooke was surprised by.

He wrapped his arm around her and pulled her in close.

17

LUKE

*L*uke had not taken Brooke to this trail by accident. He knew that if he took her anywhere near Helena, he would run into foot traffic bad enough to remind her of Los Angeles highways. If he took her east of his ranch, one, there wouldn't be as many good hiking trails, and two, his actions would be too obvious to ignore.

But taking her here provided them a scenic walk, a beautiful finishing point, and the privacy he so craved.

He couldn't say exactly what the turning point was when he knew, consequences be darned, he was ready to make a move to get Brooke back. Maybe it was telling the story of Chelsea, emotional and heart-wrenching as it was, and still wanting to be with Brooke. True, he would never forget Chelsea and would never stop loving her, but there was a difference between doing that *and* being with Brooke and doing that *or* being with Brooke.

Here, Brooke made it easy for it to be the former. Luke could not say if anyone else on God's Earth could have made him make that distinction, but he felt pretty sure that was the case.

All along the trail, he kept wondering if that moment was

the time to make a move. Under the trees? Out at one vantage point? No, it had to be the highest point on the trail. There was a reason it was called Highview Vantage.

As soon as he came to that highest point, it was as if God gave him the OK. Everything felt at peace. Everything felt perfect. He felt sure as he could in his heart that now was the time to make a move.

He wasn't sure if Brooke felt the same, and if she refused, he would step back. The thought, despite being fourteen years older and more mature, still sat in the pit of his stomach as it had the first time he'd asked her out. But he just saw it as a sign of how much he cared about her, not a prophecy that suggested he would fail.

When she got within range, he made the first of what he hoped were increasingly bold moves. He wrapped his arm around her waist and pulled her close. For a split second, she did not move. But then she leaned into him, and Luke felt more grateful than ever that things were going to work out just fine.

He could have kissed her right there, but what was the rush? In fact, Luke thought, the slower he went, the more rewarding it would be. Had the good Lord not taught him the importance of patience in all things?

"Pretty nice, isn't it?" Luke said.

Brooke nodded against his chest. Lord, his heart rate was rapidly increasing. If he waited too long, he might not make the move, and then—

"Can I ask you a question?" Brooke said.

Oh, heavens. Any time someone prefaced the actual question with permission for a question, it usually wasn't to ask to pass the salt and pepper. Luke gave the OK.

"Why are you doing this?"

Luke gulped. That didn't sound like a pleasant question. That—

"I mean... there are other women in Greenville that don't

have a permanently disabled mother or a shared history with you. To say nothing of the complications of teaching your daughter. Why... why?"

Brooke did not sound like she was looking for an excuse, at least not to Luke's ear. It sounded instead like a fear bubbling to the surface that she could not help but ask.

"You're safe, Brooke, and I mean that in the best way possible," Luke said, squeezing her even closer. "I didn't do any dating in Spokane after Chelsea died, but even though that was a decision, I could see the looks women our age would give us when they realized I was a single dad. Sure, some thought it was sweet, but others, rather than being open-minded like you are, assumed the worst."

It had never bothered Luke; between knowing he would move as soon as he could and caring for Montana, time and desire to date had never ventured beyond "might as well be open to God's will." But God had never put a woman that interested Luke in front of him before Brooke, and if He had, then Luke was oblivious.

"The life I have isn't for everyone, either," he said. "At some point, my brothers and I are going to take over the ranch. Papaw has lung cancer, and he plays it off like he's fine, but he won't be forever. Some women talk about loving ranch life until they realize how physically taxing it is, how dirty it is, and how early or late you can be up. Some women won't even entertain the option."

He shook his head. He realized he was approaching this from the wrong perspective. It made Brooke sound like she was the best of what was left over, and that was so far from the case, it just felt wrong to say.

"Brooke, I'm sorry, let me rephrase that. It doesn't matter if a million and one cowgirls lined up right now and promised to love Montana. No one has ever made me feel the way that you feel."

"Luke..."

"I'm serious, Brooke. Yes, I know I was married before, but that was only because I never thought I'd find myself back with you. And why would you want me? I treated you like dirt. I will always be grateful to Chelsea for giving me Montana, but standing here today, on the Lord's day, I swear to you that no one makes me feel like you do."

Luke tried to catch Brooke's eye, but she was looking down. Luke smiled and almost kissed the top of her head but restrained, only because he wanted his first kiss to her in fourteen years to be on the lips.

Then he heard...

Sniffling?

"Brooke?"

She looked up, and her eyes were welling. She opened her mouth to say something, to explain why she was crying, but she never said anything. Her eyes locked on his, their gaze unbreakable.

This... this was the moment. Yes, it was.

Luke moved his head slowly forward, as slowly as he could, in case he had misread the situation. Brooke never moved. She sniffled once, but a smile formed on her face. Her eyes fluttered close.

And Luke pulled her in for a kiss.

Oh, how he delighted in the feeling! How the kiss electrified him, both exciting him and bringing him to awe. Fourteen years had never felt both so long ago and just like yesterday.

He pulled her in tighter against him, their kiss remaining intact, as she ran his hands over his cheeks. He held her back in, not wanting to end this kiss as long as he could help it.

Finally, the kiss ended, but they remained a breath's distance away from each other.

"Luke..." Brooke whispered.

"Brooke, I missed you so much," Luke said.

They resumed their kissing. God was truly good. Over a decade of heartache, and—

"This is crazy," Brooke said as she pulled back, laughing. "What are we doing?"

Luke waited for a beat, trying to see if Brooke was regretting her action or just relishing in the long odds they had overcome. It was hard to tell—perhaps a bit of both?

"What do you mean, what are we doing?" Luke said, hoping nerves weren't clear in his voice.

"That's exactly what I'm asking!" Brooke said, her tone still unreadable. "I... I don't know what to make of this. It's both joyful and... unsettling."

"Unsettling?" Luke asked.

Brooke nodded and drew in a breath.

"You're one of the kindest men I have ever met, probably the kindest," Brooke said. "You are the only serious boyfriend I ever had. I loved you, and I suppose in some ways, I still do. And it's exactly for that reason that I feel unsettled."

"OK?" Luke said, not sure what to make of this.

"All of those things mean you can hurt me again worse than anyone else I know. Even my mother's memory is fading, so I know when she says mean things, it's not her, it's age. But that hurt I felt fourteen years ago, Luke. It doesn't fade. Just like the good times are worth celebrating, the painful times are worth remembering. I... it scares me."

Luke understood well. Breaking up once had changed him for the better, but he took no pride in the harm he had done Brooke. He could only imagine the damage that would come now if they failed.

And the further they went...

A nightmare scenario came to Luke just then, in which he dated Brooke so long, only to fail at the end, that she did not have time to meet someone and start a family. Or, perhaps not as bad but still awful, their failure and his commitment to his family's ranch would force her to find less distressing pastures as Greenville, her hometown.

A part of him hated to ask the question, but if he'd learned one thing from the last go-around, it was that he needed to communicate better, even when it was extremely painful.

"So what do you want to do?" he asked. "Should we... should we not pursue this?"

Brooke shook her head immediately. At least she wanted what he did.

"No, I feel the same way about you, Luke, but there's a lot to unpack. It's not like we broke up because of circumstances outside our control. We broke up because..."

"Of me, you can say it."

Brooke nodded.

"And I'm happy the Lord blessed you with a lovely wife and child. I truly am. But those are things I will be walking into. Can I replace Chelsea? Could I be a good mother to Montana?"

It dawned on Luke that Brooke was talking too much—she had had a habit of speaking and writing more than the usual person when she got anxious. Fourteen years, apparently, had also not changed that.

"Brooke," Luke said, gently placing his hands on her shoulders. "Those are questions neither of us have the answer to right now. We don't have to decide them right now. I didn't come up here to kiss you and then drop to one knee, nor did I come up here to kiss you and insist you now be Montana's stepmom. We're not lovestruck teenagers anymore, but adults. We can take our time."

"We can?" Brooke asked, not because she didn't understand, but because she seemed to want to make sure.

Luke nodded. A part of him, without question, wanted to say he loved her. A part of him wanted to fast-forward to a proposal so she could be part of his family and he wouldn't make the same mistakes as before.

But he wasn't going anywhere; if he was, it would only be to visit his brothers and bring them back to Hope Valley Ranch. He certainly wasn't going anywhere for the next four years. They wouldn't need to write letters to each other because they could drive down the road to each other.

Luke could not pretend the mistakes in his first semester in Washington had not happened. But he also had good reason to think they would not repeat themselves. He had the luxury of letting this second chance breathe and grow organically.

"Yes, we can," Luke said. "We don't even need to call ourselves dating right now if it helps. I—"

"No, don't say that," Brooke said with a laugh. "I'm not going to kiss a man and say we're not dating. I'll admit this is faster than I would go with anyone else, but I guess you're not anyone else."

Luke was wise enough not to make a smart crack there. And even if he wasn't, he could not overlook what Brooke had just said.

They were dating again.

Brooke was his girlfriend.

He couldn't help the huge smile that came to his face. This, of course, was not his final goal with Brooke. He allowed himself to imagine sometime in the future, maybe not even the distant future, proposing, getting married, and living out his life under God and with her.

But that was yet to come, and he did not pretend to know His will. He knew, however, that the present felt mighty fine.

"I guess not, and you're not anyone else either," Luke said. "Let's just take it slow. The good Lord will tell us the answer. And if, for whatever reason, this does not work, I promise to treat you better than I did before."

But Luke had no plans to allow this to not work.

"Sounds good, Luke," Brooke said, her voice finally coming to an even state.

She kissed him one more time, and a short while later, they started making their way back down the trail.

18

BROOKE

*L*uke Walker and Brooke Young, a couple once more.
It felt surreal to say.
It also felt... childish, almost?

Brooke knew anxiety had caught her in a cycle of nerves once again. She feared it would not work, which made her ask or say dumb things, which increased the odds it would not work, which made her say even dumber things, and so on and so forth. Luke, bless his heart, had brought her back under control of herself and in a more stable frame of mind. She felt blessed to be back in this spot.

No, childish wasn't the right word, but perhaps overly simplified was correct.

Being a couple in high school meant all the good and the bad of young love, and often, a trait or aspect could be both. The incessant yearning for each other meant every moment of being together was special, yet it often made it difficult to focus on life outside the relationship. The promises of being forever with the other made daydreaming beautiful, yet it also made the end even more painful than it otherwise would be.

Perhaps, then, calling him and her a couple wasn't so much

childish as it was just different. As an adult couple, they were more grounded in their faith, families, and wisdom than before. They would still do fun things together, but Brooke knew there would be a long—hopefully not too long—transition phase of sorts where she would need to become comfortable with Luke again.

And what about him with her? He'd initiated everything, even after sharing the story of Chelsea. But when he went home tonight and saw his daughter, would he also see the spirit of Chelsea in Montana? Would the sight and the ensuing memories pull him away from Brooke?

"What are you thinking about?" Luke asked as they descended, now a couple of hundred feet from the lookout point where they'd kissed.

Brooke promised herself to always tell the truth, but unlike before, to share it in a judgment-free way, to be as fair as possible.

"Just that this will need time," Brooke said. "I'm ready to give it time, but we can't rush anything. We're adults now."

"I know," Luke said. "Don't forget what I said back there. I didn't come up here to surprise you with a ring. I came up here to see if we might take the next step. You don't bound an entire flight of stairs in one step."

"Not unless you can fly," Brooke said, drawing a much-needed laugh from both of them.

Brooke said nothing more. They'd had enough intense, heavy conversation for the day.

And so, for the remainder of the hike down all the way to when Luke got back to The Homestead, Brooke deliberately kept the conversation light, never once mentioning the future or their minutes-old relationship. Instead, she talked about some of the funny stories from the first two weeks of teaching school, which fortunately meant she did not have to mention Montana's name. He, perhaps picking up on the same cue, only talked about Benny, their sheep that apparently was destined to eat Montana's homework throughout the year.

The ride was full of laughs, snorts, and giggles, just as it had been fourteen years ago. That's as far as Brooke let the thought go, not willing to go back to "but maybe this time..."

When Luke pulled into the lot of The Homestead, there were two other cars there—Brooke's and what looked like Jon's, given the military bumper stickers on the back.

"I had a great time today, Brooke," Luke said, and Brooke "hated" how his smile could make her swoon so much. "For all that we said, I'm excited to see what happens next."

And so was Brooke. She didn't want to be the party pooper all the time; she just needed to balance her strongest desires with a dose of reality. But that didn't mean that the weight was tilted toward being back with Luke.

"Agreed," Brooke said.

"Can I kiss you before we go?" he said. "I don't think you'll want me to do so in the school line."

"The kids would never stop teasing me or Montana," Brooke said, "so, sure, why not?"

Her smile grew and her eyes narrowed as Luke leaned forward. That first kiss on the mountain had been so intense and so rewarding, she'd darn near forgotten to hold herself back. This time, being in the car and in a public place, she had a little more control, but she still couldn't believe she was kissing Luke Darn Walker.

This time, she held the kiss longer than he probably expected. If she figured to see him like this next weekend, yet would see him professionally many times over the next week, goodness, she needed something to tide her over until that point. At the last part, she pulled back and gave him one more peck on the lips.

"Let's see where this goes, Luke," she said. "Just always promise to speak the truth to me, no matter what."

Luke nodded.

"I promise."

While Brooke often dreamed about the magical three words, those two words, in this context, meant more and were more genuine than if he had said the magical three words. With one more kiss on the cheek, Brooke got out of the truck and headed to her car, feeling elated.

When she got into her car, she just sat in the driver's seat, feeling the excitement course through her. She even yelled "yes!" like a teenager that had just gotten asked out by the most handsome boy in school. Luke pulled out of the lot first, waving as he drove by. Brooke reciprocated, and once he was out of sight, she collapsed against the back of her seat.

She knew she'd had the same thought countless times, but goodness, in the name of the Lord—this was really, truly, honestly, sincerely happening. She and Luke Walker were a couple again.

And while she was going to take it slow, Luke wasn't going away to college. There were no physical barriers to their relationship working. They seemed to have a real chance.

So long as the emotional barriers and the scars of their past didn't get too much in the way.

∽

BY THE TIME MONDAY CAME, Brooke realized she hadn't even scheduled the official reason for her and Luke's meeting—to schedule a time to tutor Montana in writing.

Fortunately, the young girl had taken to writing so much that she didn't need encouragement to see Brooke during lunch and in the minutes before and after school. Already she had written the first chapter of her book, "The Little Sheep That Could." Of course she named her main character Benny after the funny animal on her father's ranch, and while it would not win a Pulitzer Prize anytime soon, it was pretty good for a second grader.

Throughout her tutoring, Brooke remained professional and slightly distanced from Montana, not wanting to give her false hope about becoming more a part of her family than just being a teacher. But she couldn't help herself, occasionally thinking about what it would be like to be this young girl's stepmother. Generally, kids who came from a safe home environment behaved well in school, which boded well for Montana.

But more than that, Brooke had always wanted to start a family, and while she still wanted children of her own, she would be more than happy to consider Montana part of her own family. The thought, a silly one in the first week of school, progressively became more and more a concrete idea in her head as time passed.

When Friday came, Luke didn't bother to hide his excitement at seeing Brooke in the drop-off line. When she approached with Montana, he leaned forward and dropped his voice.

"Come by the ranch tomorrow at ten a.m.," he said. "I'll pay you if I have to. Montana won't stop talking about your teaching."

Brooke nodded. She had nothing else going on, and this was just one more step forward in her second budding relationship with Luke. *Even if I had something else going on...*

She didn't even need to contact Lola for assistance, as her father had gotten in on Wednesday and was providing care to her mother for the next week and a half. She was as free as she had been since the school year started.

"I'll be there," she said.

"Can't wait to see your pretty face."

Brooke could only hope that her blushing wasn't that obvious as she went back to finish her job as line monitor for the day.

COWBOY'S HOMECOMING

∼

BROOKE WOKE up at the crack of dawn the next day, which for her was sleeping in.

She had gotten so used to waking up at six a.m. to get to school just before seven, an hour before classes started, that her body could not go much past sunrise—which at this time was about fifteen till seven. It was strange, Brooke thought, what remained so similar and what changed so much in nearly a decade and a half. Here, Brooke knew the days of sleeping past ten a.m., sometimes even eleven a.m., were long gone.

The only regret she had waking up this early was that she still had another three hours to go before Luke wanted her to come tutor Montana, and with the drive only taking about twenty minutes, she had two and a half hours of her own time—much too long to go without daydreaming about seeing Mr. and Mrs. Walker once more, their various animals, and, of course, their ranch.

She passed the time by making coffee and breakfast for her parents, making sure that they started their day appropriately. Her father, an ardent fan of Bacon & Bakin', got, what else, bacon with eggs and toast; her mother, needing to watch her health, got some yogurt with strawberries and blackberries. Brooke made herself a quick omelet with mushrooms and ground beef, then put the plates out on the table for whenever her parents woke up.

That got her all the way to half past seven.

She sighed. She was just going to have to sit with the discomfort of waiting for ten a.m. But compared to the discomfort of not knowing where she stood with Luke, it was a benign discomfort.

She prayed to God for help with making the right decisions in this new relationship—she still almost could not fathom, after six days, that this was what they were in now—and that

139

they would know the right way forward. She still wanted some sort of clear sign from the Lord that Luke was the one, that she would get a "happily ever after" and not a "happy for a year and then morose over the loss of Chelsea and the burden of running a ranch and being a father." But she knew better than to demand from the Lord; she didn't need to see Pastor O'Connell or seek anyone else's guidance to know to have patience and faith.

Then she read one of her mother's books, still in the living room where her mother was still sound asleep, and passed the time until her parents woke up around half-past eight. At that point, she made small talk with them, but did not mention her new relationship with Luke.

A part of her feared their judgment, which was odd considering how much they loved Luke back in the day. Would they think her foolish for going back to a former lover? Maybe a part of her, out of fear of having things end badly a second time, did not want to go to the effort of informing everyone they were back together, only for her to then have to reverse course.

People had been so kind to her after the first breakup, but it wasn't hard to imagine them questioning her judgment.

Finally, the time came to leave, and Brooke only said she had tutoring to run to—a truth, but perhaps not the full one. She sped so fast over to Hope Valley Ranch that she had to remind herself there was a speed limit in Greenville of thirty miles per hour. Fortunately, the perks of a small town meant that there were few pedestrians at this time of day on a Saturday.

Finally, she saw *it*—the overarching sign, with the two stone pillars and the engraved overhang, announcing the entrance to Hope Valley Ranch.

She was stunned to see that not only did it look exactly as she remembered it, it also looked fresh. She had assumed that with everyone away from the ranch now for at least a couple of years and the age of Mr. and Mrs. Walker, the ranch surely would have at least showed some neglect.

That thought became even more evident when she arrived at their homestead and saw a porch with wood that didn't show a single crack and sported a fresh coat of brown paint, too fresh to have been done any later than within the last couple of months. Certainly, it would not have survived the harsh Montana winters.

Has Luke been working on this place?

She tried not to get ahead of herself, but the thought endeared him to her even more. He would not have put so much effort into taking care of the home if he didn't have long-term plans for it, right?

Unless he planned to sell it to someone like the Chamberlains, another Montana rancher, or even someone wealthy from out of state.

She pushed the thought aside as a sheep came up to her.

"Well, hello there," she said to the sheep. "Are you the official greeter of the Hope Valley Ranch?"

The sheep then, casually and without hesitation, tried to bite her clothing.

"Woah!"

"Hey! Benny! No!"

The sheep scurried off at the sound of Luke's voice, and Brooke looked up, half-embarrassed, half-thrilled to see Luke standing there in a light brown cowboy hat, a white button-down shirt, and light blue jeans. It wasn't as formal or crisp a wear as their previous dates, but the man had a way of making anything in the figure of a cowboy look sharp.

"Sorry about that," he said, "but at least now you know we weren't kidding about Benny eating Tana's homework."

"No kidding," Brooke said, putting her hand on her chest as Luke stepped down toward her. With no hesitation, he wrapped his arm around her and planted a firm kiss on her lips. "Aren't your parents—"

"As if they've forgotten who you are, and Tana's in the back.

She has an idea, but I haven't confirmed or said anything more to her. It's nothing against you, but I don't want her getting overly attached to anyone until I'm sure."

It was an entirely reasonable take. It also felt like a sucker punch to Brooke, as irrational as that sounded. Was he not sure? How could he not have been after everything?

"Come on now," Luke said, taking her hand, "let's go teach Tana, shall we?"

The smile remained on Brooke's face, though as soon as Luke turned the other way, she let it slip a little. Nevertheless, she kept it on upon entering the homestead of the Walkers.

"Papaw is resting upstairs. He might come down, but not sure. And Mimi is—"

"Mimi is preparing food for the lovely Brooke and her granddaughter!" she shouted from the kitchen.

Mimi may have now been in her fifties, but she still had the vigor and spunk that Brooke remembered her having.

"Come give me a hug, dear," Mrs. Walker said as Brooke beamed in nostalgia, embracing the mother who once said she was so happy to finally have another woman in the house. The two embraced, squeezing each other with the kind of love and appreciation that no amount of time could dissolve.

"You know Ms. Young?" Montana said, suddenly appearing at the screen porch door.

Brooke froze, her smile in place but fear rising in her. Did Mimi know not to reveal everything to Montana? If not—

"It's a small town, sweetie. We all know each other," Mrs. Walker said.

Brooke hoped the relief on her face wasn't too obvious. Montana didn't look like she completely bought the line, but she said nothing else.

"I'll bring the food out to you. You all just learn to write well, OK?"

"OK!" Montana shouted, hurrying out to the porch. When

Brooke turned to thank Luke and his mother, she saw both had already turned away, Luke seemingly to go upstairs and Mrs. Walker to finish cooking. Taking the cue, Brooke came out to the back deck.

She had forgotten just how *gorgeous* this view was—arguably the best she knew of in Greenville. It captured the best of all of Montana—vast skies, white mountains, green plains, and wildlife as far as the eye could see. It was the heaven of heaven, the spot where she and Luke had spent so many years talking about their future.

And now we can do it again.

Brooke smiled, grateful that, for once, the sudden thought in her head was optimistic.

"What are we going to learn now, Ms. Young?"

Brooke looked down at the little prodigy of writing. She knew just what to say.

"Today, we're going to learn to describe beauty with all five senses."

19

LUKE

Another week and a half passed, and things seemed just about perfect on the ranch.

He and Brooke continued to date, and while Luke always felt that there was just something holding Brooke back from fully being herself, they still went on two more dates—one fly-fishing again on the Missouri River, and another watching a movie at a theatre in Helena, about an hour north. A part of him yearned for them to just leap forward, but he understood relationships were not like movies, where you could skip ahead to the scene you last left off at. He needed to let this be its own relationship, not a continuation of the last one.

And as much as he felt that way for personal reasons, he also felt that way because of how much little Montana raved about her teaching skills. The last thing he wanted to do was to push the relationship too hard, making Brooke resentful and possibly bitter toward the two of them, ruining Montana's chances of learning from the best writer he knew.

But that was not why things were only "just about" perfect.

On Thursday, September 14th, almost exactly one month had passed since Montana and Luke had returned home.

By the way his father seemed to decline nearly every day, it seemed like there wouldn't be many more months where Luke could expect to have with his father. He didn't get worse every day, but Luke also didn't need a chart to know comparing him week to work showed a steady decline.

He helped Montana into the car just after seven a.m. and found himself unable to speak. Montana, wiser than her years suggested, picked up on her father's distress and grabbed a book for class. Luke was just at the center of Greenville, only about five minutes from school, when his phone rang. He answered, the phone connected to his truck's Bluetooth.

"Jesse," Luke said, his voice neutral.

"Well, dang, big boy, I know you're not a coffee drinker, but can you at least pretend you're excited to hear my voice?"

Luke let out a chuckle that, surprisingly, did not feel forced. That was usually the case around Jesse.

"That would require more acting than they put on in Hollywood."

"The only man more handsome than me out there is John Wayne, and you're acting like I just pulled you over for going thirty-six in a thirty-five."

"Says the boy who got pulled over for going thirty-seven in a thirty-five."

"Sheriff Lane has it out for me, I swear!" Jesse said, drawing a laugh from Montana. "Hey, Tana! Daddy spoiling you well enough?"

"Yes! Mimi makes great chicken and biscuits, and he's bringing over Ms. Young to help me tutor?"

"Ms. Young? Young…"

"Anyway," Luke said before Jesse could connect the dots. "What are you calling for, Jesse?"

"Letting your lazy butt know that I'll be at the ranch around noon. Make sure you've had your coffee by then."

Luke laughed again. And then the humor and jostling in Jesse's voice vanished.

"How's Papaw?"

Luke drew in a deep breath, saw there were no cars in front of him, and closed his eyes as he exhaled.

"It's best if you see for yourself. Noon?"

"It's a long drive from Casper, but nothing I haven't done before. These roads can't keep Jesse Walker from walking all over them."

The joke fell flat. Luke pulled into the school and saw Brooke was not working the drop-off line.

"Shoot, that bad, Luke?"

"We'll talk about this later, Jesse. I need to drop off Montana at school."

A pause came.

"Alright," Jesse finally said. "Tana, treat Ms. Young well. Don't make me be the enforcer for your lazy Pops."

"I will," Montana said, but even she sounded muted compared to her normal self.

Jesse hung up a second later after some goodbyes, and Luke exhaled.

"Is Papaw that bad?" Montana asked.

Luke closed his eyes again, telling himself he could not break down in front of his daughter this early.

"The Lord is calling to him," Luke said. "He's not on the doorstep yet, but he's not far down the street. My guess is… within the year, Montana."

And that was the best-case scenario, Luke thought. It wouldn't surprise him if they were planning a service by Halloween.

"Like Mommy?"

COWBOY'S HOMECOMING

Oh, did Montana have to say the most painful words possible?

"Yes," Luke said.

Mercifully, they pulled into the drop-off spot a second later. Luke leaned over and kissed his daughter on the head, telling her to focus on school and that he loved her. He only wished that he could take his own advice.

When he got home, he made his parents cups of coffee each. Mimi was already up, preparing to check on the livestock. Papaw was sitting up in bed, reading a book, and thanked Luke for his coffee. His voice sounded stronger than the day before, perhaps promising a better day, relatively speaking.

The sight was enough to bolster Luke's spirits for the next couple of hours; enough that he could continue to do the hard manual labor of repairing the other physical structures that had fallen into disarray over the last few years. He'd already fixed most of the homestead, though a few minor issues on the roof remained. Now, he looked at the fence, a task that wouldn't be difficult but would be time-consuming.

Going post by post, he found that most of the fencing was still in good shape, but some of the posts on downhills, where precipitation runoff would be at its worst, had developed cracks and rotting wood. Nothing was imminent, and neither Mimi nor Papaw had said anything about losing livestock or animals, but Luke welcomed the chance to focus on something that wasn't his father's health.

This continued until Jesse Walker showed up about fifteen minutes after noon.

If Luke was the even-keeled, wise elder of the Walker brothers, Jesse was more like the jester of the bunch. At just a little over two years younger, about to turn thirty, he was always the one trying to play silly jokes, like dusting spicy chicken with cinnamon or putting his horse behind Papaw's pickup truck. He also was easily the best dresser of the group, sporting a nice coat in the winter and often a tie when he wasn't on the ranch.

Though he could be flippant, sometimes to a fault, it was not lost on Luke that he was the first of the brothers to come when he'd mentioned Papaw's condition.

"They put you in charge of cleaning up the posts?" Jesse said with a smirk, sporting a white cowboy hat, light blue jeans, and an impeccably ironed black button-down shirt. "Shoot, they'll be calling us Walkers soon, because we'll be walking to grab our livestock!"

"I liked you better in Casper," Luke said with a broad smile, standing and embracing his brother tightly. "Thanks for coming up."

"No problem. I needed an excuse to get away from the craziness of the town."

"Oh?" Luke said, arching an eyebrow in mock suspicion—Jesse liked to portray himself as the descendant of the outlaw Jesse James, but he was more like Jesse from Full House.

"Yeah, this one cat kept hunting me, trailing me like you wouldn't believe," Jesse said, and as if on cue, the sound of another truck pulling in reached Luke's ears—followed by another grin. "Son of a gun. He followed me all the way here!"

"He," of course, was Luke's other brother, Weston, who apparently had come just behind Jesse as a bit of a surprise. Though the middle child, Weston had by far the fiercest facial hair of anyone on the ranch. He also had a quieter demeanor compared to the rest of the brothers—he was far from mute, but he also would not be nearly as talkative as Jesse or even Luke.

"Weston!" Luke said.

"Had to come when I heard how Papaw was," Weston said as he stepped out of the truck and embraced Luke.

"Well, I appreciate it, and I'm sure they do too," Luke said, which Weston responded to with simply a one-off nod—unlike Montana, his one-off nods meant he was *not* hiding anything more. "Papaw is having a good day today. I'm not terribly optimistic about the long term, but the good Lord has blessed your arrival with him being coherent."

"Yeah?" Jesse said. "Well, shoot, let's go see him, shall we?"

The three brothers abandoned their ranch work and headed back to the homestead, where Luke's father sat at the kitchen table waiting for them.

"You boys only come to visit when I've got one foot in the grave," he snapped, drawing laughs from the Walker boys and a stunned rebuke from Mimi. "Come here and give your Papaw a real hug."

After embracing all three of them, they sat down and spent all day together until Luke had to pick Montana up from school at the kitchen table. Luke and Weston had always had a strong relationship with their parents, though Jesse sometimes struggled with Papaw. That became very obvious in the way Jesse shut the heck up and Weston asked probing questions. Papaw never went into his cancer or his fatigue, only speaking about the ranch and how those darn Chamberlains kept thinking they had a shot at buying it.

"I'd say over my dead body, but they'll take that too literally," Papaw said with a snort.

Luke laughed, told himself that he needed to grab Montana, and excused himself from the table.

By the time he returned home with Montana, things had already begun taking a turn for the worse.

~

AT THE MOMENT of arrival at the homestead, Papaw had gone to take a nap, and all seemed normal.

But the rasping and gasping for air that followed when he awoke a short time after dinner put fear into all of them—even Jesse, who masked his fear with awkward jokes.

Luke sent Montana to the back porch to work on her homework, barely engaging in conversation about Benny and her writing assignment. He hurried up to Papaw's room, where he saw Mimi and his two brothers standing on opposite sides of the bed.

"He's barely breathing," Mimi said. "We need to take him to the hospital."

Luke gulped, but the order had been given.

"I'll drive," Luke said. He wasn't a huge fan of leaving Montana alone at the ranch, but there was no safer place for her, and he did not anticipate being gone for more than a few hours. "Jesse, Weston, head to the hospital and do whatever needs to be done to prepare for our arrival. Mimi, you can ride in the back of my truck. We'll put Papaw in the front."

Calling nine-one-one and paying for an ambulance was out of the question. While money wasn't the issue, Papaw's pride was; even in what sure seemed like his final days, he fought the idea of even going to the hospital.

Montana put herself inside at the kitchen table, promising not to go anywhere until Luke returned. He believed her and kissed her on the top of the head. Everyone hurried to their respective trucks, and Luke began the long drive to the hospital, which was on the university campus grounds.

Being in such a small town meant that they didn't have access to the best healthcare in the state, let alone the country, but Papaw had always dismissed such concerns, saying if God wanted him to heal, he would. That was fine, but Luke still felt they needed to ease Papaw's pain, if not actually heal it.

Thankfully, mid-September was not a busy time for the hospital, and even on holidays, Greenville wasn't exactly known as New Orleans during Mardi Gras. Papaw got admitted immediately, and the three brothers were left to themselves as Mimi followed them back to a room.

Luke slumped in his chair, exhausted. The whole ordeal

somehow seemed to both pass by in an instant and stretch on forever. The ride to the hospital, with a bit of speeding added in, took a little under fifteen minutes—quick by their standards, but still not an instant, split-second action. Jesse had stopped talking. Weston was rubbing his thumbs together, a twitch he had that signaled nervousness.

A part of Luke almost wanted Jesse to say something, *anything* that could break the tension, but another part of Luke knew this was going to somehow be a life-defining moment. It wouldn't be the first time Papaw had gone to a hospital, but in his heart, God told him this time was different. Luke needed to gird himself for the worst.

Nearly an hour later, a doctor walked out with Mimi. It was a bad sign that she was in tears.

"Hi, I'm Dr. Stephenson. Are you all the Walker brothers? Howard's sons?"

Everyone nodded.

"Your father's lymph nodes have swollen badly, making breathing difficult. We can treat him, but…"

But...

"I think you should look at hospice."

"Hospice?" Jesse said.

"Making him comfortable until the end," the doctor said. "We prescribe hospice to those patients that we believe will only live, at most, another six months. In full transparency, most patients do not make it to another two weeks. The focus would be on quality of life and less quantity of life."

This was it, then.

Luke's father truly was dying, and there now seemed to be a definitive and likely timeline for it.

Jesse had tears in his eyes. Weston had a thousand-mile stare to nowhere. Mimi had surprisingly stopped crying, though her cheeks were still streaked with tears and her eyes were still stained red.

"Thank you, Dr. Stephenson," Mimi said, and her voice was as strong as her posture and face right now. "Let me speak to my boys and God, and we will figure this out."

Dr. Stephenson nodded, added that he would make sure Papaw was comfortable through the night, and took his leave.

"Boys," Mimi said, gathering them to sit together in a circle. "We knew this day would come. We know it comes for all of us. Put your faith in God—Papaw will soon go to a better place, a place where cancer cannot reach him and he will not suffer."

Luke heard the words. He even knew someday he would understand them. But right now, it just hurt. There was always a chance a miracle would occur, and Luke supposed God could still bring a miracle to them.

But as much as he was a man of faith, he was not oblivious to medical realities, and he knew Dr. Stephenson would not have lied to them.

"We should give thanks that all of us are here for your father's last days."

"Most of us," Weston said.

Mimi nodded. They'd try to get Sawyer home soon, but him being deployed overseas made that a guessing game. And as for Carson…

Lord, help him return home before it's too late.

"While we know the Lord will take Papaw in the coming months, if not weeks, we all must acknowledge we cannot know the hour He calls for us. It could be tonight; it could be tomorrow; it could be in fifty years. All we can do is give thanks that we are still present with him and that we can still show our love to him."

All we can do is give thanks that we are still present with him and that we can still show our love to him.

For the first time all night, those words turned Luke's thoughts, however briefly, to Brooke. His father's impending death made him feel like he would need to make a more definitive move on Brooke soon; what if so much time passed that something like this happened to one of them?

However unlikely that was, Luke was in a place of desperation. He shook his head free of the thoughts of her, knowing that he needed to stay focused.

"Let us pray," Mimi said.

The four held hands, bowed their heads, and closed their eyes.

"Dear Lord, give us the strength to be there with Papaw in his last days on this Earth. Give us the strength to continue as a loving family and to continue to show that love. Give us the strength to get through each day, and to carry out your will. In your name, Amen."

Luke nodded, thanked his mother, and then stood and walked down the hallway. He had no destination in mind; he just needed some time alone to make sense of this gut punch. Behind him, he could hear his brothers discussing how Sawyer could get bereavement leave for thirty days, but Carson would take some work.

Luke, however, could only think of his father. He could only think of how grateful he was that he was getting to spend time with him in his dying days. He was thankful that Montana was getting to make some powerful, beautiful memories with him.

Luke felt his phone buzz and looked down at the screen.

"Looking forward to seeing you Saturday for Montana's tutoring. Maybe we can do something after :-)"

Luke hovered his fingers over the keyboard, but no words came to mind. A mixture of grief, gratitude, and heaviness weighed on him right now, leaving no space for creativity or banter.

And so, without responding to Brooke, he put his phone back in his pocket and returned to his family, praying that they would have more than two weeks together before the end.

20

BROOKE

*L*uke always texted back.
Always.

The man could be busy on the ranch and go to bed early, but it also wasn't even nine o'clock yet, the earliest that Luke would head to bed. It was only a little past eight o'clock.

Brooke had just finished grading that week's writing assignments so that she could hand them back to her students tomorrow with instructions on how to improve one's own writing after the first draft. As usual, Montana's first draft was significantly better than any final draft that would come from the rest of the class, but she still had things she could improve. The assignment this week, to write about what your home looked like, had produced some amusing lines.

One student had written that the sky in his backyard "was as blue as the ocean," an interesting choice of simile, and another had said that his backyard smelled like poop, a line that was tough to decipher as boy humor or actual Montana life.

But what had started as worry that something was going on with Luke turned into fear that maybe he just wasn't that into her. Was it really so surprising? Life had been good with him since that first kiss, but it hadn't escalated at all; sure, both had explicitly said that they weren't seeing anyone else, nor would they dare to even consider it, but things just seemed stuck in neutral.

Maybe Brooke was overthinking things. Both of them had good reason for taking their second chance slowly, and in such a spot, "slow" could easily be confused with "nothing." But still…

For as much as she thought of Luke as different, so much gnawed at her. Maybe she was putting too much pressure on herself. Maybe she was expecting too much of Luke, especially with him having a daughter, a wife taken by cancer, and a sick father.

Maybe they just weren't actually meant for true love.

Trust in God's will, not chance or fate.

"Blake! I'm thirsty!"

Oh, and that.

Mom was having such a bad day, she had forgotten Brooke's name.

That was a new low for her mother, who may have forgotten Brooke's nickname but never her actual name. The first time she had heard her mom yelling for Blake today, she thought her mom had somehow gotten a hold of the phone and called an old friend.

But when she realized "Blake" was her, it brought her to tears on the spot—a sight that her mother was only more confused by, which made things only worse.

Suffice to say, it was not a good day, and her pillar of strength in the face of so much trouble was not responding to her. He surely had a good reason, but… maybe that good reason was more important than her.

"Blake! Hurry the—"

Brooke had *never* heard her mother curse. Until then.

Without a word, Brooke hurriedly made her mother a glass of water, barely stammered out that she would be upstairs, and then took the stairs two at a time before reaching her bedroom, burying her head into the pillow and sobbing uncontrollably.

What a fool she was, trying to bring love into the picture when her mother was losing her mind, and Luke had other things to worry about! Her mother deserved her full attention when she was home, her kids while she was working. What in the heck did she think she was doing, trying to give it another go with a man it hadn't worked out with before?

The compassionate side of her tried to ask, "If not now, when?" But her emotions were too volatile at the moment, too rough for her to make sense of much of anything.

The only thing she promised herself, as she sobbed miserably, was that she would not make any rash decisions tonight. She would not text Luke for the rest of the night and would wait until morning. If he still had not responded in the morning, well, she would cross that bridge when she got there.

She knew she needed to be more mature and stable than to say "when he texts me." But she also prayed to the good Lord for her mother to get better, because…

Because this was just so difficult to deal with.

～

Brooke barely slept that night, multiple times glancing over at the clock and seeing the hour at one, three, four, even five a.m. If there was any silver lining in the matter, it was that it was Friday, and if she could just survive this workday, she would have the entire weekend to rest and recover.

It was a faint silver lining, however. When Lola arrived at six a.m., Brooke did not even bother to hide her haggard look, warning Lola that her mother had had the worst evening that she could ever recall. Of course, that probably meant she'd remember everything with perfect clarity today.

Brooke headed to school, pounding coffee and even stopping at The Homestead for a cup for the classroom. She tried to avoid bringing coffee into the classroom, as she understood not everyone enjoyed the scent, but today, she hoped others would forgive her for her possible sharp tongue.

Although the fourth grade teacher, a woman in her fifties who had taught Brooke years ago named Mrs. Roberts, was in charge of the drop-off line, Brooke volunteered to take over. She wanted to see Luke; even if all they did was lock eyes, say hello, and wish each other a good day, it would do much to assuage her concerns. Just something, anything, to get her to the weekend.

However, after seven-twenty had passed—the usual time Luke dropped off Montana, roughly twenty minutes after they would have left the ranch—and Brooke saw no sign of either, a greater worry than their relationship took hold. Luke not showing up was one thing, but Montana? Fear ensnared Brooke. Was she sick? Was Luke sick?

Had Papaw had something terrible happen to him? Of all the scenarios…

Finally, she saw a pickup truck she didn't recognize pull up. The window rolled down, and a smirk appeared on a very familiar face.

"I thought when Luke said that my niece's teacher was Ms. Young, he might be referring to you," Luke's brother, Jesse said. "And lo and behold, the good Lord has proved my suspicions true! Although I have to ask, he's calling you Ms. Young? Really?"

Brooke laughed, although a different anxiety had taken hold. Why had Luke referred to her that way? Why was he not telling his brothers, of all people, the truth about their situation?

"It's as weird to me as to you, Jesse," Brooke said. "Is Montana with you?"

"Oh, yeah! I suppose I should let her out. Hey, kiddo! Ms. Young's ready to teach you today!"

Brooke saw the passenger door open and Montana step in front of the car. But the usual bubbly, cheerful young girl was not present, replaced instead by a look that told her something had happened.

"Montana?"

But the young girl kept walking. Brooke grimaced.

"She learned about Papaw," Jesse said, his voice flattening some.

"Papaw?"

"Never mind that," Jesse said. "But hey, give your man a call if you get the chance? He's a bit in the dumps."

The two had to be connected. At least it had nothing to do with them, at least as far as Jesse knew. But Papaw...

Had he passed away last night?

"Is your father still alive, Jesse?" Brooke asked pointedly.

"For now," Jesse said, "but like I said, never mind that. I'm just happy to see Luke's lovely lady is the pretty girl who came over when I was in high school."

Brooke smiled politely. Jesse could be a flirt, but one stern warning from Luke in their youth had ensured that Jesse's flirtations never got serious.

With that, Jesse nodded and drove off, the last car to drop off a second-grade child. Brooke turned back to the school, only to see Montana had not even entered the building yet. Instead, she sat on the steps, seemingly waiting for her to come sit by her.

"Montana?" Brooke asked gently as she sat next to her. "What's going on? Do you want to talk about it?"

Montana said nothing at first, resting her chin on her hands and staring straight ahead at nothing. Brooke knew the other kids would see her, but she decided the young girl needed company. If the other kids said something, she'd put a stop to it faster than she'd stopped the teasing over her name on day one.

"Daddy said Papaw is going into hospice."

The words struck like a dagger, even as Montana continued

to talk about being confused about the difference between hospital and hospice. This was... this was the end, wasn't it? A legendary Walker, a figure not just to his and Brooke's families but to the entire town of Greenville, was in the end stages of his life.

"Ms. Young, I'm... I'm scared."

Montana's lip started to quiver. Brooke pulled her in for a hug and closed her eyes tight as the young girl bawled into Brooke's shoulder. At that moment, even though they were on school grounds, Brooke didn't think of herself as Ms. Young or Montana's teacher; she just wanted to be her comforter, her confidant of sorts.

If this made her a mother figure of sorts, so be it.

"It's not fair!" Montana finally said, still continuing to sob.

"I know," Brooke said, squeezing Montana tight. "God has a plan for all of us, Montana. We must learn to trust in it."

"I don't like that plan!" Montana said. *Lord forgive her, she's young.* "First, Mom, and now Papaw!"

It took a second for Brooke to realize she was not talking about Luke's mother, but his deceased wife. The way Luke had told the story, Montana had been too young to fully grasp what was going on, but the implications of her mother's death sure seemed to be reaching much more deeply than before.

It left Brooke wondering even more if it made sense for her and Luke to date. The two of them, as tough a spot as they were in, could handle emotional turmoil and caring for elderly parents, but if Luke also had to be that much more present for his daughter, what could Brooke do? She could never replace Chelsea, she knew that much.

And what if Montana came to hate her with time? It was easy being the teacher's pet. It was much harder when the teacher was your stepmother.

Stop it. Be present for Montana.

Lord, give me the strength.

"I'm sorry, Montana," Brooke said, continuing to soothe Montana with strokes of her hair. "Do you need this weekend by yourself?"

Montana vigorously shook her head no.

"Please come tomorrow!" she said, still sobbing but in a little more control now. "Uncle Jesse and Uncle Weston are here. They want to meet you!"

Both Jesse and Weston? How interesting. She wondered where Sawyer and Carson were, though with everything seemingly happening in the last twelve hours, maybe they just hadn't gotten into town yet.

"If you and your father want me to come—"

"Daddy said you should come if I want you to, and I want you to!"

Well, who was Brooke to argue with a determined second grader?

"OK," Brooke said with a smile. "As long as I don't step on anyone's toes."

"We'll watch our feet," Montana said with a slightly confused look.

The miscommunication brought a much needed laugh to Brooke. She imagined that all the Walkers would welcome some semblance of normalcy, even if things could literally change by the hour.

Lord knew that with how her mother was, she would welcome it, too.

21

LUKE

*A*s rough as Thursday night had been—to where Jesse volunteered to take Montana to school, seeing that Luke would barely sleep that night—Friday was actually a day of some normalcy.

True, their father's diagnosis of hospice hung over them like a rumbling storm cloud, threatening to burst at the seams into a storm of death at any moment, but today, he seemed much better. Maybe it was the drugs, maybe it was the finality of it all, or maybe the good Lord had given their father peace in his final days. Whatever the reason, when Papaw started cracking jokes about finally not having to watch his diet at a late breakfast, everyone burst into laughter of relief, and Luke's anxiety eased ever so slightly.

Jesse asked if he or Weston needed to go pick up Montana from school, but Luke said no; he not only needed to do his fatherly duty, he needed to see Brooke in line. He still had not responded to her text, and by the time it came to get her from school, he felt talking to her in person would be the best bet. He left the homestead in a much better mood than he'd woken up, and he was determined to pass that on to Brooke.

Unfortunately, Brooke was not at the pickup line. It was only about twice a week that Brooke handled drop-off, so that was not a red flag, but Luke still felt disappointment. Still, seeing his little girl's face looking like she'd had a great day at school lifted his spirits, and when she got into the truck, she reached over and gave him a hug.

"How's my little Tana?" he said as he kissed on the forehead.

"Feeling better," she said. "Ms. Young still wants to come over tomorrow."

Luke couldn't help the rush of excitement that coursed through him. As old as he was and as many other responsibilities as he had, the thought of seeing Brooke still made him as giddy as a teenager whose crush said yes to a prom date.

"Great!" he said. "I'm sure Ms. Young will continue to help you."

"And see you!" Montana said with her tongue sticking out.

Luke chuckled, thanking the Lord for ever so briefly making life feel somewhat normal again.

"What assignment are you going to work on this week?" he asked.

"Well, we were supposed to edit our last assignment, where we described our backyards with the five senses, but she told me during lunch that she wanted me to try to write about something harder."

"Which is?"

"She said it's describing relationships with other people."

Oh, Lord.

Luke's mind flashed back to all the letters he and Brooke had sent each other when one vacationed and when Luke went to college. Luke had never felt comfortable writing, and while he loved Brooke's letters, he sometimes had to remind her that, yes, one page of a well-written letter could hit home just as well as a five-page novel of a letter. Montana, he suspected, was going to

COWBOY'S HOMECOMING

be a much better writer than he was, eventually closer to Brooke than he ever was.

Maybe I'll take some lessons from her.

"Does this mean writing a letter? Or just like a description?"

"She said just a description."

Luke wasn't sure whether to feel relief or disappointment. He imagined it would still translate to writing a letter, but his skill wasn't on par with the women in his life. He worked on a ranch, not a keyboard.

"And who are you going to describe?"

"I wanted to do Mommy."

Oh.

Luke loved that Montana wanted to explore Chelsea more; she deserved to learn as much as she could about the woman who had brought Montana into this world. But why did she also have to involve Brooke at the same time?

"And how do you get started on this homework assignment?"

"Ms. Young said to either talk to the person you want to write about or someone who knows them well. And since Mommy is in heaven, I will pray to her and talk to you. Is that OK, Daddy?"

Oh, for heaven's sake.

"Yes, of course, that's fine, sweetheart," Luke said, hoping his expression didn't give away his obvious discomfort.

"What was Mommy like?"

Luke gulped. He sure as heck would not lie and say he didn't like Chelsea—although, if he was painfully honest with himself, he knew even in the weeks leading up to their engagement she wasn't *the one*. He had come to love her over the years, but…

But he also knew that Brooke would read everything that Montana wrote.

Shoot.

It was bound to come up at some point in their relationship,

163

wasn't it? Luke could play coy for a spell, but if he and Brooke were going to move forward, she'd start asking more questions about Chelsea. And she would be completely justified in doing so—had Brooke married someone named Brad only to have him pass away, Luke knew he'd have a million and one questions for Brooke.

He just hated that, whether because Brooke had purposefully planned this exercise or not, Montana was stuck in the middle of it all.

"Your mother was wonderful," Luke said. "Cheerful, sweet, and couldn't wait to have a family. She actually wanted to have you right after we got married, when she was still in college."

"How long did you wait?"

"About two years."

"You waited two years to bring me here? I could be ten now! Daddy!"

Luke chuckled nervously as his daughter stared him down, a scowl on her face and her arms folded.

"We wanted to make sure we were ready to have you. It would be mean to you to bring you into this world without both of us being ready spiritually and otherwise."

"If you say so," Montana half-sang. "Tell me more about Mommy!"

Her cheerful demeanor and attitude were softening some concerns Luke had. Even if Brooke reacted poorly to this, was his daughter not the most important person in the world?

And, he thought with some sorrow, if his father was soon to pass from this world, he needed to get better at remembering someone. It might do some good to practice with Chelsea.

"I met her at a... celebration at college. We spent our first date talking about ranch life. She was enamored, way more than I would have thought she would be. We then went for a hike on our second date. On our fifth date, we became boyfriend-girlfriend."

"Ohhhh!" Montana said. "When did you decide to get married?"

The truth was that Luke thought about if he could ever see Brooke entering the picture again in the future, only to decide that no, she would not; he had hurt her too much and would likely never see her again nor be received well if he did. But to an eight-year-old with a still innocent view of the world, that seemed too harsh and honest a statement.

"When I felt she was the one for me, I asked her to marry me."

"And when did you decide that?"

Oh, Lord help me.

"I had been with her a couple of years by that point and… I don't know how to describe it, Tana. You and Brooke are better at this word thing. It's just… sometimes, when you feel a certain way about someone, you can't put it into words, because words make it a certain way. But it's not a certain way. It can't be described. When you feel it, you just know."

Montana looked confused. Luke shrugged.

"Sorry, I told you I'm not good at this kind of thing."

"Apparently," Montana said, drawing a laugh from her father. "Do you miss her?"

Ooof.

What a loaded question.

The honest answer was yes, Luke missed her. But missed her enough to pass up Brooke? Missed her enough that he could not emotionally connect to Brooke and be present with her?

No.

Maybe he was lying to himself, and he spent far longer on any other question Montana had asked up to that point. Did the fact that he missed her make him not ready?

If he said he still loved her, did that mean the same?

Maybe he just meant that he valued her place in his life, but that he was ready to find love again—specifically with Brooke. But would an eight-year-old girl understand that?

Did Luke himself understand that?

"It's a really complicated question, Tana," Luke said as the archway for Hope Valley Ranch's entrance came into view. "I miss her in that she was a very important part of my life and your life. But I don't miss her in that I think about her so much, I'm not living my life now. I... I told you I'm not good with my words."

"I miss her."

Luke grimaced.

"But when Papaw goes to heaven, they're going to hang out, aren't they?"

Gosh, Montana had a way of asking the sweetest questions that could make Luke almost tear up.

"Yes, yes they will," Luke said. "But let's not think about that yet. Papaw is still here, and he may make jokes, but we should still be grateful to God for the time He gives us here. OK?"

"OK, Daddy."

Luke pulled up to the homestead. Papaw was sitting on the front porch, a content smile on his face and a worn-out cowboy hat on his head. Luke hadn't seen his father wear such a hat since he came back, though he also realized he just hadn't seen his father outside since he got home.

"Papaw?" Luke said as he got out of the car.

"What? A man's not allowed to enjoy God's country while he's on this Earth?" he said with a snort. "I'm not going to leave this place surrounded by air conditioning and your mother's candles."

"You're funny, Papaw!" Montana shouted.

"Go inside, Tana," Luke said. "Since it's Friday, you can wait if you have any homework due on Monday."

"OK!" she yelled as she went through the door.

Luke looked at his father, who patted the seat next to him. Luke took a seat and sighed.

"Don't be moping now," his father said. "You got the woman of your dreams coming over every weekend and a beautiful daughter, and you're going to be exhausted because an old man is in the final chapter of his life?"

"I thought she was the woman of my dreams," Luke said, hesitating, "and I still would like to think that. But darn, Papaw. Montana is asking questions that are making me wonder if I'm past Chelsea or not."

Papaw said nothing for a few seconds. Luke knew he was pondering his next words, but the wait became unbearable.

"How do you feel about Brooke today?"

"Today? I…"

Love her.

But even though he could think the words, he knew he would struggle to say them in front of Brooke. Before, the only reason had been caution, to ensure that neither of them got hurt. But now, he felt like he'd spun around in circles one time too many, dizzy and confused about the appropriate next step.

"Say it, son."

"I love her, Papaw," Luke blurted out. "But darn it, it's just…"

Papaw nodded.

"Nothing's worth having that's not also a huge risk," he said.

Luke expected him to say something more, but Papaw instead fell silent. In fact, a few seconds later, Papaw fell asleep in his chair and started snoring. Content in the relatively warm September weather to leave his father outside, Luke stepped indoors and watched from afar as Montana, to his surprise, was already writing on the back porch.

Life was simpler, really, when Luke just went with the most obvious feeling. But life wasn't simple anymore, and the older he got, the more complex it would become. If times were difficult now, what would happen when Montana was a teenager?

Or an adult, but by that point, Luke would be almost fifty years old?

He looked to the heavens and said a silent prayer, asking for wisdom. Wisdom to know if this was a risk worth taking. Wisdom to know if he could truly love again after everything that had happened with Chelsea.

And wisdom to know how to move forward without hurting Brooke.

22

BROOKE

Brooke showed up at the Walkers' homestead earlier than normal, about nine a.m. on Saturday. Though the week had been extremely difficult, she never doubted she would come once Montana had all but begged her to show up. The young girl was the teacher's pet, and Brooke was unapologetic about that. An older teacher might scorn her for playing favorites, but Brooke knew talent when she saw it.

It just so happened that said talent also had a handsome, values-driven father.

When she arrived, she found Luke's father on the front porch, reading what looked like an extremely old book about the history of Montana. He looked up at her and gave a warm smile, though he did not rise from his chair. Frankly, had he, Brooke would have told him to sit down.

"Good morning, Brooke," he said. "Luke and Montana are on the back porch. Walk on through and help yourself to anything you want."

"Thank you, Mr. Walker," she said, wondering if she should say something about the man's hospice diagnosis. But he returned to his book right after, and the content smile on his face suggested he didn't need any condolences—normalcy, probably.

She walked through the house and did not hear or see Mrs. Walker anywhere.

"Brooke."

She jumped at the voice, surprised to hear Weston. She saw him sitting at their kitchen table, a cowboy hat to the side, looking up something on a computer.

"Weston, how have you been?"

"Busy, but good."

He added nothing else. He rarely did. Luke was kind of the middle one in terms of talking, Jesse the joker, and Weston the quiet one. Sawyer and Carson were barely teenagers when they had dated, and they were too shy to be much of anything back then.

"That's good. How long are you in town?"

Weston shrugged.

"Probably as long as the old man is alive."

That was the other part. He was quiet, but he was blunt when he spoke.

"Got it. Hope to see you around, Weston."

He gave a short grunt and a head nod, and Brooke kept pushing past. She got to the back door and saw Montana at her table, writing on a piece of paper. Out in the distance, she saw two men in cowboy hats on horseback, riding away from where they were; presumably, Luke and Jesse were doing some of the ranch work. She pushed open the door and smiled as Montana looked up at her.

"Good morning, Montana."

"Good morning, Ms. Young!" Montana said enthusiastically. "I'm almost done with the first page of my story."

"Oh? And what are you writing about?"

"I'm calling it, 'When Mommy and Papaw Eat in Heaven.'"

Brooke bit her lip and tried not to show too many emotions.

Lord, how little children, despite their innocence, could produce such a strong reaction in adults. She almost hesitated to read what Montana would have written, fearing it would be too personal a story.

Yet, Montana had all but forced the story onto Brooke's lap. She sat down, focusing on her breathing to steady her emotions, and grabbed the papers.

She read the first couple of lines, and Brooke felt her eyes well up.

"Mommy is in heaven. Papaw will soon be in heaven. Daddy says he misses Mommy because she was a very important part of our lives. But soon, Mommy and Papaw will get to meet in heaven!"

Brooke's heart sank, but not for the reasons the young girl across from her probably thought.

Daddy says he misses Mommy.

Luke still missed Chelsea.

Brooke tried to see a way that this made sense, that this didn't mean she was a distraction for Luke. Maybe Montana had asked a lot of questions, and Luke was trying to be polite about Montana's mother. Maybe...

Brooke couldn't do it.

"What do you think?" Montana asked, oblivious to the rising emotions in Brooke's heart. "Do you like it?"

"I do, I do," Brooke said, but she wasn't present. A lump was forming in her throat as she looked at the previous month in a different light—the light in which she was not someone Luke loved or wanted to date, but the light in which she served as an outlet for emotional attention, distraction from how he was not past Chelsea.

Maybe she was being unfair. Hopefully, she was being unfair. She wanted nothing more than to believe that she was wrong, that she was just losing her marbles, and that Luke did indeed want to try a second time.

But... heavens...

"Keep reading!"

Never had Montana's enthusiasm felt like such a torturous trap.

"Up there, they can talk about how much they love Daddy."

"Montana, I'd like to encourage you to use more active verbs and to use more adjectives," Brooke said, but she wasn't providing nuanced feedback—she just needed an excuse to look away and put the focus back on Montana.

"Is it good?" Montana asked.

Brooke nodded, now accepting she could no longer hide her emotions.

"It's... tough to read for me. Talking about people who have died is always a sad thing. But you can write very well in a way that honors them."

"That's good!"

Yes, yes it was, Brooke supposed.

It was all too good.

"Try to rewrite those first few lines with more adjectives," Brooke said. "If you need specific suggestions, I can give them, but I'd like for you to try on your own first."

Brooke handed the piece of paper back to Montana, who stared at the page, deep in thought. The young child did not notice Brooke staring off at the horizon, where Luke and Jesse had disappeared past.

It seemed rather emblematic to Brooke. Here she was, back in Greenville, excited to see her most sincere and meaningful partner in her life, only to have him disappear with someone else. Yes, the contexts were completely different from Chelsea and Jesse, but as emotion overtook

Brooke's rational thinking, context diluted in favor of frustration.

Daddy says he misses Mommy...

Because Daddy loved Mommy so much, he's not ready to move on.

Because Daddy wants the life he had with Mommy, not the life he had with me.

Because...

Because I'm not Chelsea.

Brooke drew in a deep breath.

"Ms. Young?" Montana said, a concerned look on her face.

"I'm sorry," Brooke said, waving her hand at her face. "I've just got some allergies."

"You do?"

God bless Montana, the girl was the epitome of innocence and youth. She would have to grow up someday and face all the pleasure and pain of adulthood, but Brooke envied her for now. She just believed what she heard and saw her and her father as infallible. *And her mother...*

"Yes," Brooke said, "can you give Ms. Young a second?"

She stood up without waiting for a word from Montana and walked off the steps and onto the grass of the ranch. She kept walking, as if moving to where Luke and Jesse had disappeared to, but knew she'd never catch up with their horses. That was fine—she couldn't catch up with Luke, anyway.

Once she got far away enough, she burst into tears, "allergies" be darned.

Not only was it sad, it was unfair to Luke. How could he move on from Chelsea when he saw her face in his daughter every day? It wasn't like Luke wasn't over someone he dated for three months in college; he wasn't over the woman he had married, the woman who had given birth to their daughter, the woman who had died of breast cancer at an age when almost no woman even pondered the remote possibility.

Luke was only doing what Luke had a right to do, given the

circumstances.

But that also meant it wasn't meant to be.

Brooke had hoped that thinking those words in her mind, muttering "it wasn't meant to be" as well would have brought her a modicum of peace. Instead, it made the tears fall harder. Where else was she supposed to find love? Who else was she supposed to start a family with?

Why, God, did you curse me with such bad luck?

She felt guilty for questioning His will, but her pain was so great that she couldn't fathom any good answer. She wished, for a fleeting moment, she could be like the city women who didn't mind waiting to date until their thirties and didn't mind risking the possibility of never having a kid. Their minds didn't seem racked with sadness like hers was right now.

She sighed.

Well, at least Montana had a wonderful father.

At least Luke had a wonderful daughter.

At least Chelsea had gotten the mature Luke and had the blessing of a family before she departed.

If it wasn't meant to be for her, at least everyone else had had things as they were meant to be.

"Goodbye, Luke," she said, trying to force him out of her mind, but she knew it wouldn't be that easy. She owed it to Montana to tutor her for a good seven more months. She would see Luke at Greenville Elementary regularly, and they still hadn't had parent-teacher conferences.

She wasn't saying goodbye to Luke, the man. She was saying goodbye to Luke, the boyfriend and someday husband.

As if God was testing her, Luke and Jesse appeared in view a few seconds later, making their way back to the homestead. Brooke hurried back to Montana, checking her watch along the way. It was only twenty after nine; she still had over an hour and a half of tutoring the young girl. Could she find a way to excuse herself?

No, no. That made it about her. Today was about Montana.

She sat back down by the young girl, who was still scribbling on a piece of paper.

"Alright, sorry about that, Montana," Brooke said, still sniffling. "Let's focus on your writing."

∼

Whether Luke realized something was wrong with Brooke, had other things to do, or just wanted Montana to have space as she worked, he never bothered them for the rest of the time. Brooke was no longer the sobbing mess she had been at the start of the session, but the sadness never left her; the storm no longer rumbled, but the dark clouds remained overhead.

When it was time to leave, Brooke hoped she could sneak by without a word to any of the Walkers, however unrealistic that may have been. She made it all the way to the front door before Luke called to her.

"Walk with me and tell me how Montana did," he said.

His voice suggested he had no idea what Brooke was thinking. That felt too unlikely; he had to be pretending everything was fine. Brooke was too far past that to play along.

As soon as the door shut behind them and Brooke knew they had privacy, she stopped at the steps.

"Brooke?"

"We can't, Luke. I'm… we can't."

Recognition hit Luke's face instantly. He crossed his arms, drew in a deep breath, and raised his chin, as if preparing himself to look strong.

"Talk to me, Brooke. What prompted this sudden change?"

Did they really have to talk about it? Was it not that obvious?

"I can't take her place, Luke, and it wouldn't be fair to anyone even if I could."

Luke looked confused for half a second before his eyes widened in surprise.

"What does Chelsea have to do with this?"

"Everything!" Brooke said, surprised at the force of her words. "Your daughter is the best student in my class, and I love her to death, but she doesn't lie. Did you see what she wrote? That Daddy misses Mommy? And you should, Luke. Heck, if I had married and seen my husband die, I would miss him every day. But…"

Luke sighed.

"I miss Montana having a mother," Luke said. "And I miss having someone I can share everything with. And yes, I suppose you could say I miss Chelsea. But I'm not trying to replace her. I sure as heck don't think you're the second version of Chelsea. You know who I missed? You, Brooke."

Brooke couldn't take this. She didn't want to be sweet-talked out of the moment and into making a long-term stupid decision. She still liked—perhaps even loved—Luke, but goodness, did he not realize what he was saying?

"Even when I was with her, I missed you. If anyone is anything, Chelsea was trying to replace you. I didn't break up with you in college because I was trying to get with other girls. I just… I don't know."

Brooke shook her head, her eyes wet with tears.

"You're a great guy, Luke, and that's why this hurts so much. She's the mother of your child. You don't have to say she was a replacement for me. I know this hurts, but we'll be fine."

"No, we won't," Luke said, walking over to her and placing his hands on her shoulders. "The good Lord has given us a gift, Brooke. Fourteen years ago, I made the dumbest decision of my life. And I started dating only because I thought I would never have a chance to make up for that decision. Then, I walk into Bacon & Bakin', and the good Lord put you there.

"There's a lot to figure out, I know. Heck, it's only been a month. We both have a lot to figure out, definitely me more than you. We can't let it end at the first sign of trouble, though."

"It's not that it's the first sign of trouble," Brooke said. "It's that it's something fundamental to your life. You could have five kids with me, and Chelsea will forever be Montana's mother."

She sighed.

"I'm sorry, Luke. I truly didn't mean to hurt you, and I truly enjoyed being with you the past month. I promise I'll be a great teacher for Montana for the rest of the year. But… our chance passed in college. Life has happened too much in the last fourteen years for this to work."

She looked up into his eyes for the first time since the conversation started. Heavens, even now, her words all but severing her emotional ties to Luke, he still looked handsome. He looked wounded, hurt beyond anything she would have guessed, but the cowboy hat and the strong hands made it awfully easy for her to reconsider her decision.

"I'm sorry," she said as she brushed by, this time taking extra caution to make sure she did not look back into his eyes.

She put her car in reverse as soon as possible, darting her eyes to the rearview mirror as she did a three-point turn. When she finally pulled away, she stole one last glance at the homestead she pulled away from.

Luke had never moved.

She let out the longest sigh yet. She promised herself to be a great teacher to Montana for the rest of the school year. She promised she would tutor her before and after school and at coffee shops on weekends if requested.

But beyond that, she hoped she would never have to deal with the Walkers beyond the casual encounter. Too much had happened, too much history was present for them to ever just be friends.

I just hope he finds his one true love. I just hope he gets a second chance at love.

23

LUKE

TEN YEARS EARLIER

*L*uke might have been the only person at this party who wished that he was still back home, still at his old life.

He had turned twenty-three over the summer, just entering the prime of his life, but more notably, he had gotten married.

For some reason.

Chelsea was great. She was, really, great. That wasn't a lie.

But...

She wasn't the one.

Luke had known that from the day he met her. He had known that as they dated for two years. He knew that even as he proposed to her, doing so in part because of pressure and in part because he couldn't ever fathom getting back with the one.

But now, as he sat in the basement of his home, he was left to wonder why he had acted as he had. If he really loved Brooke, wouldn't he have made a greater effort to try to win her back? If he really wanted that second chance, why hadn't he acted like it? Why had he just gone with the flow in college, more or less just letting time pass without actively grabbing it?

He supposed this was the Lord's will, but no amount of

prayer answered any of his questions. He could have backed out at any time when they were dating; even in engagement, while it would have caused quite a stir, at least it wouldn't have been unheard of.

But now he had made a commitment to Chelsea to be her loving husband, and he knew he needed to be better for her. He could not live in regret. That was how married couples became roommates instead of lovers, with one partner pining for someone or something else while the other was left out to dry.

But how?

Luke closed his eyes in prayer and wondered what he could do to be a better husband. He did all the things a good man did; he took his wife to nice dinners, promised to start a family with her, went to church with her. But it seemed like he wasn't fully opening his heart to her.

His prayer was interrupted when he heard Chelsea coughing horribly upstairs. He had barely gotten out of his basement when he heard his wife vomiting. That was unexpected; she had shown no signs of a fever or upset stomach in the past few days.

"Chelsea?" Luke called as he hurried up the stairs. "Did Jesse's cooking get to you?"

"I woke up like this," Chelsea said, lying on the bathroom floor. She didn't look completely miserable, but it also wasn't exactly the paradigm of put together. "I just woke up this morning, and I felt…"

Her words trailed off. Something seemed to click in her mind. It clicked in Luke's mind at the same time as hers.

Is she pregnant?

Both of them acted without saying a word, Luke scrambling through the bathroom cabinets to find a pregnancy test, Chelsea rising to her feet. Luke finally found it in the third cabinet and handed it to her. He then walked into their bedroom and sat on the edge of the bed.

He closed his eyes and said a silent prayer.

Dear Lord, I know it is time to accept your will. I am not fulfilling my role as a husband. I am holding on to a past that I can never return to, and I am failing to be present for my wife in the interim. Should my wife bear a child, please, help me become a better man.

"Luke!"

The tone of her scream said everything Luke needed to know. He was going to be a father.

He was going to be a father!

Thank you, Lord.

He hurried into the bathroom to find Chelsea with her arms raised in triumph. He held her tight, laughing in joy. He was going to be a father! Oh, how the good Lord blessed him.

He cupped Chelsea's face, and—suddenly, for a flash, he saw Brooke's face. *That was our dream. Our...*

He brushed the thought to the side as he kissed his wife. No, he needed to be *here, not there,* for his actual, not imaginary, wife. He hadn't even heard from Brooke in four years.

"You're going to be a daddy," Chelsea said as she kissed him. "I can't wait to see you be a father."

"And you, a mother," Luke said.

Chelsea ate it up, but Luke silently cursed himself. Whenever he wasn't truly present with Chelsea, he just repeated what she said back to her, just in a slightly different style. Chelsea didn't recognize it, but he did.

He needed to change.

∽

LUKE NEVER MADE it to Sunday service that day, for the two of them were too busy celebrating. But he managed to sneak away in the evening as part of his grocery run, heading to the local chapel, St. Peter's.

All the services had finished for the day, and with the hour striking nearly seven o'clock, Luke found himself alone, save for one older woman cleaning some pews. He gave a friendly nod to her, and her to him; the communication was silent but conveyed the need for space.

Luke knelt and closed his eyes.

He had to accept that, for at least the foreseeable future, Brooke would remain on his mind. Even if he eventually stopped thinking about her, she would always be a part of his life history, the woman who taught him how to love and what it meant to be a good partner. Perhaps, rather than fight Brooke's place in his story, he needed to accept it.

Could he do that and be a good wife and father?

Dear Lord, he silently began, *I need your help.*

He exhaled slowly.

I know I started out with Chelsea because she reminded me of Brooke. I know that perhaps that was not the healthiest way to start a relationship. But it started, and now we are here.

I fought your will. I tried to have it both ways, having the company of someone physically present but emotionally thinking about someone else. I know this was stupid of me. But now... I'm ready to change.

Dear Lord, please give me the strength to be a great father. Give me the emotional intelligence to be a great husband.

He sat in silence for a few seconds. Try as he might, he could not help the next thought that came to mind. It felt horrible, especially with all that he had just prayed for, but it was there.

If, for whatever reason, in the future, I am a single father, and I run into Brooke Young, please give me a second chance. But if I am married from now until death do us part, I vow never to pray for anything other than good health and your will to come to pass.

In your name, Amen.

Luke opened his eyes. He wasn't convinced he was in a better place now. He knew only time and God's will would make him better.

But perhaps admitting the truth was the first step to becoming a better man. Anything to be the best father possible for his future child.

24

BROOKE

That Friday, Brooke had just finished grading her students' revised essays—which, unfortunately, included Montana's story about her mother and still-living grandfather meeting in heaven. She felt certain that the story would make her cry.

And sure enough, it did.

It had only been a week since her second relationship with Luke had fallen apart, but this wasn't just any one-month relationship falling apart. No, somehow, despite her best efforts and her out-loud insistence that this was best, a thought kept nagging at her she could not get rid of.

He was *the one*.

Brooke did not want to be so darn sure of it, but the thought stuck in her brain like a gnat on a hot Montana summer day. In just the one month together, even the tense moments had revealed something meaningful—even the moments about Chelsea had shown Luke not so much as a man unable to move past a woman, but a man grateful for what it had done and now ready to move on. The only thing—the *only* thing—that prevented Brooke from embracing him more fully was her own hangups on it.

And apparently, that refusal to parse out the nuance was the curse to end their second chance at love.

Just like the first time.

As she stepped out of the elementary school, still with months to go in the school year, she headed for her car. As soon as she got inside, she continued to cry.

And then she paused.

She felt like she had experienced this before, just under slightly different circumstances. The déjà vu struck her as impossible to ignore, and it didn't take long for her to connect the present to how she had reacted around Christmas time fourteen years ago. Back then, she had gotten into her father's truck and just drove.

She didn't know how to handle her emotions back then, and her anger had led her to make a vow that, depending on how she defined it, she had either cracked only ever so slightly or broken entirely. She had wasted a lot of her father's gas, Pastor O'Connell's time, and likely some goodwill with the Lord for making such a tempest of a vow.

Now...

What was she to do?

First, she sat in the car until she stopped crying. It was telling that she had teared up so much, but she knew that an emotional decision, even for the right reasons, was still one she would question later.

Second, she knew she couldn't rely on herself for help. Even now, she doubted her own ability to make sense of everything; was she actually smart for pulling away from a man who still said he missed his deceased wife? Or had she blown the situation out of proportion, treating the death of a loved one in the same way a heartbroken, angsty teenager might treat losing a prom date?

Fourteen years ago, she had reached out to Pastor O'Connell. It seemed almost silly to rely on the same path that had taken her to a better place, but was it ever so silly to trust in God? Her father had often said a test of a person's faith came not during joyful times like Christmas and weddings, but during hardships of loss, suffering, and uncertainty.

No, it was not so silly.

She turned her car on and headed to St. Luke's for a visit with Pastor O'Connell.

And this time, she wouldn't burn so much gas first.

∽

BY THE TIME she pulled up to St. Luke's, though someone might have been able to tell that she had cried, Brooke no longer shed tears as she had fourteen years ago. She didn't exactly deserve a pat on the back for being more mature than she was at sixteen, but maybe, she thought, this would bode well for her making better decisions.

As she walked inside, she recalled how she had walked these exact steps and so carefully observed the fourteen stations of the cross. Fourteen years later, those stained glass windows had not changed. *Humans change, but God's grace does not.* Pastor O'Connell was still cleaning some pews, and by this time, his hair had grayed entirely, though his face remained youthful. He was closer to ninety than nine as she thought about her father's joke, but that only meant he had added wisdom to the vigor he possessed.

Brooke took a couple of steps forward. Pastor O'Connell's hearing apparently wasn't as good as it was back then because, this time, he didn't look up until Brooke was within a couple of pews of him. But his calm voice and his smile were the same.

"Brooke Young," he said, less of a question than before. "It has been good to have you back in Greenville. What brings you here, my child?"

Though it still felt slightly odd to deal with matters of relationships, at least here, the stakes felt more real than teenage love. Accordingly, she did not hesitate to speak her mind.

"Can a man love another woman after his wife's death?"

Pastor O'Connell smiled and nodded.

"That is a question that each man must answer for himself. What I can tell you, from my readings of Timothy, is that God encourages the widowed to marry and bear more children. Whether a man chooses to do so, he must take refuge in God's grace and decide for himself."

Brooke felt surprised to feel so grateful for that. If nothing else, at least the question of faith would not prevent her from being close to Luke.

But just because a man and woman of their faith *could* remarry did not answer the question of if Luke *would* remarry without constantly thinking about Chelsea.

"Thank you, Pastor," Brooke said. "You can probably guess that this has to do with Luke Walker."

"I have seen the way you two look at each other with love at The Homestead, I assumed as much."

Brooke blushed, but Pastor O'Connell's gentle demeanor removed the embarrassment of being so noticed in public.

"Do not feel ashamed. I have seen many young couples come through here, whether just for service or in seeking marriage counseling, who do not grasp what it means to love the other person or only superficially grasp it. Perhaps you did not understand this in your youth, but both of you have matured into wonderful young adults in the years since."

"You think so?" Brooke said.

"Yes," Pastor O'Connell said. "I am aware of what happened to his former wife. Such a tragedy can either break a man or turn him into a faithful, devout servant of God. It is an amazing sign of Luke that he has become a stronger man. And you, too, Brooke. I know your mother suffers terribly from her stroke. You are unyielding in your care for her."

Oh, heavens, to bring her up...

But Brooke could see the value in what Pastor O'Connell said.

"I cannot give you advice on what you should do with your feelings for each other. Aside from following God's will, the only thing I can say is to follow your heart, trust your gut, and speak the truth, no matter how uncomfortable it may be. If God intends for you both to fall in love and become a couple, then following those steps will give you what you seek. If God does not intend it, then you can depart on peaceful terms, knowing that everything that needed to be said was said."

It was everything she needed to hear. God, per the Bible, would not condemn or judge her for having interest in a man once married. Pastor O'Connell had not explicitly said she needed to pursue him, but it sure seemed that if he did not favor it, his words would have been much bolder and straightforward.

"Pray on the matter some," he said, gesturing to the pews. "Your faith in God has grown through the years, and I know that what you pray for will have more meaning."

"You heard me all those years ago?"

Pastor O'Connell smiled.

"The Lord understands that not all our prayers come from a well-intentioned place. In the moment, you prayed for what you thought would give you the most respite and the most peace. You can see that he did not answer your prayer as you may have wanted but perhaps that is the point."

Brooke blushed again. Yet somehow, the good pastor just had a way of putting her at ease. However he did it, she was grateful.

She slid into the pew closest to her, pulled the kneeler down, and knelt. It felt strange how life had a tendency to repeat itself, though perhaps not in the exact manner she had remembered it. Pastor O'Connell was right. Much had changed in the years.

And maybe this time, instead of being petulant and insistent on acting like a stubborn teenager, she would ask for something that He would consider worthwhile. She knew she was not worthy, but all the same, she hoped she was better.

"Lord, I vow to always follow your ways. I vow to always be faithful to you and follow your will."

She hesitated for a half-second. It somehow... no, she was not asking for something obscene or wrong. Her heart yearned for clarity; the mere thought of what had happened filled her with regret. She could not help herself from asking.

She needed to become more open.

"And I vow, if the opportunity should arise, to give Luke a second chance at a second chance."

And may your will be done.

25

LUKE

As the days passed, Luke found he was less and less capable of putting up a stoic front for his daughter as he had been the previous week.

The sadness over losing Brooke a second time—this time, through what felt like the fault of his subconscious instead of a conscious decision—and his father's impending departure weighed on him too heavily. He never came close to crying about Brooke, but he could no longer sing along with Montana's impromptu songs. He expressed his pride whenever she came home with words of encouragement from Ms. Young, but as soon as Montana looked away, the words stung Luke more.

Had Brooke never been as invested as Luke was in trying this a second time? Had she already gotten to where she was feeling cheerful enough to encourage his own child? *She's a teacher, it's what she's supposed to do.* But no amount of rational thought would help.

"Daddy?"

"Yes, Tana?" Luke said in a flat voice.

"Is Ms. Young coming over tomorrow? She didn't say anything this week."

Luke shook his head.

"I think Ms. Young wants a Saturday for herself and her parents," he said. "Sometimes, you just need alone time."

Permanently.

Luke never took his gaze off the road, even as he and Montana entered the more rural part that eventually led to Hope Valley Ranch. He could feel his daughter's eyes measuring him up, but he could only put his left elbow against the door, lean on it, and sigh.

"Daddy?"

"Yes, Tana?" Luke said, trying to brace himself for another exhausting Brooke question.

"Are you OK?"

Luke sighed. An eight-year-old did not need to burden his problems. But she deserved the truth, or at least some part of it.

"Life is hard right now, sweetie," Luke said, "and sometimes, there's no good reason. Bad things happen, and even if we know exactly why, it doesn't ease the pain."

Montana nodded and then sat up, her legs tucked under her.

"It's OK to say it hurts, Daddy."

Ah, shoot, she's becoming too smart for her own good, Luke thought as a small smile came to his face.

"You listen when Daddy talks, huh?"

"I try to!" Montana said, perking up, perhaps hoping that if she expressed more energy, Luke would follow suit. "Just say if it hurts."

"It hurts."

"What does?"

Lord have mercy. If his eight-year-old was this probing, what was Montana going to be like at twelve? At eighteen?

Better that, of course, than a rebellious teenager who fell into all the wrong scenes.

"Papaw," Luke said before taking a pause. Did he want to bring Montana into his relationship? He had told himself he wouldn't bring her in because of her age and losing Chelsea, but given that she was at the ranch every Saturday and saw them interacting in every car line, he didn't think he'd followed through on that promise very well. "And your teacher, Ms. Young."

"I knew you two were together!" Montana shouted in joy, but her mood quickly calmed. "Or were. I'm sorry, Daddy. Is there anything I can do to get you back together?"

Luke laughed. It was the first genuine, joyful laugh he had had since last Saturday.

"You are an angel, Tana. But unfortunately, I think this is something Daddy's just going to have to figure out on his own."

"Maybe I can write her a story, saying—"

"Tana," Luke said, his voice stern but warmer than before Montana's innocent question. "The best thing you can do is to be the best student you can be for her. Even if you were a grown-up, I would ask you to let me handle things. Sometimes, two people just have to handle things, no matter how good the advice can be. OK?"

Luke hit his left turn signal as the Hope Valley Ranch entrance came into view.

"OK," Montana said, nodding her head once. "I will stay out of the way."

"But thank you, Tana," Luke said as he pulled through the overpass. "I needed someone to pull me out of my rut. I just didn't think it would be you."

"Well, why not?" Montana said.

"Because sometimes adults can be stupid and not realize that they can learn as much from kids as kids can learn from them," Luke said with a smile. "Turns out you might be a teacher yourself someday, too."

"I can be like Ms. Young?" she said with a rising voice.

Yes, and if you did, it would make the world a better place, Luke thought as they pulled up to the homestead. Papaw was not sitting on the front steps today, but that had been an aberration anyway. Luke helped Montana out of the car, yelling at her to enjoy the Friday afternoon. She was already running for Mimi, wherever she was.

Luke paused at the truck, leaning against the hood as he contemplated the advice of his daughter. *Of all dang people.* She had a point, though. It was OK to say it hurt.

And to say it meant talking to other people.

People that Luke had not had the courage to ask for help fourteen years ago.

And he knew just who to speak to.

∼

AFTER CONFIRMING MIMI, Jesse, and Weston didn't mind watching Montana that Friday afternoon—though there were no promises made about spoiling the little one—Luke headed straight for St. Luke's Church and Pastor O'Connell. One traffic light before he arrived, he swore he saw Brooke's car pulling out of the lot; at the very least, the vehicle was the same size and color as hers. But it was probably for the best that they did not encounter each other at the chapel, for even if Luke was ready to speak to her, a house of worship did not seem the right place.

Luke parked his truck and walked inside. He had returned many times in the last month, but this was the first time he had arrived alone. It allowed him the chance to observe the stained glass windows, how Jesus had suffered during those stages, and how whoever designed those windows had a true gift. It also made him appreciate that in the grand scheme of things, some sufferings were much worse than others.

Pastor O'Connell emerged from behind Luke, seeming to appear out of nowhere.

"Ah, Luke Walker," he said. "It has been good to have you back in Greenville. What brings you here, my child?"

"Just... seeking guidance, I suppose," Luke said, now feeling slightly silly to have come here in the first place. "I came to ask how to know if someone is the one and how to know if I am ready to love again, but I feel that is not a question worth your time."

"Worth my time?" the good pastor said. "Luke, if love is not worth my time, then what is?"

Luke couldn't argue when it was put like that.

"Tell me your story."

Luke knew, surely, Pastor O'Connell had heard what had happened from other sources, perhaps even his own family. But he appreciated having the opportunity to present from his own perspective. And so, Pastor O'Connell sat patiently as Luke recounted everything from when he and Brooke broke up to the present day, including all the heartache of losing his wife and the cautious joy of being back in Greenville.

"I see," the pastor said when Luke finished his story. "I will tell you what I tell others. God does not expect widows to mourn for the rest of their lives, refusing to ever enter society again. In fact, it would be cause to celebrate if the widowed went out and had a family once more. But as to the individual, that is up to them. So I ask you, Luke, what do you think? Do you think you are ready?"

"I would like to think I'm ready, but I'm not sure. I told Montana I missed my wife—"

"Did you miss her because your daughter asked you, or because you miss her at the expense of your own life? And do not answer from the mind. Answer from the heart."

Luke nodded. He felt certain God was giving him the answer right there.

"I am grateful for what my wife did to me, and a part of me will always love her. But there is so much more of me ready to love again. I guess if that means I miss her, so be it, but I do not miss her so much that I cannot commit myself to Broo… to someone else."

Pastor O'Connell smiled.

"Whoever it may be that has your eye," he said with a wink, "I hope you give yourself the opportunity to both be there for them and to explain what you just told me."

Pastor O'Connell nodded back to the office he had emerged from.

"I will leave you to pray," he said. "God's will be done. But we must be willing to embrace and accept God's will, and you are getting there. Also, listen to your father. I can give you guidance from a spiritual perspective. But I am not a married man. There is something to be said for listening to the man who brought you into this world."

With a gentle pat on Luke's right shoulder, the pastor departed, leaving Luke in the pews. He slid into one, not noticing until he was already about to sit down that someone had put the kneeler down. He ignored the implications and began to pray.

"Lord, give me the wisdom to follow your will," he said with a breath. "Give me the courage to follow through on it. And give me the courage to speak my truth."

He paused.

"And if you are feeling especially grateful, I would love if your will includes Brooke Young being…"

Have the courage to speak your truth.

"Being my wife."

～

Luke remained another fifteen minutes, taking the time to also pray for his father and for his brothers. Jesse and Weston seemed in good spirits, all things considered, but Sawyer deploying overseas always required prayers, even if combat had declined significantly from the worst days. And as for Carson... Luke might have needed to listen to his heart with Brooke, but he desperately needed the wisdom of the mind to figure out Carson.

Of all the Walker boys, none had seemed both so eager to leave the ranch and so hesitant to return. Yes, he was only twenty-four years old, and Luke at that time had been married with a newborn in Spokane, but he had never outright refused an invitation home. Luke could only wish that Carson would return before it was too late.

At the end of those fifteen minutes, Luke felt better about himself, but was still uncertain if he would get the chance to reach Brooke again. She had seemed pretty adamant that she would not speak to him again, at least not as they had up to that point. Still, God's grace had put his heart at ease a bit.

When he got home, he was surprised to see Papaw sitting on the front porch with fly-fishing equipment.

"Papaw?" he said as he got out of the truck.

"Let's go up to the Missouri, shall we?" Papaw said. "At my age, when you feel physically vigorous, you take advantage of the opportunity. You don't know when—or if—it will come again."

Luke did not hesitate. The others could take care of each other, and something told Luke that Papaw had already told his wife, sons, and granddaughter anyway. *There is something to be said for listening to the man who brought you into this world.*

Papaw, true to his word, rose of his own accord, put the equipment in Luke's truck bed, and even got into the passenger's seat himself. His breathing was definitely heavy, and there was a slight rattle to it, but it was the most vigorous that Luke had seen him since, frankly, they'd come home.

"Mimi cook you something good that gave you vigor?"

"No, just the thought that I couldn't go without giving the

fish in the river one more reminder of who owned that place for fifty-plus years."

Luke chuckled as they pulled out of the homestead.

"The past week, you've been acting like someone kicked you in the face. What's going on?"

Luke laughed much harder, but he cut himself off when he realized his father was serious. *Have the courage to speak your truth.*

"I thought Brooke and I were going to be together again," he said. "But she thinks that I'm not over Chelsea and, perhaps even regardless of that, we wouldn't work out a second time. I hurt her so bad fourteen years ago, Papaw. She probably thinks of that whenever she thinks of me."

His father just nodded. Although he could be brusque, sometimes even crass, no one had ever said Howard Walker wasn't a fantastic listener. Just sometimes a painfully honest communicator.

"You'd be so quick to sell yourself short?" Papaw said.

"She was over here on Saturday and said that she knew it wouldn't work out. She probably thinks Chelsea will forever be on my mind."

"And you're not going to push back at the first sign of trouble?"

Luke sighed.

"It's not that simple, Papaw."

"Take it from someone that's been married over three decades. Yes, it is. You need to confront difficulties head-on."

"When have you and Mimi ever had to do that?" Luke said as they hit the early part of Greenville, St. Luke's appearing on the left. "I have never heard you two argue."

"Oh, we argued plenty," Papaw said. "You don't see it because we had our arguments behind closed doors. Whether that was smart or not, only the good Lord knows. But you know we broke up once, right?"

Luke nearly slammed on the brakes in shock. No, no, he did not know that.

"We were dating for several years. Then, our own flaws, especially with communication, led to our breakup. It didn't help that her father, your grandfather, died right after. I didn't know this, because I was off traveling the country for a year."

That's why he encouraged all of us to explore the world beyond Greenville.

History repeats itself.

"When I came back," Papaw said, and suddenly, he started laughing, "I foolishly thought we could just pick right back up where we left off. But I needed to grow up. She needed to come to terms with her father's passing. Both of us, in other words, needed to learn to confront difficulties head-on. It's going to be inevitable there will be pain in any relationship, but we had had suffering."

"Suffering?"

Papaw nodded, certain of his choice of words.

"Pain is unavoidable, suffering is optional," he said, a favorite saying of his. "We couldn't help the pain that came with initial miscommunication or her father's death. No one can. But my tomfoolery made it worse, especially when I needed to be a man."

He sighed.

"It's not like I changed who I am entirely. You still see me, a dying man, cracking jokes as if I just drank too much scotch last night. Your mother doesn't love it that much. But I changed enough and evolved enough to become a man worthy of her—and it all started by being courageous."

Papaw then poked Luke in the arm and grabbed his forearm somewhat aggressively.

"If you want Brooke, you need to show some courage. Speak your darn mind. Don't let your best chance at your happily ever after go to the wayside because of some misunderstanding."

"I get it, Papaw," Luke said, "though this is just—"

"I'd say the same whether you misunderstood if she liked her bacon crisp or floppy or if she misunderstood how you feel about Chelsea."

That stopped Luke and forced him to ponder what Papaw had said.

Pastor O'Connell had told Luke to listen to his heart. Papaw was telling Luke to stop waiting and to act on what he heard from his heart. So the question simply became... how?

"When do you next see Brooke again?"

"I think there are parent-teacher conferences next Thursday and Friday. I'll need to check when—"

"Show her you love her there."

"There? Papaw, those are for—"

"I don't care what they're for, son; you make your point. Do you think in my dying days, I'm going to say, 'Oh, well, I shouldn't say this because others are around?' No. I will forever express my love to the people I love. If I need to say I love your mother, even with her ridiculous jokes about geese causing traffic jams, then I'll do it whether in the privacy of our home or in lunch hour at Bison Brothers."

The point was made. Luke would need time to think about how, exactly, he'd pull this off.

But determination filled him. If his father could speak the truth as strongly as he was, Luke could too.

He wouldn't need a stoic front when he had courage inside him. He just needed a chance.

26

BROOKE

Brooke's anxiety increased as Friday afternoon approached, her day to host parent-teacher conferences.

With her classroom size, she would only have about twenty sets of parents to speak to, each with a maximum of six minutes, so at least she wouldn't have to stay much past dinner time. Lola, bless her, always agreed to stay later than expected, which was much needed with Brooke's father back in the air for work.

But there was the obvious concern and the one she didn't want to think about.

The obvious concern was parents—bless the good ones, who could take critiques of their children, but the bad ones... oh, Lord.

The one she didn't want to think about, well, she'd have to have sooner rather than later.

For now, though, it was only lunchtime, and as usual, once Montana had finished her lunch with the girls she'd made friends with, she came to Brooke for further help. It relieved Brooke that Montana had made friends; she knew the "teacher's pet" could quickly become the target of bullying. Luckily, kids in Greenville were better than that.

"Hi, Montana," Brooke said as Montana put her most recent story on her desk. "How are you?"

"Good!" she said. "Daddy seems happier, and Papaw doesn't seem as sick as before."

Brooke's smile showed she felt genuine happiness for Luke and Mr. Walker. Thinking of Luke still warmed her heart and brought strong feelings, but at least he was getting to a better mental place. He'd find someone who didn't bring so much baggage to a potential relationship, and he'd forget Brooke ever existed.

"Miracles do happen, don't they?" Brooke said.

"They sure do! He also misses you."

Brooke froze. *He misses me?*

"How?"

Only a second after asking the question did she realize she might have crossed professional boundaries. Luckily, no one else was in the room, and it was too late to take it back from young Montana, anyway.

"He's happier, but he's talking to himself a lot," Montana said. "When I ask him what he's doing, he said he's planning and getting more courage. Like, he's stronger?"

It took Brooke a second to realize the young girl was asking what "courage" meant.

"It means that he's getting braver," Brooke said, some possibilities coming to mind as she said the words out loud. "It means that he's becoming more willing to do or say what he believes in."

"Well, that's good! He should say how he feels about you to you."

Brooke couldn't help the smile that spread across her face, even knowing that Montana would tell her father about that smile. Perhaps, though, that was not the worst thing in the world.

"I think he loves you."

"Montana!" Brooke said, laughing to avoid the implications of what the young girl had just said. "You are much too young to be talking about love between two adults."

"What? He talks about you way more than he does Mommy."

Brooke kept her laughter up, this time as a shield for very different reasons. Now she was feeling more and more like a fool.

"He does that because I'm tutoring you regularly, and your mother has… she's in heaven now. I'm sure when Christmas comes or when the school year ends, he'll go back to talking about your mother much more."

"I don't know!" Montana said, her voice rising in a way that implied she did know—she just disagreed. "I also hear Mimi and Papaw saying your name a lot. Uncle Jesse won't say anything, but he says that's because he doesn't want to jinx you. What does jinx you mean?"

Brooke found herself lost in her head. Luke was really going to come back for her, wasn't he? Possibly as soon as this afternoon.

Maybe she had misjudged the issue of Chelsea. Maybe she had overreacted. Fine. But was *she* ready for a second time? Was she ready to take the risk of having her heart shattered and stomped on the floor?

Am I ready for the potential reward of finding the greatest love anyone could have outside of the Lord?

"Miss Young?"

"I'm sorry, Montana. What was your question?"

"What does jinx you mean?"

Brooke brushed back her hair, trying not to feel too embarrassed at missing the question.

"It means to curse someone. Like if I jinx your writing, it means you won't write well."

"Ohhh. So Uncle Jesse was saying he doesn't want to make you getting back with Daddy difficult!"

This was too much. How in the world did Brooke wind up in a spot where little Montana was the middle woman in all of this, innocently relaying private conversations she probably assumed many other adults had?

"Well, I have to agree to take him back," she said, "and at one time, your father and I were serious. But it just didn't work out. He found your mother."

"Yeah, and then he found you again."

Brooke sighed. Was the entire Walker clan convinced Luke was going to get Brooke back? The pressure seemed to grow by the moment, and yes, in a perfect world, she wanted Luke back. And yes, the world was a little more perfect than she had imagined.

But was it perfect enough?

"Let's just focus on your writing for now," Brooke said. "I need something to talk to your father about at parent-teacher conferences."

∼

THE AFTERNOON CAME, and Brooke nervously twitched her fingers as the clock approached four. She had to be at her desk until half-past six, and if a parent sat down one minute until the end, she'd still have to give them the full six minutes per parent.

She went through her notes for every student, discussing talking points, their strengths and weaknesses, and possible answers to likely questions. In her first parent-teacher conference, she had thought that she could talk simply by memory; what a mistake that was! Most parents were good, but the ones who were bad, either because they were entitled or because they were mean, never left her memory.

Where Luke fell on that spectrum remained to be seen. Would he come out cold and rude, knowing that he had some leverage over her with their courtship? Or would he be the opposite and flirtatious, charming, and almost even seductive?

Or would he just show up as a father, not as a former partner, and focus on Montana and only Montana?

All possibilities seemed on the table. And when the clock struck four p.m., Brooke took a breath as the first set of parents walked in, the Martins.

The Martins had a son, Corey, who did well in school, but when he decided he'd rather tell a joke, there was little Brooke had found that could keep him in line. Even the threat of extra homework or the dreaded d-word—*detention*—failed to keep him in line. Only following through on detention one day in the third week of school had kept him in line, but recently, he'd reverted back to some bad habits.

But to Brooke's utter relief, the Martins listened to what Brooke had to say and even admitted that Corey could be a bit much in the classroom. They said they would do better in training him to listen, and they even asked if there was anything that they could do to make Brooke's life easier.

Truly, moving back to Greenville had some amazing perks.

Including, perhaps...

She refocused before her mind drifted in an embarrassing manner, and she only said that she would appreciate the continued support from the Martins.

For the next two and a half hours, all the way until five minutes before the end of the parent-teacher conferences, Brooke continued to encounter only good parents. Maybe it was because the town still saw teachers as a group to be respected, an extension of raising the kids, but the worst that Brooke encountered was one parent asking for an explanation of extra homework. When she explained it was because of them making fun of Montana's name, the mother immediately apologized.

The last set of parents, the Browns, stood up and shook Brooke's hand. Luke had not shown up.

It might just be for the best, Brooke thought.

She sat and watched the clock, trying to ignore the rising tide of disappointment in her stomach. Four minutes till.

It definitely was for the best, she thought. If Luke was going to have this kind of conversation, then it needed to be in a non-professional setting. Right? It wasn't like anyone else was around, but still. Boundaries.

Three minutes until.

No, she needed to show courage to listen to him wherever he was. If it was here, she could close the door as she did for all the parents for privacy. No one would record her or hear her. If Luke showed the ability to talk about tough subjects, she could do the same with listening.

Two minutes until.

She must have misheard what Montana said. *How can you mishear "I think he loves you?" You know what she said.*

One minute—

She heard someone running down the hallway. Oh, heavens, it was going to be—

Luke Walker.

"Sorry I took until the last minute," he said. "I debated coming until I decided it was better to show up than not at all."

"I would agree," Brooke said.

She stood up. An awkward pause ensued as Luke took a second to realize he needed to walk fully in and take a seat. Brooke could have brushed by him, maybe even touched him as she closed the door, but her courage wasn't quite at that level.

"Anyway," Luke said as he took a seat, "how is Montana doing?"

COWBOY'S HOMECOMING

Brooke drew in a breath. *Show some courage.*

"We can talk about her, but I think you know the answer to that. I've spent the last few weekends at your family's homestead tutoring her. What is it you really want to talk about?"

Show some courage. Luke drew in a breath; she had a feeling he was telling himself the exact same thing.

"I want to talk to you about what seems to be preventing us from being together," he said. "And I need to speak to you as honestly as I can."

"Go ahead. I suppose I should say we have six minutes per meeting, but we can always talk elsewhere after."

Luke nodded.

"Brooke, you're never going to hear me say a bad word about my former wife. I didn't lose her because she was a bad person or an unfaithful spouse. I lost her because of cancer. But the only reason I miss her is because I know Montana misses her. And even then, I don't think Montana misses her, per se—I think she just wishes she had a mother."

Me...

Maybe that's why Montana has taken to being my teacher's pet so well.

"If you don't ever want me to say my former wife's name around you, I am OK with that. I cannot forget her, but I can move on and be present with you. I can do better."

Brooke nodded. She was grateful for the words, and she believed him. But there was a level of conversation they had not yet reached, something to truly show that he was committed. Words were great.

But if words were all they had, then they needed to be the strongest words yet.

"Can you love another woman after Chelsea's death?"

She'd named Luke's former wife on purpose, wanting to show that she did not treat the name like a curse. Courage meant recognizing Luke had once loved someone else and not hide from it.

"Yes," Luke said.

Silence hung over the room. Brooke had heard what she needed to. Pastor O'Connell had been right—they both had matured over the years. She could...

She could move forward, but something still held her back. Her heart yearned to go with him, to practically lean across the table and kiss him, but something still held her back.

And part of it, she realized, was because she was scared. She was scared to get hurt again. Scared to be a mom—not just a teacher—to Montana. Scared to raise a family when she had her own mother, and Luke had his father to take care of.

Show some courage.

But it can take time to build enough courage to move to the right spot.

"You're thinking," Luke said, disrupting her thoughts.

"Yes," Brooke said, "there's quite a lot to think about. I need to pray some and seek God's guidance. It's... it's a lot, Luke. Some of it is good, some of it is not."

"What about it is not good?"

Brooke sighed.

"I guess... it just feels a bit too easy. Like you come here, we talk, and then all is well. Except a part of me still wants to hold back, still wants to think about what's ahead. Words are wonderful, but..."

"Time and acts of commitment and truth make it possible," Luke said, nodding.

Brooke felt she had become more open, and she felt like she was giving him a second chance at a second chance... but it just wasn't *quite* there yet.

"It's alright," Luke said, and strangely, his face seemed to light up.

"It is?"

"Brooke, is there anything with Montana I need to do?"

Oh, right. That's why, officially, they were here.

"No, just keep encouraging her to write."

"Good," Luke said, rising from his chair.

Then, the darndest thing happened. He extended his hand for a handshake, an act that seemed incredibly goofy and awkward yet somehow endearing at the same time. Brooke took it, and her entire body filled with excitement. Goosebumps raised on her arms and even her legs.

Yet Luke seemed completely unaffected. It was almost like he was playing by pretending to be so professional.

"Miss Young," he said with a nod, "you don't mind coming to the homestead to tutor Montana tomorrow morning, do you?"

"I, um, no," Brooke said, surprised that was still on the table.

"Good. Let's do ten a.m. so you can sleep in. If you need more time to take care of your mother, just text me, but I would love to see you there tomorrow. We sure would be excited for it."

With another nod, Luke left the room, leaving Brooke flummoxed but surprisingly hopeful. What was Luke's plan? He would not have set something up if it wasn't also meaningful to Brooke.

She hoped, at least.

She looked up at the clock. She had spoken to Luke for exactly six minutes. Whether he had deliberately done so to respect her time or not, she was happy to be heading home on time.

The only question remained, would she have the courage to accept and embrace whatever happened next, knowing there were no guarantees?

27

LUKE

To Luke, the plan seemed absolutely perfect. By the time he got home, he had the most confident smile on his face he had ever worn. He saw Montana and Mimi sitting on the front porch as he pulled in, the two of them seeming to giggle about something together. He emerged from the truck with an exaggerated bow.

"You look happy!" Montana said.

"Well, Montana, your father has figured some things out."

"Like what? Are you and Miss Young getting back together?"

Luke didn't even pretend otherwise. He was feeling so good and so certain about his plan that he nodded without hesitation. Mimi looked surprised but did not say anything for now.

"Tana, I'm so glad she's your teacher, because it gives me an excuse to see her even after last weekend. Today, when talking to her, I realized I could talk all I wanted, but I needed to show her I love her. Well, I know what I'm going to do."

"And?" Tana said, her excitement growing.

"I'm going to take her on a horseback ride out here on the ranch. I'm going to show her how besides us Walkers, she's the only one I want to be with."

"Cool!" Tana said.

But as Luke looked at his mother, he was surprised to see she had not changed expression. She was leaning forward, listening closely, but her enthusiasm was non-existent, certainly nowhere near the easily impressionable young girl.

"Mimi?" Luke said. "I'm putting this all out there in front of you. Isn't this what you wanted? For me to communicate more?"

"Is this what Brooke would want?"

"What, to communicate more? Of course."

"You know that's not what I meant."

Luke opened his mouth to retort, but caught himself. Was it what Brooke would have wanted?

Well, Brooke did love horseback riding and Montana life. That much was a given. But did she love it like other things? Like, say, reading and writing and teaching?

If he sat back and really thought about it, probably not. It was a credit to the type of person Brooke was that she had still loved every moment of him in their youth and still was opening herself up for another chance.

"What do you mean, Mimi?" Luke asked, even as he had already begun to understand what she meant.

"You're doing what you think is best," Mimi said, "but I want you to think about what Brooke would think is best. It's what your father did—does—so well."

"What do you mean?" Tana asked.

Luke smiled at how invested his little girl seemed in his happiness.

"If Papaw had his way, he'd be ranching from dawn until dusk, and I'd be by his side herding cattle, branding livestock, and tagging everything. He'd dress me up as a cowgirl and have me saying all the things. But he knows that's not a loving relationship—that's just a one-sided courtship.

"No, your father sometimes makes nights for me with Hallmark movies. He sometimes asks me about the romance novels I've read. He'll play along with me when we watch Jeopardy!"

"I cannot imagine Papaw asking anyone about a romance novel," Luke said, scratching his head. The thought was akin to seeing Jesse and Weston swap personalities, or seeing himself suddenly deciding to move to San Francisco.

"You can't, because that's not what he wants to do. But a healthy relationship is based on meeting each other where the other is, not on demanding that they come to you."

Luke sighed. At least he was learning this lesson while Brooke was more open to the possibility of a reunion than otherwise. He might still have won her back if he'd followed through on his horseback idea, but he knew there would be a voice of doubt in Brooke's mind all the same.

And Luke was determined, no matter what came in the following months, to ensure that Brooke had zero doubt in her mind that Luke was there for her. Shoot, if it meant proposing soon enough…

It would have been way too fast if they had never dated before. But having been together for three years, matured over fourteen, and discussed everything? Why the heck wouldn't it make sense?

Still, he calmed himself. He would not be proposing tomorrow. He didn't have a ring, even.

"I suppose motherly advice always makes sense," Luke said with a smile. "What would you suggest then, Mimi?"

"That's for you to decide," she said. "You know Brooke better than anyone here. What would truly make her happy? Not what would make you happy to make her happy, though, of course, don't torture yourself. What would truly be unselfish and show you understand her as a person?"

Luke thought. Then a smile came as he stole a glance at his daughter.

"There's someone else here who can help me figure it out,"

he said. "Come, Tana. I know it's Friday, but we've got a homework assignment that's due tomorrow morning."

∼

LUKE AND MONTANA sat on the back porch, their chins in their hands, struggling to come up with the *perfect* display of commitment and love that would show how well Luke understood Brooke.

It was strange to see his daughter, so talkative and so cheerful, suddenly seem contemplative, practically silent since they got to the back porch. This wasn't just her thinking; this was something occupying her mind.

"What about gifting her a pony?" Montana said, but she didn't seem especially committed to the idea.

"As cute as that is, Ms. Young doesn't have the space that we do to have a pony."

"She could come here, and we could take care of it."

They could. It would give Brooke a reason to come over more often. And if Luke was to inherit operations of the ranch as he expected relatively soon, once they got married, Brooke would likely move here, perhaps even with her mother.

Even so, they were falling into the same issue that Luke had—the idea made Montana happy, but he'd never heard Brooke talk about wanting a pony at any point.

"She could, but let's try to think of something else, OK? Does she mention liking anything in school?"

Montana shrugged.

That set off alarms for Luke. Montana never shrugged; if she didn't know the answer to something, she couldn't let it go without thinking about it.

"What are you thinking about, Tana?" Luke asked.

"Is Ms. Young going to be my new Mommy?"

Luke drew in a breath. He'd thought for so long about the

dynamic of Brooke and Chelsea from his and her perspective, but he'd never stopped to consider what it would be like for his eight-year-old daughter.

"If all goes well, there's a very real possibility," Luke said.

As he spoke, he realized he'd never run this possibility by Montana for discussion. He couldn't imagine her vetoing the possibility, but if she did, he'd have no choice but to accept her request. There was nothing and no one he valued more in this world than his child.

"How does that make you feel?"

"Good," Montana said, but she wasn't smiling. "I'm just scared I'll forget Mommy."

Luke nodded.

"It's not about forgetting Mommy, it's about honoring her by continuing to love and live. Brooke, Ms. Young, she wouldn't be replacing her or trying to push her out of the way, and she doesn't want to do that herself. It's about her being a valuable addition, not a replacement, to our lives."

Montana nodded, her smile still unfortunately absent.

"Do you not want Ms. Young as a mother figure in the house?" Luke said. *Have the courage to ask for her truth.*

Then Montana finally did something Luke had hoped to see for the entire time.

She smiled.

"It would be great, Daddy," she said. "But it would be kind of weird! She's my teacher, and then she's my mom?"

Luke laughed. Comedy was a much easier situation to handle than resentment.

"It will be weird at first, yes, and, honestly, some of the other kids may make remarks. But I promise you, Ms. Young will be a great person to have in your life, especially for more than just teaching."

"I know. She wrote me a note before last weekend."

"She did?" Luke said, surprised—Montana shared practically everything with him.

"Yes, she said it was just between us, but if she's going to be family, you'd be a part of it too!"

She began digging into her backpack, and Luke's heart rapidly beat faster. Even with their unique situation, teachers generally didn't insert themselves into their students' lives, much less talk about their parents to them. Luke told himself to temper his expectations about the letter.

Finally, she found a note that she had folded twice over and opened it.

"'Dear Montana, I think you are a very special writer. I love the way you can use all five senses in your writing, and you are one of the best second-grade writers I have ever seen. I will try to culti…' cultivate? What's cultivate, Daddy?"

"To nourish and grow," he said, thinking about all the times Papaw had talked about cultivating in ranch life. *And all the times you'll end up teaching Montana in the years to come.*

"OK! Anyway, it says, 'I will try to cultivate your talent no matter what. I think it would be wonderful, near the end of the year, to write a story about your father. He is a great man and deserves to have his story told. Best, Ms. Young.'"

That was it.

"Tana, I don't know if you realize it, but you are a genius."

"I am?"

"Yes!" Luke said.

It was right there—the thing that Luke himself may not have done for himself, but that would warm Brooke's heart how she wanted it warmed.

"Tana, I know this is going to sound weird, but I need your help with something. Come with me."

He brought Tana back into the house and into the room he and she had taken over in the past month. With all the possessions they had brought with them from Spokane still in boxes, the room looked like a mess. But even with all the years that had passed, there was one possession that Luke had held onto and always knew where it was.

He pulled open a box full of papers, flipped through a couple of stacks of them, and finally found what he was looking for.

"What is it, Daddy?"

"This was the last letter Ms. Young wrote to me fourteen years ago. Brooke always encouraged me to write to her to show my affection, but I was not a great writer. I'm still not."

He smiled.

"But you are, Tana. How'd you like to help Daddy write a note to Ms. Young?"

Montana's smile was bright enough to light up a snowed-in January evening.

"Let's do it, Daddy!"

28

BROOKE

*B*efore Brooke headed home, she made a quick stop at Bison Brothers to meet with her two best friends, Clara and Danielle. She hadn't seen them since their last meeting, and while they remained up to date with regular texts, they had not known much since last Saturday, when Brooke had determined at the time things wouldn't work out.

She was quite curious to see their reactions now. Before, Clara had expressed all the empathy in the world and had only been concerned with Brooke's well-being. Danielle, on the other hand, called him "a fool who couldn't recognize the difference between gold and dog urine." The text had somehow made Brooke laugh but it also forewarned of a difficult conversation ahead.

When she arrived, Clara and Danielle were already seated. Danielle had a martini in front of her, while Clara only had water.

"What do you want, girl?" Danielle asked.

"Just a water," Brooke said.

"PTCs weren't as bad as you feared?" Clara said.

Brooke shook her head.

"I didn't have a single bad parent."

"Are these the same parents I dealt with a few years ago? Because I swear, some of these sweet next-door neighbors turn into the devil's minions when their four-bedroom house only has 2,200 square feet instead of 2,300."

Clara and Brooke chuckled as the waiter came by. The three of them ordered boneless wings with buffalo sauce and blue cheese on the side, a quick order meant to get them fed but not seated for too long at the restaurant.

"Well, surely, there must have been some excitement you're not telling us about," Danielle said. "I refuse to believe you dealt with, what, forty parents? And not one of them was a drama queen."

"Well, no, actually, none of them were dramatic."

Show some courage. Even if they hate this.

"But you know one of them was Luke."

Both Clara and Danielle arched their eyebrows in curiosity. Clara looked interested; Danielle looked concerned, almost nervous on Brooke's behalf.

"We talked about his daughter for maybe thirty seconds," she admitted. "I tutored her every Saturday at their ranch. He knows how I feel about her."

"Good kid?" Clara asked.

"Yeah, you'll see her more at the bookstore soon, I'm sure. Even all the Luke stuff aside, she's wonderful."

"So what about the other five minutes?" Danielle said, leaning forward as she rested her chin on her right hand. "Did he come crawling back to you? Say he was sorry?"

"He…"

Actually, he did not. But the thought had not upset Brooke, because truthfully, what did he have to apologize for? For honoring the memory of Montana's mother in a way that made Brooke lose her mind? Whose fault was that?

"He said that he needed to clarify some things about his

former wife," Brooke said. "Things that I had misconstrued for some time. It was good—"

"You're making it sound like everything was your fault, Brooke," Danielle said.

A tense pause came.

"I am not back with Luke, if that's what you are concerned about," Brooke said, keeping her voice tempered. "But it was a very honest conversation that we needed to have. I don't know what will happen next, but I do know that what happened was much better than last Saturday."

"I don't like how this sounds," Danielle said. "I know he was your first, and that the idea of a storybook ending is wonderful. But we know real life is more random than the stories we tell. If you get back together, maybe it will work, but I have my doubts."

"Is it, though?" Clara said. "It's random only to people who don't trust in God's will and don't follow their hearts. If you let life and others direct your actions, of course it will seem random."

"Just because I trust in God doesn't mean I don't also recognize He gives us free will," Danielle retorted. "And with that free will comes an awareness that not everything is prince meets princess, princess and prince kiss, and live happily ever after."

Brooke kept silent the whole time her two friends went back and forth with each other. She knew Danielle wasn't the most objective source; she had her own history with one of the Walker brothers. Weston, if she remembered correctly.

Granted, it was impossible to live in Greenville and not know who the Walkers were, but their connection went beyond acquaintance in a small town.

"I trust you to make the right decision," Clara said, "but Danielle is right. Please be careful. We know how the last week has been. It will be a thousand times worse if you get back together and break up in like a year or so."

"That's why I'm not with him now," Brooke pushed back. "He said all the right things, and if I just wanted to go with my emotions, I would have taken him back. But I told him I need to see something more. I don't want to be his consolation after the last fourteen years; I want to be his one true love."

That seemed to appease Clara, who nodded and drank her water.

"I don't trust the Walkers," Danielle said as she drank her martini, as if she hadn't just slid in the remark.

"I don't have to trust all of them," Brooke said. "I just have to trust Luke."

"Now that's silly," Danielle said. "You'd be dating into that whole family. Jesse's hilarious, Weston is… himself. Sawyer at least is overseas. Carson's a headcase no one can figure out. You want to be one of two women in a house of, what, six boys?"

"Don't forget his daughter."

Danielle grimaced and sighed.

"I know, I know, I'm the boring and realist of the group," Danielle said. "Just make sure you pray a lot before saying yes to anything. The good Lord is here to help, but the good Lord also gave us free will to make a bunch of mistakes."

Brooke took the advice to heart, but it didn't change much for her. Maybe fourteen years ago, when she was more concerned with how she looked to her friends, she might have been more cautious about what they said. But she had her faith, and she had maturity to guide her.

There was just one final person to talk to before she saw Luke tomorrow and, she knew, make a decision one way or another.

∼

BROOKE GOT HOME JUST as Lola poked her head outside the door. The sight nearly gave Brooke a heart attack—had something happened to her mother?

But no, fortunately, Lola exclaimed she simply was worried about Brooke and was looking outside to see if she was coming. Brooke apologized and slid her an extra twenty bucks in cash, admittedly a pittance compared to what she was normally making, but Lola could not have been more grateful.

"How is she?" Brooke asked as Lola put the twenty-dollar bill in her pants pocket.

"Good, actually," she said. "She was asking when Brookey would come home."

Those words warmed Brooke's heart. Her mother remembered her nickname. Her mother *remembered*.

"I'll get right to her," she said. "I'll see you tomorrow?"

"Of course," Lola said.

Brooke hugged Lola, surprising her mother's caretaker. But she was feeling so grateful for her mother's good condition that she would have hugged anyone standing before her—even Danielle, despite her doubts about Luke. *She's on her own journey of love. She'll have her own things to overcome and learn from.*

Brooke walked inside, shouting, "Mom?" as she took her shoes off.

"Brookey!" her mother said. "I almost finished this mystery novel, and you wouldn't believe who did it."

Brooke smiled. From a certain point of view, her mother's memory issues almost made her reading of mystery novels more interesting, because it made remembering key plot points difficult. Brooke would have felt bad for that thought if not for her mother having already admitted to it weeks before.

"Let me guess—the butler?"

"No, actually—the billionaire! He set up the butler to take the fall. Can you believe that?"

"No, I can't," Brooke said with a smile as she kissed her mother on her forehead.

"Hogwash, yes you can. Your head is just in the clouds thinking about Luke."

Did she remember everything from the last week? Brooke sat down and prepared to recap what had happened.

"You know—"

"I know you two had a misunderstanding. Do you know how many misunderstandings I've had with your father over the years? How many times we went for each other's throats? And do you know how many years we've been together?"

Brooke folded her hands, a nervous, tepid smile forming on her face. Could she really—

"I wasn't asking rhetorically, dear. How many years have we been together?"

"Forty-one, right?"

"So your memory isn't worse than mine," her mother said. "Well, one thing I can promise you is that the number of times your father and I have fought is certainly more than forty-one. And we're still here, aren't we?"

Brooke nodded, starting to see the point.

"Dear, I know it's scary. But you know what's really scary? Regrets."

She chuckled to herself, shaking her head.

"I can't use half my body, and half the days, I'm not even here, but I don't have any regrets. You know why? Because I put my life in God's hands and took what He gave me. Sure, I was terrified at moments. Walking down the aisle to your father was joyful—and the scariest thing I've ever done. All those eyes looking at you? And you don't know what can happen?"

She laughed again, a little harder than the last time.

"But I trusted God, I trusted your father, and it worked out."

"Did he ever do anything to win you over?"

"Any one thing?" Her mother shook her head. "Your father is a bit too practical a person to ever have some grand reveal. But you know what? He got the little things right so very often. He knew when I needed a foot rub after a long day. He knew when a sequel to my favorite mystery series came out. He knew what countries I wanted souvenirs from, and which ones I could've cared less about."

Brooke wondered if she had put too much on Luke's shoulder by expecting him to "show" his love for her. Was he going to think he needed to put on some big demonstration that had more potential to embarrass her than cheer her?

"If you expect Luke to do the one thing to make you fall head over heels for him—besides maybe a marriage proposal—give him some grace. Trust what he says. And for goodness' sake, stop coming home so late! Your mother gets bored hearing Lola's stories."

Brooke squeezed her mother's hand as the two laughed together. She took her mother's words to heart. Tomorrow morning, she would not hold Luke to an impossible standard.

She only needed to see something that showed he understood her and cared. And if he did, she needed to show that same understanding and care to him. She needed to not be demanding or expecting him to do something he was incapable of, but meet him where he was.

∽

THE NEXT MORNING, she drove with little thought to Hope Valley Ranch. A strange sense of hope, curiosity, and a little nervousness overcame her. She tried her best to keep her eyes on the road and Montana's gorgeous mountains and scenery—it worked to a small extent.

But once she pulled into Hope Valley Ranch, all of her ability to remain focused only on what she saw went out her window. This was it. For all the negativity Danielle had spoken with and all the positivity her mother—and even Luke—had shown yesterday, a sense of finality came over Brooke.

She could just as easily see him saying that he had thought about it and decided they needed to just be friends as they wanted to be together forever.

It would just make life easier if they were only friends. No more getting confused; no more wondering who was first in whose heart; no more concerns over the young Montana's education. Just a straightforward parent-teacher relationship.

And yet, her heart ached at that very possibility.

She stopped in the middle of the road, with the path to the homestead only about a hundred more yards. She wasn't in view of the homestead, but she knew anyone outside would hear her car. *You cannot turn back now.*

Show some courage.

"Lord, give me the strength," she said, "to accept whatever comes my way, and the wisdom to understand how to handle it."

She exhaled, gently pressed the accelerator, and drove forward.

When she got to the front of the homestead, Luke sat on the front porch, his left leg crossed over his right, something that looked like paper in his hand. On the steps, Montana sat, wearing what looked like an enormous, barely contained grin on her face.

Show some courage.

Brooke got out of the car.

"Ms. Young!" Montana shouted. "I know you came to tutor me, but I actually tutored Daddy, and he wants to show you what he learned. Bye!"

Montana went running into the house, the door slamming shut. The whole thing was cute and almost funny, but it also left Brooke even more nervous than before.

Luke stood, cleared his throat, and went to the top of the stairs.

"Brooke Young," he said, "I wrote you a letter."

29

LUKE

*L*uke's hands shook.

If that didn't show how nervous he felt, nothing did. He'd written far too many essays for school. He'd written, at Brooke's behest, a few letters that felt more awkward than meaningful when they were teenagers.

But he had never poured his heart out into any one letter like this one. Nor had he ever had as much help for one letter from someone as he had with Montana.

He was nervous not just because he was showing a teacher his best writing. He was nervous because of how badly this could backfire. Yes, it was what Brooke liked and had even asked for fourteen years ago, but what if he couldn't give her what she wanted? What if his letter got laughed at or, perhaps even worse, produced no reaction at all from Brooke?

Brooke and Luke met at the bottom of the stairs. They were close enough to kiss if they wanted to. Part of Luke wanted to toss the letter over his shoulder, pull her in for a kiss, and tell her he loved her right there.

A healthy relationship is based on meeting each other where the other is, not on demanding that they come to you.

"I hope you like it," Luke said, silently beating himself up for sounding like an embarrassed, awkward teenager.

"You wrote this?" Brooke asked, though she had not read anything yet.

"With a little help from the young one, yeah," Luke said. "I'm not a great writer, and she told me I needed to write with the five senses and write about relationships, and..."

He cut himself off at Brooke's gaze and smile. It was time for him to shut the heck up, let Brooke read, and then trust God's will.

"Does this have a title?"

OK, maybe not quite time.

"Montana suggested 'Brookey and Lukey.' And who am I to argue with her? She's the better writer."

Brooke let out what sounded like a stifled laugh, as if she didn't want to show how the letter fully made her feel. She nodded. And then she began reading the words that Luke had poured over in such careful detail, he knew them by heart.

"Dear Brooke,

Fourteen years ago, you asked me to write you a note. You said that you promised you'd like it, even if I knew I wasn't good at it. I hope that you still feel the same way.

I thought about what to include in this letter. And then, as Montana pointed out to me, I should write from the heart, use the five senses, and describe the relationship. I hope her advice is good enough for you. So, here goes nothing.

I love the way your face lights up every time you see me and Montana. You don't always realize it, but your eyes go wide and your smile grows, even in small ways, around us.

I love hearing your voice greeting my daughter and the way you laugh. Hearing that always puts me at ease.

I love whatever fragrance you wear every day. I love how,

even amongst the stenches of the ranch, I can smell you from a mile away.

I love the way food tastes around you. I could write more, but I think that might not be best.

I love the way your touch always brings me to a place of joy, how even simply touching my arm can be as meaningful as a hug. I love how your kiss always brings me from wherever I am in my head to the present moment.

Now, some relationships.

I love the relationship you have with your parents. It is a rare thing in this world to care for your parents as you do, and it is even rarer to care for someone like your mother, so much so you would return to Montana when you had a promising career elsewhere.

I love the relationship we had and, yes, that we have now. I am grateful every day that you showed me what it means to love someone. No matter what happens today and in the coming days, I love who we are and what we have.

Most of all, I love your relationship with God. You are truly a woman of faith; outside of when circumstances forced you to care for your Mom, I am not sure you have ever missed a Sunday at church. It is grounding and humbling to see what you do with the Lord.

Now, the part I am really not good at. Writing from the heart.

Brooke, I never expected to see you again. I accepted around the time I met Chelsea that I would have to live with my mistake for the rest of my life, and while I did all I could to be a good husband and father, you were so foundational to my understanding of love and relationships, it was impossible not to think of you. When I saw you at Bacon & Bakin' those first days back, it felt like the good Lord had blessed me.

But as He does, He would not give me something I wanted so easily. Because I never expected to see you again, I had no idea what to do when I saw you again. I would be lying if I said I was never attracted to you, but I knew I needed to start as friends. That led to us being boyfriend-girlfriend again, though we were not doing it well.

I was not doing it well. I was not showing courage. I was not showing honesty.

Well, it is time to do that, and Tana says writing from the heart means showing those things.

Brooke, when I think of ten years from now, celebrating Montana's high school graduation, I picture you there by my side, holding my hand as we cheer her on. I picture there being some children of our own there, maybe a brother and sister. I picture Papaw looking down on us from heaven, standing near the good Lord, giving us his blessing. I picture looking into your eyes and still seeing that same love that I saw fourteen years ago and that I saw in short moments these past few weeks.

The truth is, I love you, Brooke. I have loved you for a long time, and even though my stupidity separated us, that did not end my love for you. I know only time, acts of faith and kindness, and commitment to you and the Lord can truly show that, but please, accept this letter as proof of how serious I am.

Lord knows that it took me all night to write this letter, but I would have kept Montana up until midnight to help me if I needed to.

I love you, and I hope this shows I care about you for you, and I want to try this again—this time, forever.

Love,
Luke"

By the trail of Brooke's eyes, Luke could see she was near the bottom of the letter, and he almost passed out from forgetting to breathe. He had not only written from the heart; he suspected he had done so too much. Wouldn't it have been better to wait? To say these things in person?

Show some courage. A healthy relationship is based on meeting each other where the other is, not on demanding that they come to you.

Brooke paused when she finished the end of the letter, and time seemed to stand still. Luke truly could not get a sense of where her heart was.

"Is this... is this all true?" Brooke asked.

Luke nodded. He bit his tongue from spilling out all the words he held back.

"You really mean it?" Brooke said again.

Luke again nodded. He stuffed his hands in his jeans pocket, fearing if he had them out, he wouldn't know what to do with them and might pull Brooke in for a hug she was not ready for.

"Luke..."

The moment of truth. Luke drew in a breath.

"I've been waiting fourteen years for a letter like this from you."

She raised her eyes to him. They glistened with tears of love. Luke did not waste a second more, reaching up and pulling her into the tightest embrace he could give. She cried tears of joy; Luke even felt emotional, surprised at how stirred his soul felt by the moment.

"I'm sorry it took so long to get it to you," Luke said, remaining in the embrace. "I needed some help from a little angel. Who got help from you. Guess it comes full circle."

Brooke laughed as she cried. Luke pulled her back and looked straight into her eyes. Did he—

He didn't even get to wonder if he should kiss her, because Brooke cupped his cheeks and pulled him in for a tender kiss. He put his arms around her back and pulled her in, the kiss the most meaningful the two of them had had for all they had been through.

"Who would have thought the key to making you write

better," Brooke said quietly as she pulled her lips back, "was an eight-year-old girl?"

Luke giggled. Brooke giggled. Soon, they were laughing like school kids who had just heard the funniest joke ever.

Then they kissed again before pulling into a hug. As he held her close, Luke looked over her shoulder. The sun was just breaking past some overcast clouds, with the clouds retreating over the mountain.

The good Lord had truly blessed him with something amazing—a second chance at a second chance. Perhaps Luke was overestimating it, but it wasn't too hard to imagine Brooke at least being curious about Luke being back in town. It wasn't even that difficult to picture her, in a moment of emotion, kissing him.

But to go through the emotions of finding out about his former wife? To have to see him regularly at school? For both of them to have sick parents to care for? And for them to still emerge as boyfriend and girlfriend?

Luke smiled and silently thanked God for this opportunity. *And*, he thought, *I promise not to waste this opportunity, Lord.*

I'm not going to let this chance at love go to the wayside. I will show courage. And I will meet Brooke where she is.

"What are you thinking about?" Brooke asked.

Luke pulled back and smiled, placing his hands on her shoulders. Lord, she looked *so* beautiful. Everything about her was perfect.

"How grateful I am to have you, Brooke Young," he said, "and how grateful Montana is to be calling you something besides Ms. Young soon."

"Oh, good grief," Brooke said. "You are something else, Luke Walker."

They pulled back into an embrace. They looked into each other's eyes, and both said the exact same thing at the exact same time.

"I love you."

It was too perfect. Luke leaned forward and kissed her, his only mild regret that he interrupted her from repeating the words. But when he gave her a chance to breathe, she didn't waste the opportunity.

"I really do love you, Luke."

His heart warmed, and his whole body felt like it could melt into hers. God was truly great; this was silently all he'd ever wanted for years and years, and finally, he'd been blessed with it.

"And I truly do love you, Brooke."

The front door opened, and Montana stood, watching curiously. Luke waved her over—she was as much a part of this reason for celebration as anyone else.

"Did it work, Daddy?"

"Ask Ms. Young," Luke said, having not once taken his arms off her.

"I think you listened very well during our tutoring sessions, Montana," she said. "They do say the best sign of understanding material is to teach it to someone else. And I'd say you succeeded."

"Yay!" Montana said, and she took her father's offering for a group hug.

This, this right here, was what Luke had yearned to see again, he finally understood. Not just a second chance with Brooke, but a second chance at a family. As he stood there, one arm around Brooke and the other around Montana, he realized he had no doubts about her ability to care for the young girl.

Brooke was going to make a heck of a mom.

"I'm so happy," Montana said. "Daddy and Ms. Young, sitting in a tree. K-i-s-s-i-n-g."

"Oh, Lord," Luke mumbled, drawing a smirk from Brooke.

"First comes love, then comes marriage, then comes the baby in the carriage!"

Montana ended her song with a "yay!" before running back inside, presumably to let all the other Walkers know. Luke shook his head. When he looked down, he saw Brooke with a grateful yet curiously contemplative smile on her face.

"What are you thinking about?" Luke said.

It took Brooke a few seconds to respond.

"A lot happened in the fourteen years to prepare me for you," she said. "You know most of the story. But what you don't know is how this all became possible on what should have been one of the worst days of my life."

30

BROOKE

SIX MONTHS EARLIER

*B*rooke had hurried back home as soon as Mrs. Baker had phoned her the news from the kitchen of Bacon & Bakin'.

Her father was somewhere in the Caribbean for work, and while Brooke knew her father would hurry home as soon as he could, she would get there first. She would be the first to see her mother after a stroke that apparently looked like it had killed her. She would be the first to know how drastically life would soon change.

She would be the first to return to Greenville.

As she drove north through Bozeman, she could not help but recall *him*. How he liked to make jokes about Bozeman being "the big city" of Montana. How if Greenville ever became what out-of-staters thought of Bozeman, he would have to move to a small hut on the Missouri River.

She tried her best not to think of his name, but even after all these years, after all the prayers she had sent up to forget him, he remained lodged in her mind. Perhaps that was God's way of saying things were not over?

But how could they be anything but over? It was over thirteen years now, almost fourteen, in which she had not heard a word from him. By now, he probably had gray hair. Maybe he was even balding.

Maybe he had forgotten her.

She hoped to the good Lord not, especially considering she couldn't seem to forget him, but men got over relationships faster than women, right?

She pulled into the parking lot at the hospital, barely got her car in park before she turned the car off, and hurried through the hallways. She actually slowed down when she realized these were not like the city hospitals, understaffed and overpacked; on the contrary, this hospital actually seemed in control.

She found the Intensive Care Unit where her mother had been admitted to. Upon giving her name to the front desk, she was admitted a short time after. The doctor gave her the good news—and then Brooke soon realized it should have been singular, because it was only one piece of good news.

Her mother would live.

But everything else would change.

She had lost the use of her left hand and foot, and it was a miracle she had also not lost use of her entire left side. She had suffered brain damage that would likely lead to some memory loss or difficulties functioning. At the very least, she could no longer live on her own.

The doctor said she could either go into assisted living or have someone live with her full-time, possibly with a caretaker. To Brooke, there was no debate—she was moving back to Greenville. Yes, the place produced a lot of different emotions, but none of them mattered to her.

Family first.

Once the doctor had given her the rundown on everything, he took his leave to let Brooke be with her mother. The doctor closed the door behind them, giving them the privacy she welcomed.

The stroke had happened too recently for her mother to look like she was on death's bed, but there were definitely signs. The left side of her face drooped, not obviously, but enough for anyone to tell something was off. She had a thousand-yard stare, the kind of gaze Brooke usually saw in her students who were not paying attention. And physical capabilities and signs aside, she could just tell her mother felt off.

"Brookey."

Well, maybe not entirely off if she remembered her nickname.

"You came."

"Of course I came, Mom," Brooke said as she sat on her left side before remembering she needed to sit on her right—something that would take some getting used to. "Family first."

"That's very kind of you," her mother said. "How are you?"

"I'm fine, I'm—"

"Brookey," she said in a calm yet knowing tone.

Brooke swore her mother always seemed to know when she was hiding something.

"It's weird being back here for something other than the holidays," she said. "Not for you, of course. But like, this time of year, kids are looking forward to summer, fly-fishing is right around the corner, there's less talk of snow and more of lakes… it's all…"

"Things that bring you back to your youth."

And to him.

"Do you keep in touch with anyone from your childhood?"

"Danielle and Clara, yes. Past that, not really."

"What about that Luke boy?"

Brooke pursed her lips.

She wanted to sigh, but thinking about him now, in the presence of her stricken mother, did not cause as much angst as she would have guessed right before. In fact, it almost brought back mostly good memories—the time that they took his father's truck to Helena without warning, the time they rode horseback to the best place to see the sunrise on his ranch, the time that he tried to get her to play along with his senior prank.

Innocent moments, some more meaningful and poetic than others, but all of them pleasant.

Where was the disgust she'd once had for him? Where was the pain she always felt upon hearing his name? Was it because she now saw her mother in a hospital bed, and the sight of her mortality had made her softer?

Or, as the cliche so often went, had time healed her wounds?

"I do not know where that Luke boy is," Brooke said, doing her best to keep her voice even.

"Maybe he's grown up. Maybe he'll actually write you a letter this time."

Brooke laughed. Now? Now, he'd write a letter? Even if he showed up, why in the heck would he write a letter? If anything, his writing skills probably would have gotten worse, now that he no longer had to be in school.

"He would never do that."

"But what if he does?"

A long silence filled the air. Brooke felt like she was arguing something akin to "what if people could fly," yet her mother seemed so intent on pressing the point.

"People can change, Brookey. They don't always, but they can. I think if Luke wrote you a letter, let yourself feel whatever the letter does to you. Don't fight it. It's what you kept talking about wanting, at least in high school."

"This isn't high school anymore, mother."

Her mother smiled.

"No, but you'd be surprised how often our past remains in our present thoughts."

Wasn't that the truth?

"You still care for him."

Did her face make it that obvious?

"I don't know how I can care for someone I haven't seen in so long, Mom."

"I don't mean you think about him every day or that he controls your actions. I mean, if I mention Luke Walker, you react a certain way."

Hadn't Brooke come here to comfort her mother? Not talk about a lover she'd never see again? She refrained from sighing, but only because she didn't want to make her mother feel bad.

"He meant a lot to you when you two were teenagers. That is how your father and I started, you know. I only suggest that if he appears again, and if he shows growth, give him a chance, would you?"

"I'll tell you what, Mother," she said, hoping that this would end the conversation, "if Luke Walker, of all people, writes me a letter, I'll give him a second chance. But you know that's not going to happen, right?"

Her mother just smiled.

"I know."

There was an unnerving calm to the way her mother reacted, as if she just knew exactly what would happen. But to Brooke, she might as well have prayed to God for a billion dollars and her own country. If she didn't even know where Luke was, let alone if he was married or not, then the odds of him writing her a letter were almost miraculous.

Then again, she thought, if the good Lord had taught her anything, it was that miracles could and would happen when she least expected it.

31

LUKE

The snow always fell early in Greenville. It was one reason that Luke loved his hometown more than anything in the world—he always associated the first snow with the imminent arrival of Christmas.

Even if it wasn't even October yet.

Two weeks had passed since he and Brooke had affirmed their willingness to give a second chance a second chance, and he never wasted an hour to text her something goofy, a day to tell her he loved her in person, or a week to take her someplace different. He would say this was like being a teenager all over again, but that wasn't quite true; it felt more like being a teenager with the wisdom of an adult.

He suspected it was because Brooke had revealed that his writing a letter to her, from her perspective, was akin to a miracle. She didn't use the word lightly. Hearing her describe the impossibility of it made him refuse to take it for granted.

It also made him determined to seal his commitment to her.

But just like in getting her back, he knew he couldn't do it alone.

"Finally!" Montana yelled as they pulled into the parking lot of Green Cream.

"I told you, I promised that when something big happened, we'd get Green Cream. And here we are!"

"Even though it's snowing, Daddy!"

Luke could only shrug and half-heartedly apologize to his daughter. He suspected that even if they'd gone in the dead of January, with sub-zero temperatures and dark skies, she still would have cherished a visit to Green Cream.

It was about seven o'clock on a Friday night, so the store was relatively quiet, except for the one employee behind the counter. As soon as Luke opened the door, Montana hurried over to the glass display of flavors, looking like she could eat the entire row of flavors.

"Hello there," the employee, who looked to be a young girl in high school, said, "What brings you here?"

"Daddy got his girlfriend back, and we're celebrating!"

"Oh, congrats!" the employee said with an awkward laugh, as uncertain about how to react as Luke was. *Oh, Tana.* "What flavors would you like to celebrate?"

"All of them!" she shouted, and once more both Luke and the young woman were left to wonder just how to handle the overjoyed eight-year-old.

"Tana, you get to pick up to two," he said, though silently he knew if his daughter pushed for three flavors, he wouldn't say no. Life was too good right now for him to say no to anything, even if he might regret the sugar bomb that would ensue.

"Aw, Daddy! What are you getting, then?"

The sly look on Montana's face told Luke he was not about to be the only one trying his ice cream.

"I'll get two scoops, one with mint chocolate chip and one with strawberry," Luke said. "And Tana?"

"Can I get three scoops?"

Luke surrendered to his daughter, nodding his head.

"Yay! How about chocolate chip, vanilla, and peanut butter?"

It was quite the combination, but Luke decided Montana would best learn by tasting herself. After paying for the ice cream and heading outside, Montana shivered.

"Daddy, can we sit in the car? It's so cold!"

"You're really pushing my good mood, aren't you?" Luke said with a playful rub of Montana's shoulder. "Sure. But you know what we came here for."

Montana nodded as she headed over to his truck. He unlocked the door, and she was already taking scoops of her ice cream—much too big for her to eat without dripping some on his seat—before he had even opened his door. But indeed, he was not only in a great mood, he needed Montana's help to prepare for his next major step.

"I hope you are feeling creative and the ice cream helps," Luke said, "because this isn't going to be every day."

"I know! But you said it's a special occasion!"

"It is," Luke said, "and it's time to capitalize on that special occasion. Montana, have you ever written a poem before?"

Montana looked at him for a couple of seconds, scaring him into thinking that she hadn't, before she nodded vigorously.

"And has Brooke taught you how to write poetry?"

"Not really, but that's OK! It'll make it more fun when Ms. Young sees it."

There was some truth to that—plus, maybe it would make Luke look like he was doing more work than he usually did.

Actually, it would look that way because that's how it really was. He didn't need to fake going above and beyond or trying to do things that Brooke liked. He had had more than enough guidance from his parents and his daughter, of all people, to make him authentically and lovingly do that.

"What is this poem for again, Daddy?"

"It's for my proposal."

"Proposal for what?"

It warmed Luke's heart even to talk about this with Montana.

"To propose to marry her."

"Aww!"

"And your part in all this is to help me craft good writing."

"Do I get more ice cream out of it?"

Luke laughed.

"I'll tell you what. If she says yes, then we can get ice cream either right after or the day after. OK?"

"OK!"

Montana went right back to her ice cream, apparently lost in the thought of more delicious flavors she could try. Luke would eventually bring her back to talk about the poetry side of things, but for now, he just let her be. So much of the past couple of months had been spent wondering "what if" or "how will this affect Montana or Brooke" that he was happy to just let things be.

He was only preparing to propose because he felt sure that Brooke would say yes. While there was always the possibility of something incredibly unusual disrupting their plans, Luke felt sure that after all they'd been through and the time it had taken to get to this point, the last thing Brooke would want was *more* time spent as just boyfriend and girlfriend.

When the Lord told you it was time, it was time. And for as much as Luke had prayed about it in the two weeks since that emotional reunion, he always felt certain God was telling him it was time.

And while he wasn't proposing specifically for this reason, he knew well that his father could go at any moment. He'd already surpassed the average life expectancy of someone in hospice by still being alive beyond two weeks. It would only take one bad night for things to change forever—and Luke was determined to make sure his father and her mother would go to heaven knowing their oldest had found his forever love.

"Are you enjoying your ice cream?" Luke asked as Montana got down to her last two bites.

"It's sooooooo good," Montana said, exaggerating a swooning motion. "I can't believe you made me wait two months to get this! We are not waiting two more months!"

"Then you better make sure I have the best poem ever," Luke said.

"Oh, right!" Montana said. "Well, poems have really good lines. Hmm... like what about saying she's like a flower?"

The thought was nice, but to Luke, it felt a little unrelated. Brooke had never expressed an insistence on having flowers, and while she'd never been ungrateful to receive them, they didn't move her like good writing or hiking did.

But then his thought turned to the state that allowed him to hike so much. The state that he had named his daughter after. The state that was *home*.

Luke's thoughts turned. There was something there. He just needed a bit of time to think about it.

"That's not a bad idea," Luke said, referring to the flower idea. "But I have a different thought. Montana, what did you remember most when we came in from Idaho? Remember two months ago?"

"Yes!" she said. "Well, hmm. It is my state."

My girl.

"The mountains were so green."

Her eyes so brown and beautiful.

"It's home!"

Being with her is being home.

"I think you're giving me some good ideas, Tana," Luke said. "Let's keep discussing. But now, I have one more assignment for you in preparation for tomorrow."

"What's that?"

Luke smiled.

"I need everyone in the family at the Missouri River right by your school fourteen minutes after eight a.m. And I want you to tell everyone where to be."

32

BROOKE

Brooke woke up at six a.m., prepared to go about her day caring for her mother, going to the homestead around nine, and then spending the rest of the day with Luke.

So it was of great confusion to her when she went to her mother's bed downstairs, only to see that she was gone, with just a note left behind.

"Dear Brooke, had to go do something important today. Will see you later this morning! Love, Mom."

The handwriting definitely belonged to her mother, but she didn't even have a car she could drive—was she trying to test her capabilities by walking on one foot somewhere? It was a credit to Greenville that she did not even assume someone had kidnapped her mother.

Is Luke doing something?

She called her mother, and her mother answered on the first ring.

"Did you not see my note, Brookey?"

So she was alert and in a good mental state today.

"I did. I was just... surprised."

"You act like your mother isn't capable of moving for once," she said in a joking voice. "Relax. I promise I'll see you before noon."

"OK, sounds good Mom, love you."

They hung up right after, leaving Brooke even more confused. So it wasn't that Mom was in a bad space, but past that, she had no further answers.

Well, so be it. She trusted that her mother, especially when she had her wits about her, knew what she was doing. Brooke went about the rest of her morning for the next hour and a half when she got a call from Luke at seven-thirty. Alarms went off in her head again; was Montana sick? Luke never called this early.

"Hey babe?" she answered, concern in her voice.

"Hey, so Montana actually wants to do something at the school today. She said something about being inspired by being in a school setting? I don't get it, but you might."

That was… unusual.

Now Brooke was wondering if something bigger was going on. Either her mom going out or Montana requesting something different would have been unusual, but not necessarily suspicious. Now…

She tried to think if it was anyone's birthday. Luke's was in January, Montana's in July, her mother's in May. Maybe Luke's father? His hospice diagnosis would at least give credence to the idea of doing something big, since he wouldn't likely live another year.

But Brooke swore October was not when Mr. Walker's birthday was; it felt like she'd celebrated that more in the colder months of winter than this time of year.

Wait.

Was Luke going to…

Do that?

No, that seemed impossible, outright absurd. He loved her, and she loved him, and there was no doubt about the commitment on either side, but Brooke did not want to presume anything. The time would come when it was appropriate.

Even if, she privately thought, if he proposed now, she would say yes. It wasn't like she needed to see anything else from him or the world at large to know he was the right man.

"Brooke?"

"Sorry, Luke, got caught in my own head. Um, yes, sure, what time do you want me there?"

"Maybe a little after eight. Montana pushed this on me pretty late, so it'll take me a second to get ready, but she was pretty adamant about being there sometime between eight and eight-fifteen. Are you good with that?"

The way Luke asked suggested Brooke didn't have a ton of say, though it wasn't a hardship by any stretch, especially with her mother seemingly winding the clock back before this past April.

"Sure, I'll start making moves to leave here around eight. I'm not too far from the school, so that should get me there around then."

"Perfect, see you then! Love you, Brooke."

"Love you too, Luke."

They disconnected almost too quickly, again leaving Brooke smiling with some level of suspicion. Perhaps this was some sort of corny one-month reunion; granted, the short but brutal breakup in between kind of made timing tricky to figure out, but it wouldn't have been the first time Luke did something sweet yet surprising.

She put herself together, combing her hair, putting on a nice, thick white coat and dark blue jeans. She thought about wearing a cowgirl hat, her way of being playful with Luke, but with it still snowing outside, Brooke decided she wouldn't need it.

She headed to her car, dusted off her windshield wipers, quickly shoveled enough snow to give her space—though that wasn't necessary, she also used it as a chance to kill some time—

COWBOY'S HOMECOMING

and pulled out of her driveway at about four minutes after eight. According to her GPS, it would get her to school about fourteen minutes after eight.

Just like fourteen years. Funny how that works.

Her mind continued to race with various possibilities as she made the short drive over. Maybe this was exactly what Luke said it was; her mother really did just want to get out, and this was all just a giant coincidence. Brooke didn't believe in coincidences per se—that was just God's work—but to someone else, it could have seemed that way.

Maybe Luke, to rebuild his relationship with Brooke's mother, had brought her alone for this tutoring session. Unusual, but Luke had talked about the need to regain the trust of her parents. Still, it seemed unlikely that would take place while she tutored Luke's daughter.

Maybe it was the p-word.

Stop it, Brooke. Don't get presumptuous now.

But once she crossed the bridge over the Missouri River and turned right into the school parking lot, and once she saw her mother, her *father*—her father?—Brooke, Luke, Luke's parents, Jesse, and Weston, she began to suspect she wasn't being so presumptuous after all.

"Luke?" she said. "What's going on?"

Luke stepped forward and smiled.

"Fourteen years ago, I made the mistake of not listening to other people, most of all you. Today, I decided to make up for it. Jesse? Weston?"

Jesse and Weston turned around, both of them holding guitars. They strummed a gentle tune, soft background noise, as Montana went up to Brooke with a huge smile on her face.

"Dear Ms. Young," she said, her voice sounding like she was reading a script, yet without any paper in front of her. "You have taught me so much about how to write. But, more importantly, you taught my Daddy to believe in hope again. You taught my Daddy to believe love could be had again. And so, I taught him how to write."

The gentle guitar strumming filled the air behind them as the snow fell at a gentle pace. Behind Luke, his parents and her parents—she still could not believe her father had shown up—came together. They wore huge smiles on their face, and both of the mothers had started to tear up.

Brooke started to tear up, too.

"Allow me, Brooke, to read you a poem."

Luke cleared his throat and pulled out a piece of paper.

"Sorry, I'm not as good at memorizing as Tana is."

Brooke laughed, her eyes still watering as the realization of the moment hit her.

> *"Brooke Young, the most beautiful woman I know,*
> *Not just that I know, that I love.*
> *Her eyes so brown and beautiful,*
> *I would never say no.*
>
> *Tana says Montana is home,*
> *But with you, I am truly home.*
> *Once I may have been lost,*
> *But now I will never roam.*
>
> *God's will is great,*
> *He has blessed me with you.*
> *He has tested me in many ways,*
> *Now He has given me chance number two.*
>
> *Brooke Young,*
> *I love you.*
> *Forgive these cheesy poem,*
> *And what I am about to do."*

COWBOY'S HOMECOMING

Brooke wasn't thinking about the quality of the poem or the structure or anything academic. She was too mesmerized by the entire sight, that Luke, the man who once claimed he didn't enjoy writing private letters, would now share a love poem in front of his family, her parents, and his own daughter. She laughed, she cried, and she trembled in excitement.

Luke came up to her and took her hands in his. His voice lowered, and even though no one had left, she felt alone with him, in almost a halo of snow.

"Brooke, you told me that as wonderful as words are, you needed action. I have thought long and hard the past two weeks, and ultimately, I realized you are right—whether those words are written on a piece of paper or said out loud. I should have done this before I went to college, knowing what I did then, but I thank God every day for this second chance. Brooke Young, I love you, I have always loved you, and I want to love you forever."

Then he dropped to one knee.

"Brooke, will you marry me?"

Brooke laughed. She cried. And then she squeezed Luke's hand and nodded.

"Yes, Luke," she said as tears streaked down her cheeks. "Yes! Yes!"

"Yes!"

Luke lifted off his knee and lifted Brooke into the air, twirling her through the snow as everyone cheered. Montana let out a "yay!" as she clapped her hands. The guitars briefly stopped so Jesse and Weston could applaud, but as soon as they stopped, the tune picked up in pace and electricity, their strumming accelerating.

Luke let Brooke down and planted the longest kiss of Brooke's life on her. Heavens, had it really been fourteen years since they'd kissed like this? *May it not even be another fourteen hours.*

"I'm sorry for everything, Brooke," Luke whispered into her ear as he pulled her into a hug.

"You have nothing to be sorry for," she replied. "It was all God's plan. I'm just grateful that it ended with us back together."

"With us blessed with a second chance."

"With us blessed with happily ever after."

EPILOGUE

Much as Luke tried to keep things quiet for the time being, word spread fast throughout Greenville.

The next day, after both the Walkers and the Youngs went to church together, Pastor O'Connell pulled them aside to congratulate them on their engagement. Neither Luke nor Brooke had even said anything about getting engaged, but at least this was news Luke didn't mind spreading. There would, of course, be questions about Brooke marrying the father of one of her students, but their job wasn't to explain themselves.

Their job was to love each other, put the good Lord first, and, when necessary, help each other's families. The day would certainly come when Luke would lean on Brooke for emotional support with his father's passing, but in the very short term, he actually looked as healthy as he had in months.

This allowed for an afternoon trip with his brothers Jesse and Weston to Bison Brothers, his first moment with just the three of them since well before he'd gotten engaged.

"I'm telling you, it won't be long before you live with Ms.

Young," Jesse cracked as they waited for their loaded french fries to come.

"You know we will not do that until we're married."

"And you know that's not what I mean, dummy," Jesse said, smacking Luke's arm. "The only thing more romantic than two lovebirds are two lovebirds getting back together a second time, this time forever. You two won't be able to look at each other in the school driving lane without going goo-goo ga-ga."

"So supportive," Weston quipped, drawing chuckles from both brothers.

"You'll be living over there in no time, watching movies three times a week, cooking dinner two times a week, bringing Montana over two times a week, and, oh, look at that, there's only seven days a week. Guess me and Whispering Weston over here are gonna be running the ranch."

Jesse's voice had started in his usual jestful tone, but by the time he finished the last line, the weight of what could come had dulled his humor. The three of them had vowed not to talk about Papaw today; his will outlined everything that would happen financially and operationally, so there wasn't much in the way to talk about logistically.

Given that, no one, most especially Jesse, wanted to talk about Papaw's hospice condition.

"You think I can leave you two fools alone?" Luke said, trying to interject levity into the situation. "Jesse, Lord knows that if I don't keep an eye on you, you're likely to make all the women hide themselves in their homes."

"You're out of your mind," Jesse said, back to his usual self.

"Uh huh," Weston added. "Is that why you haven't said a word about Clara Reed since we got here?"

Jesse's voice fell silent for a very different reason this time.

"Oh, snap!" Luke chuckled. "The comedian and the librarian. Doesn't that sound like the beginning of a great comedy?"

"A slapstick one, maybe," Jesse murmured. "Listen, Miss Reed's a lovely lady—"

"You say that like she was your teacher, but she was your classmate."

"A nerd of a classmate," Jesse countered. "If you told me in high school Clara Reed would be running a bookstore, I'd one hundred percent believe it."

Luke knew the next line carried a little risk, but he couldn't help himself.

"Careful what you say, Jesse," Luke said, "you might need to become a nerd yourself if you're going to handle finances, accounting, suppliers, and all the other stuff cowboy movies never show you."

Jesse harrumphed and shook his head, a sign that at least the words hadn't reminded him too much of Papaw. Luke and Weston shared a look and a soft chuckle as the loaded french fries came out.

But before digging in, Luke did not miss that Jesse, looking over Luke's shoulder, was clearly looking at the bookstore just southeast of Bison Brothers.

He had a hopeful look in his eye that the very Clara Reed might soon come out of the store and, perhaps, into his life.

∼

If you want to see how Clara and Jesse come together, check out "Cowboy's Dream" at the link or QR code below.

Cowboy's Dream

You can also turn the page to get a sneak peek!

∽

Want to connect with Sierra Hart? Check out our Facebook page!
Click the link below to do so.

Sierra Hart FB Page

∽

Do you want to read how Mimi and Papaw fell in love? Check out the link or the QR code below to get your free story!

Cowboy's Calling

SNEAK PEEK: COWBOY'S DREAM CHAPTER 1

*J*esse could laugh, Jesse could joke, Jesse could make anyone in the room smile, but all the quips and cracks in the world could not hide two facts creeping into Jesse's life.

One, the time was coming for him to give up the bullrider lifestyle and move back to Hope Valley Ranch.

And two, that was because his father was dying.

"Jesse!" his mother shouted from downstairs in the kitchen. "Can you come help me prep the potatoes for tonight?"

Jesse grimaced and drew in a breath. Alone in the family office, trying to learn how to use Excel, he would never say no to his mother. But as he stood and the aches of his muscles and the stiffness in his bones started to settle in, he knew he needed something to change.

Namely, his career.

The two facts of his current life conveniently went hand-in-hand, of course, but even had his father been of perfect mind and body, Jesse knew the lifestyle of a bullrider did not lend itself to a long-term career. The physical strain on his body, even at just thirty years old, was starting to catch up to him.

Muscle cramps magically appeared after a supposedly good night's sleep, scars didn't heal as quickly as they used to, and the lifestyle of enjoying perhaps a beer too many was weighing more heavily on his Sunday church attendance than he cared to admit.

And that didn't even account for the money side of things. The most famous bullriders, like the peak of any other profession, made darn good money, but Jesse was not a household name. His wit and flair for the dramatic made him a favorite, but for some reason, he had just never broken that barrier needed to elevate to the highest level of notoriety.

Perhaps, he feared, he just wasn't the true daredevil that some of the elites were. Those men were playboys, partiers, and shameless in every sense of the word. Jesse had his moments, but he still had values built from Greenville, Montana, that he would never let go, even on hard Sunday mornings.

Whatever the case, Jesse had used his father's deteriorating condition as a legitimate and convenient excuse to take a self-described sabbatical from bullriding. He knew, however, that such a sabbatical was likely to last a lifetime.

"Coming, Mimi," he said, trying to mask any difficulties from his voice.

As he exited the family office, he stole a glance at his parents' bedroom. His father lay resting on his side, snoring loudly but otherwise looking comfortable. The snoring was new; it was perhaps a sign that the lung cancer had gotten worse. Jesse couldn't say for sure, and he didn't feel comfortable looking it up.

As long as he's at peace, then the good Lord is blessing us.

Jesse shut his father's door. He made his way downstairs and found only his mother working in the kitchen.

"Hi, sweetie," his mother said as she poured salt on some pork.

"Hey, Mimi," he said, "where's everyone else?"

"Well, Luke and Tana are doing homework on the back porch, Weston is out on the ranch, and your father is resting upstairs."

Jesse chuckled, readying another wisecrack.

"I guess a man gets hitched, and he turns into a professor, huh?"

"Someday you'll have kids, and you'll realize all the things you swore you'd never do are things you'll do every day," Mimi said.

Jesse had already begun to feel that way. There was a reason Excel was open on the computer upstairs, and it wasn't so Jesse could make jokes about excelling.

"You mean someday, I'll be changing diapers, being attentive and serious, and working at a desk? Mimi, I love you, but I think even the good Lord would have a laugh at that one."

"On the contrary, my dear, I think you'll have a good laugh at this one sometime down the road," Mimi said. "We all change at some point, or at least grow. Doesn't mean you need to give up being the class clown."

"Ah, Mimi, you know I'm thirty years old and haven't been in a classroom in a dozen years!" Jesse said, aware that once, he had taken a couple of online classes on launching his own YouTube channel. He'd ultimately decided against it, figuring he wouldn't last long enough to make it as a bullrider to get a big enough following, but the clarification went unspoken.

His mother said nothing, smiling to herself as she continued to work on the pork. Jesse gave up the dialogue and went to making mashed potatoes.

Occasionally, he'd glance out the window and see Luke and his daughter, Montana, working on the young girl's next story. Much as a prankster as he was, Jesse never wanted to stir up trouble with the wrong words, but it was painfully obvious that Montana had not gotten her good study habits from her father.

Still, Brooke would only nurture the young girl's gift for learning.

What it would be like to settle down, Jesse wondered. *Would it really be the worst thing in the world?*

But he laughed at the thought, drawing a side glance from his mother. Coming to Greenville meant largely giving up dating and flirting, and since it meant taking care of his father, he was OK with that.

Jesse finished making the mashed potatoes with enough time to spare so that he could run upstairs and continue watching a video about Excel. When he clicked the Play button, however, nothing happened. He fussed around with the web page before getting an error message informing him the internet had failed.

Because, of course, it had. This wasn't the town center or the middle of a well-packed venue full of options for Internet access. This was Hope Valley Ranch—a beautiful place in many ways, including such little internet access that Jesse had to look to nature and his family for love and companionship!

He sighed. Quietly, he wrote down the name of the video, "Excel Accounting for Adult Dummies," and pocketed the note. With an early dinner about to come, Jesse could make an excuse to head into town to watch the remainder of the video. So long as Luke, Weston, or his parents didn't know, it didn't matter too much where.

"Jesse! Wake up your father and let him know dinner is ready!"

Jesse bit his lip, yelled, "Of course, Mimi," and slowly got out of the chair, grunts following the stiffness of his knees. He headed to the bedroom and knocked once, hoping that his father had already awoken. Seeing that Papaw had not, he walked inside and, as gently as he could, put a hand on his father's shoulder and stirred him.

"Papaw."

His father's eyes slowly fluttered open.

"Have you come to tell me a knock-knock joke?"

Jesse bit his tongue from saying something scathing to a dying man and just shook his head.

"Mimi said dinner is ready."

"Oh, good, did you add a dash of pepper?"

"Of course," Jesse said, knowing he could beat his father downstairs to add it.

"That's my boy," Papaw said. "I like you when you're not trying to be Johnny Carson."

Jesse brushed off the half-insult and headed out of the room without another word, trying not to let Papaw's words linger too much. He hurried down to the kitchen, added a dash of pepper, and sat down at the same kitchen table seat he'd had since he was just a tot. Montana and Luke entered a second later.

"Uncle Jesse!" Tana said. "Do you have a good joke for me?"

Glad someone wants to hear them.

"Your daddy."

"Hey!" Luke shouted, which of course only encouraged Montana to giggle harder.

"Naw, your daddy's a good man, even if he can't cook a lick," Jesse said. "Maybe you can teach him that as well, Tana."

"I don't know how to cook!" Montana said as she shrugged in an almost theatrical manner.

"And I don't know how to do a lot of things, but that hasn't stopped your Uncle Jesse from doing things anyway!"

Left unsaid was "because he teaches himself how to, since he's not very good at listening to others teach him." But that would defy who Jesse was to his family, and someone needed to provide some comedy these days.

"Food's out," Mimi shouted.

"And Papaw's here," his father said, "so let's say grace and enjoy a good meal, shall we?"

Even Jesse knew better than to find the joke in something as meaningful as family dinners.

∼

AFTER DINNER WRAPPED UP—A dinner in which Montana revealed that Brooke would soon be focusing more on math, much to her disappointment, and that Weston said they had a better-than-expected harvest of apples and potatoes—Jesse took his leave, announcing to his family that he was going to see how Greenville had changed in the days since he'd moved back.

Only Luke seemed to catch on this was a ruse, an obviously doubting expression painted on his face. Jesse brushed off the look, knowing Luke wouldn't say anything, and got into his red Ford F-150—most of the brothers had the same truck.

Most except Carson because, honestly, no one knew what Carson drove these days or if Carson even had a car. Only Weston probably had an idea, and no one broached that subject with him for the sake of family harmony.

Still, as Jesse pulled out of the ranch and made his way right toward Greenville, he found himself calmed by the place he'd called home for his entire childhood. He was always struck how, despite there being plenty of beautiful places in the trifecta of Idaho, Montana, and Wyoming, nothing ever just felt like home. He'd spent plenty of time on the road, certainly more than big brother Luke, so he knew what he spoke of.

And now, going to The Homestead? With Jon, the owner, and all the regulars who kept to themselves while others worked? What a perfect opportunity to prepare for the things that Luke had once described as "all the other stuff cowboy movies never show you."

So, of course the good Lord just wouldn't allow the evening to go off without a hitch.

"What in the world?" Jesse said as he pulled up to the coffee

shop and saw no one—not even Jon's truck—in the parking lot.
"Did someone get indigestion from Jon's baked goods?"

He parked his truck and quickly jogged out of the car to the front door. Posted there was a handwritten sign informing Jesse that Jon had given the employees an early out today and on the first because he was keeping the shop open late on Halloween.

Well, bah.

"Jon, Jon, Jon," Jesse said to himself. "Don't you know ol' Jesse Walker's got to surprise some folks? Maybe I'll surprise you!"

He thought back to his younger self, how he would have played a prank of some kind—maybe thrown toilet paper over the coffee shop, maybe written something on the chalk. Some kids talked about spray painting, but to Jesse, there was always a difference between pranks and damage.

And in any case, age was mellowing out Jesse. Now, instead of thinking of how funny such a prank would be, he thought about the work the poor barista would have to do in the morning or the frustration Jon would face. He also thought about all the responsibilities beckoning to him and the opportunity cost of spending time on a sophomoric prank. Age was mellowing him out and making him more empathic.

Jesse didn't like it. He wanted to be a kid at heart forever, not have his heart age with the rest of his body. *Shoot, Luke might be right. I might be more Jesse from Full House than Jesse James.*

Just can't ever let him know that!

With a chuckle, Jesse headed back to the car. The university had the town's only library, and Jesse didn't much feel like hanging with a bunch of college-aged kids—and he swore it had nothing to do with the age difference but their rambunctious nature. The only other option, he realized with a smile and a grin, was the bookstore.

Because, of course, it would be the place where Clara Reed was, the one woman in high school he had never managed to get to go on a date with him. The one woman that, in some ways, represented everything he wanted to be—put together, sure of her future path, studious...

Well, she was also beautiful, but at least Jesse knew how to flash a smile and wear nice clothes.

But dang, she was *quite* beautiful.

Jesse needed only to recall looking over Luke's shoulder at Bison Brother's at a recent outing and seeing her come out of the bookstore wearing a black suede jacket, her blonde hair pulled up to her shoulders, and, bless his soul, boots. Jesse always had a thing for a woman in boots, and that Clara had also always had an affinity for them yet never went out with him drove him mad.

It was strange, really. Jesse never lacked for attention from women at rodeos, and yet she, of all people, made him nervous.

But Jesse was getting caught in his own head too much. He had studying to do. *Bet Clara would lose her marbles if she heard that.*

He drove to the bookstore and pulled into the small lot just behind the bookstore. There was one other car—surely Clara's, a black Honda. He thought about peering inside before deciding first impressions after twelve years did not include "being a creep" and headed to the front. By now, he did not pause, not wanting to make his attraction—

He opened the door and gawked. Clara had on cowboy boots, a red sweater, and dark blue jeans.

"The good Lord is good indeed."

—obvious.

SNEAK PEEK: COWBOY'S DREAM CHAPTER 2

*C*lara heard a truck pulling into the back lot of her bookstore and smiled.

The perk of owning a bookstore was that no matter how she spent her time, she got to do something she enjoyed. Mostly, she buried her nose into a novel of the week—in this case, it was "A Prayer for Owen Meany;" last week, it was a historical fiction novel by a local author named Grayson Drury. But when she had to interact with customers, she made an effort to learn their stories.

Clara had owned the bookstore for over four years now, and she saw it as her gateway to eventually becoming an author. She didn't like admitting that to many people because compared to authors like Drury, Irving, and Dangerfield, she felt like small potatoes. But she trusted the good Lord would give her a meaningful idea for a novel someday, likely through the story of someone that she encountered here at the bookstore.

Even if that never happened, opening the store in 2019 and giving her hometown access to books she'd read online and elsewhere provided her a level of joy and meaning she had never gotten and, outside of church, could not imagine getting anywhere else.

She put down "A Prayer for Owen Meany" and headed out from the front desk to the bookshelves. Clara had employees, but they only worked part-time, and in any case, a town like Greenville did not really create the need for employees; she only did it to give college kids some money and a chance to immerse themselves in literature. Tonight, she was on her own.

Perhaps Luke and his daughter were finally making their way over here. If Brooke was to be believed, Montana would soon have reading assignments at the bookstore. Maybe it was Mrs. Baker, who couldn't pass up the chance to enjoy a good mystery novel after closing Bacon & Bakin'. Heck, even Sheriff Lane enjoyed a good thriller novel.

And then, of all people, *Jesse*, not Luke, Walker had to enter.

"The good Lord is good indeed."

Clara put her hands on her hips and tried to compose herself. On the one hand, yes, but on the other hand, surely Jesse didn't mean it in a faithful way. When had Jesse ever said something that wasn't meant as a jest, insult, or meaningless quip?

"What the heck is that supposed to mean?" Clara asked, her voice stern.

"I think it's pretty clear, don't you?" Jesse said with a smile. Lord, she hated that smile. How perfectly straight and white and charming and handsome and *oh, get it together, Clara.*

"If it's referring to the books, then yes. If it's referring to the Lord in general, then yes. If it's referring to you?"

Jesse shrugged playfully, as if "surprised" to have gotten caught.

"Are you here to read or flirt?"

"Both," Jesse said.

Clara shook her head. The problem with Jesse wasn't that he was flirtatious; it was that he was flirtatious and handsome and bad news. He always dressed impeccably, always had a perfectly groomed five o'clock shadow, and always carried himself like he knew he was the best looking man in almost every room he walked into.

Clara would never dare admit it to Brooke, but she considered Jesse the most handsome of the Walkers, hands down. Unfortunately, of the three brothers that she knew relatively well, she also considered Jesse the least mature of the Walkers.

"If you want to flirt, I'm sure that there'll be someone at Ranchers or Shooters by the college," she said, thinking of two bars she'd never be setting foot in anytime soon. "If you want to read, then I suppose we are open for another hour. What do you want to read?"

"Something that teaches me accounting."

She folded her arms and waited. Something about "accounting for your looks!" or "accounting for the money I need to save for our date!"

She waited.

And waited.

And... waited?

What was going on? Jesse Walker... *wanted* to learn about something that wasn't humor or women?

"Where is this going?"

"To whatever aisle of yours has books about accounting."

"Be serious."

"Why? I'm telling you the truth, but why?"

Clara sighed. She still braced herself for some stupid joke that Jesse always, *always* delivered and motioned for him to follow her to the non-fiction section of the store. The Jesse she knew—and so far, had no reason to change her perception on—could pull elaborate ruses and pranks for a good joke.

Maybe he had changed, though? Maybe he really had come here to learn? Did his father's condition have anything to do with this? Clara felt a stroke of shame that she'd judged Jesse so harshly; maybe he needed to learn accounting to help his mother with his father's estate.

Then again, he had asked "why" in response to her asking him to be serious. *Never mind.*

"Here," she motioned without turning around. She headed to the far end of the aisle, largely out of view of the street, and grabbed the first book she saw, "The Ace Accountant." When she turned to him, she nearly jumped at how close he had gotten.

Heavens, he wore some sort of cologne that just melted her brain and made her feel and come near to acting stupid. Who needed to go to Shooters or Ranchers when a scent like that could intoxicate your brain?

He was close enough to put his arm around her, pull her in, and…

She laughed. Speaking of things to laugh at.

"Aw, shoot, did I forget to clean my teeth?" Jesse said, but his smile almost looked uncomfortable.

"Nothing, it's nothing with you, I promise," Clara said, meaning how he looked, not what he could do.

"Oh, whew!" he said, and the smile became warm. But Clara had not overlooked the surprisingly tender smile on his face; it suggested a man who was going through something that could easily be triggered by a memory. What, though? And was Clara just giving this Walker the benefit of the doubt because of how Luke was now engaged to Brooke and how handsome Jesse was?

Clara thought herself a good judge of character, if not a talkative one, and she suspected that there was more to Jesse Walker than his high school goofball image had suggested.

"Well, since I don't have your number, I guess the ones in this accounting book will suffice."

Oh, Jesse, she thought with a sigh.

"I'll be in the back if you need help with anything," she said, trying to keep him on business. "It's a small town. I don't mind if you knock on my office."

As she walked away, she immediately regretted her choice of words. She could practically feel Jesse grinning ear-to-ear behind her, and this would not be an uncomfortable or nervous smile.

But the perks of a small town were real. She could leave the front desk unattended. She could leave her office unlocked. The worst that happened here was someone staying in their parking spot past their allotted two hours, and until the day came where that prevented other customers from visiting her store, she wouldn't care.

She went into an open entryway, took a right, and opened the door, with only an "Employees Only" fading sign adorning it. She barely pushed it open and sneaked in before she felt the other office resident running up to her in excitement.

"Clifford! Clifford!" she said in a quiet but bemused voice.

Though her dog was neither big nor red, the energy of her black-and-white border collie meant that he could cause more than enough chaos to mirror the fictional children's story dog. The only way to get Clifford to remain calm was to leave the room or have the patience of a priest; Clifford thrived off social interaction and saw all humans as play toys. Clara, though, loved Clifford, having adopted him three years ago, and she used store owner privileges to bring him into the office often.

"Hi buddy, good boy! Sit!"

Clifford looked at Clara like she'd just asked him to leap from Greenville to Colorado. Clara laughed and pulled out some treats. Sure enough, Clifford sat so fast it looked like he might hurt himself.

"Oh, Clifford, I'm glad someone can be a good boy here," she said with a smirk. "You see, sometimes boys just never grow up.

Oh, sure, they might look older, they might grow beards, they might still make you laugh…"

Her voice trailed off. There had to be more than met the eye with Jesse Walker, right? He wasn't destitute, and the Walker family didn't have so much money that they could pay all the expenses of their five boys for life. And yet, what would someone with Jesse's study habits and desire for learning have done in the twelve-plus years since graduation?

Clara hated that the question gnawed at her more than she cared to admit. Her insatiable curiosity for learning about stories compelled her to find out, but her strong will to not indulge Jesse's humor in the slightest overpowered that curiosity. But to go ask Jesse himself?

Fortunately, there was someone who might know the answers.

She picked up her cell phone, scrolled barely through her contacts, and dialed Brooke Young.

"Hey Clara," Brooke said, her voice at ease—it seemed like her mother was having a good day. "What's up?"

"Question for you. What can you tell me about Jesse Walker? Luke's brother?"

"Jesse? Why do you ask?"

Brooke's voice carried an air of suspicion. Clara ignored it.

"He came into the bookstore just now, on a Monday night, and asked to read some accounting books. That seems nothing like the Jesse Walker I grew up with. Curious if you know anything."

A pause came.

"Well, you know what I know in terms of his humor and his silliness."

"I know, he made a crack about not having my number," Clara said, but she was surprised to find herself smiling as she thought about the joke.

"And you didn't give it to him?"

Wait, what?

"I, uh, no?"

"I'm pretty sure he's into you, Clara."

Clara laughed at that, trying to do what Jesse did best—wield humor as a shield against discomfort.

"What in the world makes you think that?"

"Luke's suspected it. He won't tell me why, and I'm not even sure he knows why, but Luke's been big on better communication with me. If he thinks he's into you, I know he's telling me the truth."

"I... see," Clara said, unsure how to react to that.

Him, into her? Did he not remember anything from high school, how she all but hated him? Did he also have a crush on any single woman under the age of forty in this town—up to and including Brooke before the last month or so?

It was flattering to be seen as attractive by a man as handsome as Jesse, but Clara also couldn't see how that distinguished her from any other woman.

"Luke also said that he thinks Jesse is hiding something, but he can't figure out what."

"Bad?"

"He doesn't think so. Jesse keeps disappearing to their family office, and he even sent me a text maybe an hour ago saying Jesse was heading to The Homestead for something. I guess he found his way to you, which probably makes the idea he's up to something even higher."

"Something stupid and whimsical, no doubt," Clara said, even though she had plenty of doubt.

"In any case, Clara, just keep an open mind to him. I had my doubts about Luke at first, and we even split apart for a week in there. But look where we are now."

Except, Clara thought, Brooke and Luke had a romantic history. She and Jesse had no history, at least none that Jesse was probably aware of. The way he chased girls and acted a fool, she doubted that Jesse knew anything more than her name and what she looked like, especially in high school.

Still, people could change. What was the point of a story if not to show that people could mature, become better versions of themselves, and sometimes even share that better version with their spiritual other?

"I don't think we'll get there," Clara said, "but I'll do my best not to judge him so early."

"You might be surprised. But then again, it is Jesse."

The two women shared another laugh before Brooke hung up a short time after, saying her mother needed some food. Still, Clara had gotten…

Well, maybe she hadn't gotten clarification. She'd called Brooke for knowledge about Jesse, and all she'd learned was that he was into her—but possibly only her, possibly not—and that she should keep an open mind—but possibly only about him as a person, possibly much more.

With her friend unable to provide clarity, she closed her eyes and said a prayer.

"Dear Lord," she began, "please give me the wisdom to handle all who walk through that door with grace and dignity. Help me open my heart to love to whoever may best cherish it."

She sighed. Did she dare specify Jesse? She certainly wanted to. But God had his own plans, and to expect Him to tailor them to her particular desires seemed ludicrous.

But was there harm in asking if it was done with noble, faithful intentions?

"And if Jesse has changed, please help me keep my options open. In your name, Amen."

It felt… not wrong. But certainly weird.

Jesse Walker might very well have been the last man in her graduating class she ever would have considered as a partner.

And now he might very well be the first man in some time she would consider romantically.

Funny how stories sometimes went.

~

Click to continue reading Cowboy's Dream.

Or use the QR code below.

ABOUT THE AUTHOR

Sierra Hart is the pen name of a married couple who got to experience their own real-life, second-chance sweet romance story. They met in 2019, broke up for nine months, then rekindled their love for each other after much prayer, reflection, and growth. Today, they live in a small town in the South, where they seek to craft love stories similar to the one they try to live up to on a daily basis.

To learn more about Sierra Hart, visit her website at:

sierrahart.me

Copyright © 2023 by Sierra Hart

All rights reserved.

No part of this book may be reproduced in any form or by any electronic or mechanical means, including information storage and retrieval systems, without written permission from the author, except for the use of brief quotations in a book review.

Editing by Florence Petock

Cover Design by Blue Water Books

Created with Vellum

Printed in Great Britain
by Amazon